ONE MORE DAY OF US

SHARI LOW

B
Boldwood

First published in Great Britain in 2025 by Boldwood Books Ltd.

Copyright © Shari Low, 2025

Cover Design by Alice Moore Design

Cover Images: Shutterstock

The moral right of Shari Low to be identified as the author of this work has been asserted in accordance with the Copyright, Designs and Patents Act 1988.

All rights reserved. No part of this book may be reproduced in any form or by any electronic or mechanical means, including information storage and retrieval systems, without written permission from the author, except for the use of brief quotations in a book review. This book is a work of fiction and, except in the case of historical fact, any resemblance to actual persons, living or dead, is purely coincidental.

Every effort has been made to obtain the necessary permissions with reference to copyright material, both illustrative and quoted. We apologise for any omissions in this respect and will be pleased to make the appropriate acknowledgements in any future edition.

A CIP catalogue record for this book is available from the British Library.

Paperback ISBN 978-1-83518-480-6

Large Print ISBN 978-1-83518-481-3

Hardback ISBN 978-1-83518-479-0

Ebook ISBN 978-1-83518-482-0

Kindle ISBN 978-1-83518-483-7

Audio CD ISBN 978-1-83518-474-5

MP3 CD ISBN 978-1-83518-475-2

Digital audio download ISBN 978-1-83518-478-3

This book is printed on certified sustainable paper. Boldwood Books is dedicated to putting sustainability at the heart of our business. For more information please visit https://www.boldwoodbooks.com/about-us/sustainability/

Boldwood Books Ltd, 23 Bowerdean Street, London, SW6 3TN

www.boldwoodbooks.com

To my very own Posh Pal – the magnificent Emma Vijayaratnam, my friend from the instant we met in Hong Kong back in the nineties, when we were barely in our twenties, loving life and looking for adventure.

And to our families and our husbands, who didn't mind that we left them behind to go off on our reunion trip last year, meeting up again in Hong Kong after decades apart.

Carina, Lisa and Moira's stories are not ours – their lives and choices came from my imagination – but we sure had a good time researching them.

Emma, this is for us... so we'll always remember that there was so much laughter, a few tears, and those steps on Lantau were worth it.

All my love, Shari x

ON THIS TRIP, WE MEET...

Moira Chiles – former pub, club and cruise ship crooner, has returned to her home town of Glasgow and is ready to create the next chapter in her life – just as soon as she's decided what she wants that to be.

Ollie Chiles – Moira's son, star of the global hit TV show, *The Clansman,* all round good guy, co-founder of a theatre school for underprivileged kids, called The Moira Chiles Academy of Music and Drama. And yes, his mother is MORTIFIED that he named it after her.

Jacinta McIntyre – Moira's lifelong closest friend, actress and wearer of floaty chiffon kaftans.

Nate Wilde – The first love of Moira's life and the boyfriend she left back in Hong Kong in the nineties – a free spirit who dreamt of a life of travelling and surfing.

Carina Lloyd – Wife to Spencer, mother of Imogen and Erin, hostess extraordinaire, has lived as an expat in Asia for the last three decades of her impeccably curated life, but now based in Dubai.

Spencer Lloyd – Carina's very suave husband, CEO of Lloyd

Asia Trading, an international company with offices in several countries, dealing in global imports and exports.

Ben Lloyd – Spencer's brother and Carina's reliable, caring friend of thirty-five years. Has lived in Hong Kong since the nineties, never married.

Felicity Bateman – Carina's mother, setter of standards, believer in etiquette, snob.

Lisa Dixon – Long-ago friend of Moira and Carina, divorced, mother of one daughter, Stevie, works in a care home for the elderly.

Stevie Dixon – Lisa's daughter, named after Stevie Nicks, she has the blonde hair, the throaty voice, everything except the wild ways and the rock and roll lifestyle. Born and brought up in Ireland, she came to Glasgow to do her radiography degree and stayed. Now a radiographer in the Emergency Department at Glasgow Central Hospital.

Caleb Henry – An ED nurse, Stevie's colleague and best mate since they both started work at Glasgow Central Hospital on the same day, straight from university.

Keli Clark – The third friend in their trio, a nurse on the elderly ward at the same hospital, and the kind of solid, loyal pal who can always be relied upon to help in a crisis.

Gilda Clark – Mum to Keli and her three siblings, straight talking, warm-hearted, and always happy for anyone to join her family for Sunday dinner. Has a special place in her heart for Stevie.

PROLOGUE
MOIRA

Rose Cottage
Weirbridge
Scotland
1 April 2025

Dear Lisa and Carina,

I'm sending this letter to both of you, so that we're all on the same page – quite literally. And yes, I thought about sending an email, but since I've been asking Lisa for an email address for the last ten years without success (seriously, Miss Technophobe – come join us in the 21st century), I'll stick to snail-mail for now.

How are you doing, ma darlins? It's been a while. Hope you're both loving life and surviving all this middle age rubbish that no bugger warned us about. My body seems to have entered its landslide era. I'm now considering putting flashlights on my nips so that they illuminate my feet when I'm walking down dark paths at night.

Anyway, enough of my woes. Since we're apparently the

only people on earth who still communicate via letters, I send this missive with glad tidings – after sixteen years, I've finally hung up my sea legs. Yes, I've left the world of the cruise line cabarets and returned to Glasgow to take up a post teaching music and theatre to aspiring teenage stars as part of a new project to give kids from deprived areas access to training in song, dance and drama. My Ollie is one of the driving forces behind it and I couldn't be prouder. I'm already working there, getting everything ready for the grand opening which should be early Autumn.

Which brings me to my second reason for writing...

Chums, do you realise that this summer, it will be exactly thirty-five years since we met in Hong Kong? July 1990. Oh my, what a time to be alive that was. And it did get me thinking... Aye, brace yourselves for this one. Now that I'm no longer constrained by my sea schedule and have developed a 'f*** it, life's too short' attitude (that came with the landslide situation, the menopause and the arrival of a new credit card), I'm going to take a trip back to Hong Kong. I want to explore it again, I want the nostalgia, the memories, and I want to see if the twenty-three-year-old me is still there, because lord knows, I lost her somewhere along the years.

Here's the crunch part. I'd love some travel buddies, but there's no one I'd want to do this with other than the two friends for life I met there. So how about a wee trip down memory lane, ladies? Hong Kong, the three of us, for one week in July. I know at first glance, that seems crazy, but why not? It's been over three decades since I saw your faces in real life, so surely it's time for an encore? Let's do it. Let's just bloody do it. Lisa, I don't want to hear all the reasons it's not a good idea. And Carina, I couldn't care less if you already have glamorous plans with far more important people. The twenty-

something us deserve this. And the fifty-something us deserve this even more.

I've already looked into it, and here's my plan... The Harbour Lights Hotel. Arriving 1 July. Let's not go back and forwards on this because, well, I don't want to pressure you or guilt you into coming along. I'm going anyway – whether you join me is your decision. All I'll add is that thirty-five years ago the fates made our paths cross and I'm just going to trust (and hope) that they'll do it again.

So, ma darlins, I'll sign off now. Sending you all my love as always. Hope you're happy and healthy and kicking life's arse. And hope I'll see you both soon.

Love you until the band stops playing,

Moira xxx

P.S. Here's my favourite photo of us just to remind you why this is a bloody brilliant idea. xxx

1

JULY 1990 – HONG KONG

Moira Chiles

Jesus, it was bloody roasting. Moira wiped the sweat from her forehead with the hem of her T-shirt, hoping that allowing a slight breeze to go up her top would help stop the rivers of perspiration that were oozing from under her boobs. This bra was going to have to be boil washed to get it clean again. It was brand-new, as well – straight out of Marks and Spencer's the weekend before. Her mum had insisted on the underwear-shopping trip, extolling dark warnings that if 'the plane went down' or she was 'knocked over by a double-decker bus... Do they have double-decker buses there, Moira?', then at least her parents weren't going to have to suffer the indignity of identifying a twenty-three-year-old body that was adorned in greying knickers or a bra that had seen better days.

She'd only landed in Hong Kong a couple of hours ago, but she'd already realised that this was about as far from the lukewarm streets of a Glasgow summer as it was possible to get. It wasn't just the volume of people. Buchanan Street on the first day of the January sales was wall-to-wall folk, and there was a fair amount of jostling for position, especially when you got near the House of Fraser perfume department. No, this was different. The packed streets here came with noise, and shops selling things she couldn't identify, under signs she couldn't read, and a hundred different smells from food vendors and drains and traffic. She'd heard about something called humidity, but she couldn't even have imagined that it would feel like this. Her hair was now the size of her mother's rhododendron bush, and her lungs felt like they could explode at any minute from trying to catch her breath. It was chaos. Hot, sweaty, frantic, gob-smacking chaos. And Moira didn't think she'd ever felt more excited in her life.

As directed by the woman from the talent agency, she'd got off the bus from Kai Tak Airport outside a big hotel on Nathan Road, and now she was following the next steps in the instructions. Walk about a hundred yards down Nathan Road, going towards the Harbour, then turn left into Middle Road, and the guest house is about fifty yards along the street, on the left-hand side. 'It's just a doorway, so you'll have to ring the bell, and someone will come and let you in,' she'd said, as Moira had scribbled it all down on the back of a Rice Crispies box that she'd snatched from the middle of the breakfast table when the phone on the kitchen wall had rung only a week ago.

Her mother hadn't been impressed by the vandalism of Snap, Crackle, and Pop's image. Or by the fact that Moira was contemplating travelling thousands of miles, to a country they knew nothing about. Their family holidays had never taken them further than Benidorm and even then, they'd taken their own teabags, bread, and five packets of chocolate digestives in case of emergencies.

'It all sounds so dodgy, Moira,' she'd fretted. 'I mean, you hear about the things that go on when they lure these young women away from home.' Her dad hadn't got involved in the discussion. Unless it concerned his work, the pub, or the bookies, he tended to keep his opinions to himself.

'Mum, it's a proper entertainment agency. I checked them out with Calvin, and he says they're all above board.' Calvin was the talent agent she'd signed with back in Glasgow when she was still at college and already booking singing gigs at weekends in pubs, clubs and theatres across the city. She'd done the panto at the Kings Theatre in Glasgow's city centre five years in a row now, rising through the ranks from the chorus to the giddy stardom of an Ugly Sister in last year's *Cinderella*. She'd even auditioned and had a callback for a dream job playing Magenta in the new national touring production of *The Rocky Horror Show*. In the end, she hadn't won the role, but it was the closest she'd got to theatre stardom. She'd been in the depths of disappointment over that rejection when she'd been flicking through the job adverts in a stage magazine and spotted this opportunity. Six months in Hong Kong, with guaranteed work, singing six nights a week in a five star hotel. Flights and accommodation paid by the agency. Sounded like a huge, fabulous, glamorous adventure.

But now, looking at the sign above the door, she was beginning to wonder if her mum had a point. The tatty wooden proclamation of: *The Kowloon Star Guest House* wasn't filling her with confidence, and neither was the chipped paint on the door frame, or the fact that the door appeared to have a large, boot-sized dent in it where it had, presumably, been kicked. Her first thought was, *oh, bollocks*. Her second thought was that even if this accommodation was down there with the seventh circle of hell, she was going to tell her mother it was perfectly nice, otherwise there would be a middle-aged Glaswegian woman barrelling down Nathan Road as soon as a flight could get her here.

Moira rang the bell as directed, then waited, hoping that whoever came spoke English. She'd already sussed out that most people here did. When she'd gone to the library to fax in her application letter in response to the advert, she'd done a bit of research while she was there, and learned that Hong Kong was currently a British colony, but it had already been agreed that it would be handed back to China in 1997. She'd then, on the advice of the librarian, taken out James Clavell's *Noble House* and well, that had sealed her decision to come. It had all seemed so glamorous and cosmopolitan. Clearly, that exotic glamour didn't extend to the kicked-in door that was opening in front of her now.

'Hello,' said a voice her mum would describe as 'pure posh'. The girl was obviously English. About the same age as her. Tall. The kind of thick dark, flowy hair that shampoo adverts promised but had yet to deliver to Moira's red, curly, rapidly expanding bob.

'Hi,' Moira replied. 'I think I'm booked in here. I'm with the Night Stars Talent Agency.'

'Oh, dear God, another victim. Are you vaccinated?'

'Against what?'

'Everything.'

Moira wasn't sure why that was important or what her answer should be, so she shook her head.

'In that case, I hope you have travel insurance because this place is a germ factory.' With that, she stuck her hand out. 'I'm Carina. A fellow hostage of Night Stars Talent. There's still time for you to run.'

'I can't. My lungs gave up working about ten minutes ago.'

Moira shrugged, feeling the friction rash beginning to bubble under the damp straps of her bra.

'Fine, but don't say I didn't warn you.' The other girl (what had she said her name was?) stood back to let her past, then followed her up a narrow, rickety staircase. At the top, there was a small reception desk with a wall of key slots behind it.

'If you bang on that bell for long enough, someone will appear with your key.'

'You don't work here?' Moira asked what she thought was a fairly reasonable question, but the other woman looked horrified by the suggestion.

'No, I only answered the door to make you stop ringing the bell. I was trying to sleep before I go to work.'

'Oh. Right. Sorry about that,' Moira said to... She suddenly remembered the name. *Carina, that was it.*

'Oh, it's fine. Just a little hiccup in yet another day in paradise around here.' Carina turned to go down a nearby corridor, when another girl about their age came the other way and blocked her. Moira's eyes widened, and she thanked the universe for the third or fourth time that her mother wasn't here right now. Unlike Carina, this girl was short, with blonde, shaggy hair, and the fringe that was falling over her eyes was definitely a fire risk, given the cigarette that was hanging out of her mouth. But it was the Clash T-shirt, the tiny denim shorts, the leather Doc Martins, and the bottle of beer in her hand that grabbed Moira's attention.

'Lisa, this is— sorry, what was your name again?' posh Carina was asking her now.

'Moira.'

'Moira,' Carina repeated, completing that half of the introduction before going on, 'And Moira, this is Lisa. She's with

Night Stars Talent too. There're loads of us here. It's like a cult, but without communal sex or free food.'

That made Lisa laugh, as she lifted her beer bottle in greeting. 'Hi. Singer or musician?'

Moira didn't have much experience with accents, but she guessed Irish, then got distracted as she felt a very attractive rivulet of sweat run down her cheek. She quickly brushed it away. 'Singer.'

'Me too. I'm in the Fleetwood Mac cover band over at the Harbour Lights Hotel with our Princess here. She's Miss Fancy Fingers on the piano too though, so we worship at her altar of talent.'

Moira watched as Carina responded to the teasing with a roll of her eyes and a snarky, 'I prefer you when you're six drinks down and close to comatose.' For a second, Moira wondered if she was going to have to break up a domestic incident, but Lisa just grinned.

'Yeah, me too. Give me another few hours.'

Any further conversation was interrupted by the arrival of a guy who slid in behind the reception desk. 'Sorry. Delivery at the back door.' He eyed Moira expectantly. 'You must be...' he checked some kind of paperwork on the counter in front of him. 'Moira Chiles. British. Here with Night Stars Talent.'

Moira nodded, transfixed. What were the chances that Michael Hutchence from INXS, one of her favourite bands in the whole wide world, had a part-time job in a dodgy hotel in Hong Kong? Slim. So this guy must just be his identical twin.

'I'm Nate. Australian. Here with no other job, so I'm forced to work in this cesspit.' His smile revealed the most gorgeous white teeth she'd ever seen, and Moira felt her temperature go back up to where it had been a few minutes ago, when she was outside in 90-degree heat.

'I'll just get your paperwork – give me two minutes.'

Carina gave her a quick wave. 'I'm in room 19, just along here, if you need help, advice or antibiotics.'

'And I'm in 17 if you need beer or cigarettes,' Lisa added, before they both headed off down the corridor, letting Moira turn her attention back to the guy in front of her, brain whirring to take all this in. This hotel was a dump. She hadn't even seen where she'd be singing yet, but that could be awful too. The city was way too hot. And crowded. And far from home. And if this was an example of how her new agency treated their talent, then it could be an absolute nightmare. Maybe she should take the advice and run.

'Okay, they've already sent all the paperwork, so I just need your signature here and you're good. If you definitely want to stay, that is. I'd say we're at about fifty-fifty with people doing a runner when they see this place.'

Moira could definitely understand why. And she could also hear her mother's voice telling her to run like the wind.

However…

It was only six months of her life. And she'd get paid to live her dreams, singing six nights a week in front of a live audience. And so far, she'd encountered a deeply sarcastic but apparently friendly, piano-playing, posh bird. A rock chick with a fondness for day drinking. And a guy who looked like Michael Hutchence and was so attractive he was making her soggy bra straps itch.

She took the pen he was holding out to her. 'Where do I sign?'

2
JUNE 2025 – GLASGOW

Moira

Moira Chiles stood in the middle of the newly soundproofed recording studio and opened her mouth, to let the opening line from one of her favourite songs belt out from somewhere deep inside her soul. Lulu's 'Shout' had been in her repertoire for forty years, since she'd started singing in bars and clubs at eighteen, and she still got a kick every time she sang that intro. Moira held the last note until a lovely man in a hard hat on the other side of the studio glass gave her a thumbs up. Testing the acoustics and the efficiency of the soundproofing today had been an absolute blast. Especially as it worked both ways and gave her a merciful break from the relentless construction noise she'd been subjected to over the last few months. She couldn't remember the last day she didn't go home with the sound of a jack hammer reverberating in her brain. Not that she minded, because she loved every other thing about her new working environment.

She adored the exposed stone bricks on the walls of the old church in what was commonly regarded as one of the more impoverished areas of Glasgow. She adored the incredible team of actors, musicians, admin staff, cleaners and construction workers, who were grafting to turn it into an academy of music and drama, one that would give access to the arts and free classes to nurture talent in this part of the city. She even loved the cheeky young buggers who'd been hanging about these streets drinking and getting up to all sorts of mischief, before they'd been offered their first jobs, working with the building team.

'Ma, you should come with a health warning. I think you just blew out my eardrums.'

And she especially loved spending time with the man who'd just entered the studio and who was now coming towards her, his gorgeous grin already making her smile too. The very best thing about this new project was that her son, actor Ollie Chiles, was the biggest investor, and one of the co-founders of this whole project. Moira had grown up just a couple of streets away from here, and she'd brought Ollie up here too, so this was personal for them both. Although, his plan to call this place The Moira Chiles Academy of Music and Drama made her flush to her toes with embarrassment. She'd been trying to talk him out of it since he'd suggested it, mortified in case anyone thought she was blowing her own trumpet and becoming some kind of grandiose, self-promoting diva.

'Don't mock my pipes, son. They've got us this far in life,' she replied, laughing. It wasn't strictly true. She could only take credit for supporting Ollie until he got his big break. Everything else he'd achieved in life, the leading role on *The Clansman*, one of the biggest shows on worldwide TV, playing a Scottish warrior from bygone days, was all down to his talent, his determination, and aye, his good looks hadn't harmed his chances.

He gave her a hug. 'You're so right. I'm just in to say goodbye. I'm heading to the airport and back to LA. Need to go earn some bucks to pay for all this.' He was joking, but there was a hint of truth in there. Ollie had teamed up with her old friend and former agent, Calvin Fraser, to make this place a reality. Calvin had been her agent in her younger days, and then again in her thirties, right up until she'd gone off to sing for her supper on the cruise ships. He'd been a lifelong mentor for Ollie too, so when Calvin had the idea for the academy, her son had been happy to get on board. Ollie had put up the cash for the building and funded most of the renovation out of his own pocket, his way of giving back to the area he grew up in. He and Calvin had then recruited a squad of well-known faces in TV, film and music to help them raise a hefty sum for the day-to-day operational costs. The plan was to put on regular shows starring both the young students and the household name talents, with the aim of becoming self-funding. A lottery grant had helped too, and they'd also got an unexpected boost when they managed to get a documentary team onboard to film the whole thing for Netflix. That would bring in revenue and give the centre the publicity it would need to keep going and raise more, at least for the foreseeable future. Thankfully, she hadn't encountered the film crew today – she made a point of avoiding them as much as possible, having no desire to see herself on screen or subject herself to public scrutiny. Her days of dreaming about TV stardom were long behind her. This was Ollie's world now.

'I think I've got a bargepole lying around somewhere in case you see that ex of yours when you're over there,' Moira quipped. Ollie was in the process of divorcing his wife of six years, American actress, Sienna Montgomery, after she'd been secretly filmed snogging one of her Broadway co-stars on a red-eye flight from New York to Los Angeles a few months back. Turned out they'd been having an affair for months. And not that Moira held a grudge... Actually, she definitely did bloody well hold a grudge, but she kept telling herself that this was for the best, because Sienna was a spoiled, entitled horror, who'd grown up as the beautiful granddaughter and daughter of two generations of acting legends and become a Disney child star before turning to theatre in her twenties. Her upbringing and adult life revolved around deep wealth and shallow people, but of course, Ollie had been too smitten to see that when they were young, daft and falling in love. Thankfully, he'd now seen the light, and he knew he was far better off without her.

He nodded thoughtfully. 'Good to know. Might be tricky getting it in my hand luggage though.' That cheeky mega-watt grin and the twinkle in his eye was why he had one of the biggest fan clubs in the business. Apparently, he had over fifty million followers on the Instagrams – not bad for someone who had always loved acting, but not the fame and attention that came with it. 'Anyway, I just wanted to say goodbye and I'll see you in a few weeks. I'll be back for the opening.' The launch was scheduled for September 1st, which was why she was squeezing in this week off now. Once the place was up and running, it would be all hands on deck for months to come. 'When do you leave for Hong Kong?' he asked.

'Day after tomorrow. You know, I couldn't be more excited, son. I still can't quite believe I'm going.'

'I'm happy for you, Ma. You deserve this. Although, if you want to change your mind and come to LA with me instead...'

On any other day, she'd have jumped at an offer to go hang out with her son, but not today. She'd been saving for this trip for months and it was so much more than a holiday.

'Me and my bargepole will definitely take you up on that, but not this time. Ask me again next time you're going – but give me a bit of notice so I can lose fifty pounds, get my roots done and my teeth whitened, otherwise they won't let me into LA. A wee facelift probably wouldn't go amiss either.'

'Nope, you're perfect just the way you are,' he said, laughing as he hugged her again, blissfully unaware that she wasn't entirely joking. Decades of working long hours and late nights, stressing about money, taking care of her parents in their last years, juggling to keep all the plates of their lives spinning just in time for middle age and the bloody menopause to come along – it had all taken its toll, and she saw it every morning when she looked in the mirror. She remembered the days when her confidence was on the inside, in every bit of her, and not just part of the act she put on for the outside world.

'And so are you, son,' she replied, entirely serious now. This man made all the graft worthwhile, and she wouldn't change anything about the last thirty years if it meant she wouldn't be where they were now. 'Safe travels and remember to call your mother. I'm needy in my old age.'

'Will do, Ma. Love you.'

'Love you, too. I'll see you soon.'

Off he went, with a wave behind him, just as the studio technician's voice cut through the air. 'Moira, we're all good,' he relayed from the sound desk. 'Construction are happy with the soundproofing and the acoustics – we're just going to break for lunch now.'

She gave him a thumbs up. 'Thanks, Charlie.'

Moira picked up her water bottle, one of those ridiculously expensive, posh Stanley cups that Ollie had bought her a few weeks ago. Fifty quid! She could have got ten water bottles for that at Home Bargains. Although, much as she'd objected on a point of principle and frugality, secretly she loved the baby blue container, and it hadn't left her side.

Dodging joiners, electricians, and a load of other workers in the corridors, she made her way to the tiny room that the management team had commandeered as their staff room, office, eating area and, occasionally, quiet space to have an afternoon nap if they curled up on the old, battered sofa that sat against a wall, between a mini-fridge and a coat stand they'd found in a charity shop.

After flicking on the kettle, she retrieved a ham sandwich from the fridge and a packet of cheese and onion crisps from her bag, then finished making a cuppa. She carried it all to the table in the middle of the room. Or rather, the old door that had been propped on a couple of wooden crates to form a makeshift eating space. It was a far cry from the five-star cruise ships she'd worked on for the last sixteen years. Five days a week, three performances a day: an afternoon session in the lobby bar, a show in the theatre, and then a late-night croon in the piano bar. Her cabins were never up to much, but at least her contract had stipulated meals in the ships' restaurants, as opposed to the huge staff canteens in the bowels of the boats. On the outside, it seemed like such a glamorous job, but the truth was it was a grind. Groundhog Day. Up, eat, sing, bed, repeat. And there were few holidays and strict rules about not fraternising with guests, so even though she'd been friendly with other performers and crew members, it had been a pretty lonely existence. Still, she'd been grateful – the sad reality was that regular, decent jobs for singers of her age were few and far between. That's why she was now so delighted to be here, on home turf, with family and friends, starting a whole new chapter.

'What are you smiling about, doll?' Jacinta, her lifelong pal, academy colleague and semi-retired actress, had wafted into the makeshift staff room, one of her ever-present ornate, floaty chiffon kaftans trailing in the sawdust behind her.

'I'm just thinking how happy I am to be back in Glasgow, with a full-time job here.'

'One that you're leaving for a week to go off galivanting to Hong Kong,' Jacinta pointed out, as she gracefully took a seat opposite Moira at the table. 'You know, on that holiday I wasn't invited on.' Jacinta drawled, topping it off with pursed lips of disapproval, while popping the lid off a Tupperware dish she'd brought with her, then fishing a plastic fork out of her kaftan pocket. 'It's okay. No reason you'd invite me really. It's not like we're close. I'm only your best pal and trusted confidante of thirty odd years so we barely know each other.' The sarcasm oozed from every word.

'You're right. Sometimes I wonder if I'd be able to pick you out in a police line-up,' Moira deadpanned, refusing to bite, and at the same time, cracking Jacinta's faux disdain and making her cackle. She leaned over and put her hand on Jacinta's arm. 'Ma love, I'll miss you every day and I'll bring you back the most over the top, feast of a silk kaftan you've ever seen.'

Jacinta rolled her eyes. 'I'm so easily bribed. You're lucky to have me.'

Much as they joked about it, Moira did feel a twinge of guilt that she hadn't invited her best friend. Or her son. Or anyone else from her current life. And that was deliberate, because, just for one week, she didn't want to be Ollie's mum or Jacinta's age-old pal, she wanted to be the Moira Chiles who'd lived in Hong Kong at twenty-three, who'd had a wild adventure with her friends there – ones that sadly, she hadn't seen since then. The Moira she'd been before all her hopes and ambitions of stardom had been derailed a couple of years after she'd returned home, when a holiday romance in Tenerife had resulted in her gorgeous Ollie.

Motherhood had brought duties, responsibilities and commitments. The dream of a life on the West End stage had been abandoned, so that she could stay in Glasgow and be the best mother for her son. Not for one second did she regret it, but she'd gone from raising Ollie as a single mum for sixteen years, while also taking care of her parents in their final years, to a life on cruises where someone else told her where to be and when to be there. It had all been so regimented – everything done to a schedule, decisions made by other people. Now, in her late fifties, she was experiencing her first ever period of freedom. She was finally the only decision maker in her life… and she didn't know what to do with herself. Over the last few months, working in the Academy and creating something new and exciting had fuelled her fire again, but it had also made her realise that – outside work – she had no idea what made her happy. She was looking forward to helping the young ones who would come here to make their dreams come true, but what were her dreams now? When it came to her personal life, she'd lost all her spirit. Her boldness. Her confidence. And she couldn't remember the last time she'd even contemplated a relationship, love, or even a casual fling with some bendy sex. Although, she might have to work up to that because decades of shimmying on stage had played havoc with her knees.

The reason she wasn't taking anyone from her present life was because she truly hoped that when she got to Hong Kong, she'd find the one person she'd lost touch with thirty-five years ago who could change all that. It was someone that Carina and Lisa knew well, so Moira had invited them along, fully aware that she needed all the help and encouragement she could get.

Yes, now – knocking on the door of her sixties – she

reckoned this was her last chance to track down the carefree, bold, ambitious, optimistic dreamer who had been twenty-three-year-old Moira Chiles. The one who'd been so open to adventure, to risk, to dreams and to love.

And if Moira could find her younger self, then maybe she could remember how to live her life like all those things were still possible.

3

JUNE 2025 – DUBAI

Carina Lloyd

The air was thick with the scent of the jasmine wafting in from the garden that Carina and her gardeners had spent two years cultivating. Even in the suffocating Dubai heat, her favourite place was her garden, but having the party out there wasn't even a possibility at this time of year. Instead, this was the compromise – an evening soirée on the air-conditioned terrace of their home, overlooking the beautiful landscaped grounds that led to their private beach on The Palm.

Carina's gaze scanned the adjacent tables from her position at one end of the centre table, her smile never faltering, even when she spotted that the guests seated to her left hadn't yet been served their lobster starter.

Without missing a beat, she subtly gestured to her house manager, who had long since learned that his job included keeping one eye on his employer at all times, then pointedly directed her gaze back to the other table. He saw the issue and immediately beetled off in the direction of the kitchen, where she had no doubt he'd have the situation remedied within seconds.

Tonight was an intimate dinner party to celebrate the thirty-fourth anniversary of the day that she'd walked up the aisle into the waiting arms of Spencer Lloyd. Or at least, it had started out as that, until her husband had, as always, invited a few key business contacts that he wanted to schmooze, impress or reward. The logistics of tonight's event and every other special occasion were Carina's department. The invitations, the food, the entertainment and helping Spencer to woo potentially profitable clients all fell into Carina's field of responsibility, where they sat with her everyday responsibilities of their adult children, their home and their staff. In Spencer's piece of the workload pie was his career and earning the income required to give them the life they'd enjoyed for every one of those thirty-four years together.

'You've done an amazing job, as usual, Cary,' said the person to her left, the only one who ever shortened her name from Carina.

'Thank you. And you're trying to make me feel better, as usual, Ben.'

Spencer wasn't the only man who'd become a permanent fixture in Carina's life after they met in the busy bar of a swanky Hong Kong hotel thirty-five years ago. She'd also gained a brother-in-law, who'd become the dearest of friends.

Moira and Lisa had been with her, and Spencer's brother, Ben, had been by his side that night. It was a life-changing moment, one that she had thought back to when the letter had arrived from Moira a couple of months ago, proposing they all meet up for a week to revisit their youth. It was a lovely idea, but Spencer had booked a trip to London for their anniversary, leaving tomorrow, 1 July, causing a schedule clash that she couldn't get around. She'd meant to write back to Moira and explain, but she'd been caught up with organising tonight and it had completely slipped her mind. She'd do it tomorrow, and send a note along with a gorgeous bouquet to the hotel. Moira would understand that she could hardly tell Spencer that she was unavailable for their anniversary celebration because she was going off galivanting to Hong Kong. First thing on the list after she got back, though, was a visit to the UK to see Moira and Lisa. It was ridiculous that they hadn't managed to get together in all these years, but with Moira away on cruise ships, Lisa being reluctant to travel, and her being a full-time wife and mum, mostly in Asia, the time had just slipped by. Somehow, life with Spencer had always come first.

Her eyes were drawn to her husband at the other end of the table, their daughter, Imogen, and her friend, Arabella, on one side of him, and two senators from Texas on the other. These men, she knew, were his main targets tonight. Something to do with new trade routes, but she hadn't delved into the details. She'd done her job. She'd greeted them when they arrived, charmed them, and now they were being wined, dined and entertained – anything else was down to Spencer.

'Erin couldn't make it?' Ben asked, and Carina's smile masked a wave of sadness that their younger daughter wasn't here to celebrate with them tonight.

'No, she's still in Shanghai. It's driving Spencer crazy, but she's stubborn.'

Ben took a sip of his Champagne – it was Spencer's favourite Veuve Clicquot – then topped up her glass. 'I'll stop in on her next time I'm over that way.' Ben still lived in Hong Kong, so Shanghai was only a short flight away. He was also free of ties, time constraints or family commitments, because he'd never married. His choice. He'd had a couple of long term relationships over the years and Carina was rooting for him to meet someone just as kind, decent and lovely as he was.

Ben put his glass back down on the white linen table cover. 'That kid is good for the soul. I bet she doesn't give a damn that she's pissing Spencer off.'

For the first time tonight, Carina's smile was genuine. 'Not even a little bit.' Erin was a law unto herself. Unlike Imogen, she genuinely didn't give a toss what her father thought about her, her life choices, or her decision to teach English in Shanghai instead of following her sister into the family business.

Erin had always been drawn to Asia because that's where she'd spent most of her childhood. They'd lived in Hong Kong, Singapore, Beijing, Shanghai – moving every few years as Spencer's role and the expansion of the business required him to set up offices and supply chains in each new location. And every time, Carina would pack up their lives, and move them – new house, new school, new friends, new lives. She'd do it all with a smile on her face and a sympathetic shoulder for the kids, who invariably pushed back at leaving their lives, attributing half the blame and directing all of the resentment at Carina, because she was the more present parent. Her determination to show a united front with Spencer left the girls unaware that it was never Carina's choice to move. She'd dreaded every relocation, hated the upheaval, but she'd put a smile on her face and got on with it. Wasn't that one of the responsibilities that still fell in her piece of that pie too? Smile and get on with it. Hold it all together. The transient life had shaped both girls in very different ways. Erin was a free spirit who wanted no part of a traditional family life. Whereas Imogen had been intoxicated by her father's success and the rewards that came with it. She'd joined Lloyd Asia Trading straight from university and would undoubtedly take over from Spencer and Ben one day.

At least the kids were adults now, so she hadn't had to reorganise their lives when they'd relocated to Dubai from Singapore a couple of years ago. Once again, she hadn't wanted to move, but Spencer had promised her it would be the last time. Dubai had become a crucial location for his business and Imogen had agreed, so Carina had called in the packers and made it happen.

The ding of metal against glass interrupted her thoughts and took her attention to the source of the noise. At the other end of the table, Spencer was standing now, rapping his spoon against his vintage Stuart crystal champagne flute. Carina bristled, wanting to say that those glasses cost over £100 each, so would he please stop doing that.

'Ladies and gentlemen,' he began, and Carina felt the sheer power of the way he so effortlessly commanded his audience. He was still the most handsome man in any room. Well over six feet, his dark hair peppered with grey now, but it only made him look more distinguished. He worked out every morning at 5 a.m., with his personal trainer and he'd recently started playing pickleball with Imogen and her friends after work. Add a Savile Row suit and skin that had been lightly bronzed by the Dubai sun, and he could overshadow and out-suave a man twenty years his junior. It was a standard that Carina worked hard to match. The duck lips of fillers and frozen foreheads of anti-wrinkle jabs weren't for her, but not a grey hair survived her monthly visit to the salon, and her face and body were kept youthful by weekly facials, daily yoga, and twice-weekly Pilates. She had accounts at Chanel, Prada and Valentino, and Spencer expected her to use them, so that she was, at all times, the chic, elegant wife on his arm.

'First of all, I'd like to thank you all for being here tonight to celebrate the anniversary of the day I married the beautiful lady at the other end of the table.' That evoked a round of applause that made Carina blush. The centre of attention wasn't a place that she'd craved or enjoyed for a long time now.

When the room settled again, Spencer went on. 'And Carina, I'd like to thank you for being the core of our family for all these years...'

Carina felt her face redden again, this time with a sudden flush of attraction that had been missing for the last few years. It was difficult to pinpoint exactly when the passion and the closeness had faded. Or when the resentment she felt inside had begun to bubble and become impossible to ignore. Maybe around the time that the girls had left home and she'd realised that they'd taken her identity and her purpose in life with them. All that was left was her service to Spencer: a life of arranging his dry cleaning, making sure his golf shoes were polished, managing their home, planning their trips, smiling as she hosted yet another dinner for his business associates, wondering if she could recall the last time she'd actually had fun. Of course, it had never been discussed. This was the life she had chosen, and it was too late to change it now. *Smile and get on with it. Hold it all together.*

'And for your patience, and strength and love...' Spencer was still speaking.

Maybe it wasn't too late to get things back to the way they once were. Perhaps she just had to give herself a shake. Weren't these things cyclical? Didn't all marriages go through ups and downs?

'...and for being so great at spending my money.'

A titter of laughter reverberated around the room and Carina fought with every ounce of discipline she possessed to keep smiling at the joke that had very obviously amused Spencer. Spencer. The man who only ever travelled first class.

Who thought nothing of dropping ten grand on a watch. Or hospitality at a Grand Prix. Or a fricking dinner at Nobu. And he was saying *she* spent his money?

'Prick...' Ben hissed under his breath.

'No, but seriously, Carina, thank you for my family and for the wonderful thirty-four years you've given me. To Carina...' He raised his glass.

'To Carina,' everyone echoed, joining the toast. 'To Carina,' Ben said beside her. He was the only one she believed.

Smile and get on with it. Hold it all together.

Carina somehow managed to keep up the façade of the perfect hostess until dinner was over and it was time to bridge the half-hour gap between the string quartet that had just finished, and the evening DJ who was currently setting up in the corner of the room that the string quartet had just vacated. When she'd run through the details of tonight with her husband, Spencer had suggested that she play piano for her guests during the crossover between acts. Carina had been reluctant. Her love for music had never wavered, but her inclination to share it with the world had lessened with every passing year. Her music was her safe space, her refuge, the place that soothed her soul, where she could still feel emotions like passion and tenderness and belonging. But of course, Spencer had coaxed her to play tonight, as always. It was all part of the image he wanted to portray – his beautiful wife was talented too and weren't they just perfect. That's why he was now standing beside her, his hand outstretched towards hers. 'Darling, are you ready to entertain our guests?'

No, she wasn't. In her head she was screaming a rebuttal to his jibe about spending his money, and all the resentments were in full flow, reminding him that she'd raised his kids, run his house and facilitated his whole life... But of course, she kept that inside. The only thing worse than having a husband make cheap jokes at her expense would be to make a scene. Her toes curled inside her Louboutin sandals at the very thought of that. They'd been a gift from Spencer for their twenty-third anniversary. Or was it twenty-fourth? She couldn't remember, but it was back in the days when they truly enjoyed spoiling each other and celebrating their love. This year he'd bought her the large, diamond studded gold bangle that was on her wrist and, not to be ungrateful, but it wasn't her style. Too showy. Too flash. Too gaudy. He'd had his secretary deliver it this afternoon, so of course she'd worn it tonight to make him happy.

Reaching out, she accepted his hand, and he walked her over to the grand piano in the centre of the terrace. Her performing days were long behind her, but she still knew how to entertain an audience. This wasn't a classical music crowd, so she kicked off with a Beatles medley. Carina had never had Moira's raucous power vocals or Lisa's sexy, intoxicating tone, but her voice was clear and pitch perfect as she encouraged everyone to join in. Imogen was the first to oblige. Both her daughters had gorgeous singing voices, and they'd spent endless days of their childhood at the piano, but neither had any interest in making music their career. Those memories faded into the background right now because, as always, Carina got lost in the music, feeling each word of the lyrics, each emotion of the melody, as the Beatles merged into Oasis, which then went into a bit of Coldplay and Snow Patrol, before a Motown compilation rounded off her set. After the last bars of 'Superstition', she stood and took a bow to rapturous applause.

Imogen, so tall and confident like her father, came towards her for a hug. 'That was amazing, Mum,' she whispered, and Carina felt a very uncharacteristic swell of pride. Maybe taking centre stage again every once in a while wasn't so bad after all.

Over her daughter's shoulder, she glanced around for Spencer to see his reaction. No sign of him. Probably buttering up the senators somewhere.

Catching the eye of the DJ who was now set up and ready to go, she gave him the nod, and the sound of an old favourite dance floor filler, George Michael's 'Too Funky', blared from the speakers. Imogen was, of course, the first one to head for the dance floor they'd had installed for tonight, and she tried to pull her mum along, but Carina slipped out of her hand and made a gesture saying she'd be back in five minutes. She just wanted to check on the clear up in the kitchen, ensure the bar staff still had ample booze on standby, and have a peek at the toilets to make sure they were still pristine with plenty of toilet rolls and disposable towels for hand drying.

The downstairs loo was the first one she came to, and it was fully stocked and just needed a quick tidy and a squirt with her favourite Jo Malone Myrrh and Tonka room spray.

Her heels clicked on the marble stairs as she made her way up to the second guest bathroom on the first-floor landing. Her hand was an inch away from the door handle when she heard a noise coming from inside. A low, urgent groan. Her first thought was a medical emergency, but the 'Oh baby, yes,' that came right after it changed her mind, and her eyes widened. In the name of all that was unhygienic, someone was having sex in her bathroom! And she'd just had the countertops replaced. If their antics took her cream travertine sink unit off the wall, she'd damn well send them a bill.

They were obviously getting to the crunch of it, because the groans became more and more urgent and before she could even retreat to a safe space, she heard the unmistakable sound of an enthusiastic orgasm. Her first thought was that she'd never look at her travertine sink unit the same way again. Her second was that she had to get out of there to spare her guests' embarrassment.

She'd barely managed to duck into the doorway of the spare room, just a few metres away, when she heard the bathroom door open. *Don't look,* she told herself. Rise above. It's none of your business. But then... she had to know who to strike off the guest list for future parties. She wasn't risking a scandal or her furniture.

Straining her neck, she very carefully peeked forward, and had to clamp a hand over her mouth. That was a shocker. Her money had been on her loud, brash and obscenely wealthy neighbours – he was a former premier league footballer for one of the London clubs, and she'd been a glamour model – but no, there was no mistaking the back view of Imogen's friend, Arabella, as she walked in the other direction, towards the stairway. Arabella and Imogen had been friends for ten years, since Imogen had gone back to the UK to study economics at Cambridge, so they had a long history. Carina immediately realised she might have to keep this to herself so as not to be viewed as a prude. Unlike her, Imogen would probably think this was hilarious.

However, Carina was now deeply curious to see who she'd been in there with. One of the waiters? No, like Imogen, Arabella was ruthlessly ambitious. If Carina was a betting woman, she'd put money on one of the senators from Texas. Or maybe the footballer from next door was playing away from home. Peeking forward, she saw no one there. Had she missed him? There was a noise. A toilet flushing. A tap running. The door opening. Steps on the marble floor...

And then Spencer Lloyd, her husband of thirty-four years, walked out of the bathroom.

4

JUNE 2025 – IRELAND

Stevie Dixon

Stevie pulled into the driveway outside her mum's house in a tiny seaside village on the outskirts of Galway, on the West Coast of Ireland, and sat for a moment, just staring at the front door. Fleetwood Mac's 'Landslide' was playing on the car sound system. Her favourite song, written in 1973, long before she was born, by the woman she was named after. This all felt so strange. Sitting outside her mum's home. Driving her mum's car. Listening to words and music that she'd first heard when she was a child. Just another minute, until the song ended, she decided. As soon as Stevie Nicks sang the last line, she'd get out of the car and go inside. Until then, she'd sit here, putting off the moment she'd been dreading for the last three weeks since a call had brought her back to Ireland.

The game plan was holding up until a rap on the window made her scream. Caleb's gorgeous face then appeared at the windscreen, accompanied by a thumbs up.

She rolled the window down. 'Jesus, you scared the crap out of me there.'

'Sorry, I thought you saw us pull up. How are you doing?' Before she could answer, his attention went to the song he could now hear. 'Oh no. "Landslide". Is the emotional crisis happening or imminent?'

She sighed. 'Both. And I really hate how well you know me. If I was your type, I'd marry you in a heartbeat.'

It was an often used joke, but there was a grain of truth in there. Caleb was funny, kind, smart, with a killer physique and face that made every head turn when he walked into a room. He was also only interested in Stevies of the male variety.

He had been her best mate since they started working together in the Emergency Department at Glasgow Central Hospital straight out of university. Leaving home, and Ireland, to study in Scotland had been a shock to the system and was only supposed to be a temporary adventure for an eighteen-year-old who wanted to try something new, but it had turned into a permanent move after university, when she'd found a job, a flat, and Caleb, a new friend she'd instantly adored. Long days and nights at the hospital had bonded them and they'd forged a friendship that had seen them through the last ten years of work, love, broken hearts, good times, terrible times and disputes over whose turn it was to cook. But this... what they were dealing with today... this was new.

Another face appeared beside the car. 'Come on, hon. We can do this. We'll be with you the whole time.' Keli was the third friend in the group and she'd travelled in Caleb's pickup from the B&B on the seafront that they were all staying in. Mum's house was only a two bedroom, and moving in here, letting anyone sleep in Mum's room, hadn't felt right, even if it was

Stevie's closest pals. Keli was a nurse on the elderly ward at the hospital, but they'd struck up a conversation one night about two years ago in the staff canteen, and had been a gang of three ever since. Sunday night dinner at Keli's parents' house had become a regular fixture, because her Ghanian mother, Gilda, made the best food Stevie had ever tasted. Keli and Gilda had flown over from Glasgow two nights ago and looking back, Stevie could see Gilda on her phone, deep in conversation, in the passenger seat of Caleb's pickup.

'I'm so grateful that you and your mum are here, Kel.'

Keli shrugged that off with a soft smile. 'We wouldn't be anywhere else. My mum's just taking a quick work call, then she'll be right in.'

Stevie felt a lump begin to form at the back of her throat and swallowed it back. Not now. Not here. Time to move. Now that her friends were here, there was no putting this off any longer. Stevie Nicks would have to finish the song later. Leaning forward, she switched the car engine off, then grabbed her handbag and the large roll of black bin bags that were on the passenger seat.

Caleb opened the car door for her. 'I've got the boxes in the back of my pickup, so I'll go grab them too.'

'I'll help you,' Keli offered, walking back down the drive with him to his vehicle.

Stevie got out of the car and went alone to the front door, her keys in her hand. She was thirty-three years old, and she hadn't lived here since she was eighteen, but she still thought of it as home because it was where she'd grown up. Eight-year-old Stevie had made a tent out of old sheets on the grass in the front garden. Twelve-year-old Stevie had brought a dog home that she'd found in the street and smuggled it through this same front door. Fifteen-year-old Stevie had climbed out of the bedroom window above her, and slid down that drainpipe to go meet the boyfriend she'd fallen in love with. And no, she couldn't remember his name now. This was the home that had shaped her – for better and for worse.

Pushing the key into the lock, she held her breath and fought the urge to retreat and leave this for another day. As soon as the door swung open the familiar smell of her mum's favourite 'clean linen' diffusers assaulted her senses. Her mum's jackets hung on the row of coat hooks in the hall. One of her handbags sat on the console table below them, next to the bowl with the spare keys, a couple of pens and some mints.

'I'm home, Mum,' she said, but only in her mind, because Lisa Dixon, her mother, had walked out of this house three weeks ago today, and she hadn't come home again. The woman who had spent her whole life being scrupulously careful and measured, avoiding risks and refusing to do anything out of her comfort zone, had, in a brutal irony, been knocked down by a bus. A mini-bus, to be completely accurate.

Stevie still struggled to accept that this wasn't some terrible joke being played by the universe, but no. To her horror and disgust, a local newspaper had shown the CCTV footage of the accident on their website. They'd stopped it a few seconds before the moment of impact, but it left nothing to the imagination. Her mum had been walking along the main street of the village, just a couple of miles from where they were now, when she'd stopped opposite the post office. Then, ignoring the pedestrian crossing only fifty metres or so away, she'd taken advantage of a gap in the traffic to walk hastily across the road. She was almost there, when a minibus came around the corner, the sun glaring off its windscreen. Stevie had read the driver's statement. The sun was in his eyes. He hadn't seen the woman who was dashing across the road right in front of him, only a few steps from the safety of the pavement. Stevie had spoken to the paramedics who treated her mum at the scene, but their professional opinion was that Lisa had died on impact. She, quite literally, hadn't known what hit her. The poor minibus driver, a family man from Connemara, was haunted by what happened and Stevie's heart went out to him. She'd spoken to him on the phone yesterday, after her mum's funeral. He'd asked the Gardaí to pass on his number to her, and she'd been glad to call him and tell him that she bore him no ill will or blame – it was just a heartbreaking, tragic accident that he couldn't have avoided, a split-second fluke of timing that had ended one life and changed so many others. The Gardaí had thought the same, so no charges were being pressed. It was over.

'You okay there, Stevie?' Keli asked, coming in the door behind her, carrying a stack of flatpack brown boxes.

Stevie flicked on the kettle and pulled a carton of milk from her bag, glad that she'd remembered to stop at the little supermarket in the village for supplies so that they could have tea while they worked.

'Kind of,' Stevie answered, not sure whether she was telling the truth. 'It's just so...' she searched for the word and settled on, '...surreal. I keep waiting for her to walk in the door. Or to shout to me from upstairs.'

Keli put down the boxes and wrapped her arms around Stevie. 'That's to be expected. The funeral was only yesterday. You have to give yourself time.'

The funeral. It couldn't even really be called that. After the Gardaí called her to tell her about her mum's accident, Caleb had sprung into action. He'd packed a bag, taken some leave he had owed to him, then he'd picked her up and they'd driven down to Holyhead, in Wales, to get the ferry to Dublin. After that, they'd motored across country to Galway, to her mum's home. The first thing Stevie had done was go into the sideboard cupboard where her mum kept all her important documents, and she'd found what she was looking for – the folder her mum used to mention on a regular basis. 'If anything ever happens to me, all you need is in there,' she'd say, and Stevie would dismiss her. 'Mum, nothing is ever going to happen to you.'

But there it was, a whole folder with a sticker on the front that said:

If I Die…

Inside was all of her mum's legal documents: birth certificate, her parents' divorce papers, Mum's insurance documents, her will (leaving everything to Stevie), and a note saying what Stevie should do with Lisa's possessions. Stevie was to take whatever she wanted, then donate anything else of value. She was to keep the car if she wanted it, or sell it if she didn't. Stevie had felt her stomach clench when it came to the section about the house. This had been her great gran's home, the house where her mum and gran had grown up, but Lisa's instructions had been clear:

Put the house on the market – it's not worth much but there should be enough there to make your life a bit more comfortable.

Stevie had contemplated keeping it and renting it out, but the reality was that she had no ties to this area any more. She knew she would never come back, so having a commitment over here didn't make sense. She'd called the local estate agent the day before the funeral and he was coming round in a couple of weeks to take photos and get the ball rolling on the sale.

'I mean, who does that?' she'd said to Caleb at the time. 'Who actually puts together a whole book, at the age of fifty-something, with express wishes on every detail of both their life and their after-life? She's even put in explicit details about the kind of funeral she wants.'

Actually though, it had all been invaluable, because it had taken all the decisions out of her hands, including yesterday's farewell. Her mum had specified a direct cremation. No service. No mourners. They had no other close family – it had just been the two of them since her mum and dad divorced when she was five – and Mum had never been one for socialising or having close friends. She liked the people she worked with at the care home but she didn't have 'out of office' friendships with them, so no one was going to be devastated that they weren't getting an opportunity to pay their respects. In the end, the only people present had been Stevie, Caleb, and Keli and Gilda. After they'd witnessed the cremation, they'd gone for a picnic in the park and toasted her mum with wine out of plastic cups.

Now, tea was going to have to suffice. There was another noise at the door, and Caleb came in, followed by Gilda, whose outstretched arms Stevie gladly walked into.

'We'll get through this, sweetheart,' Gilda said, holding on to her. It was strange. This woman gave out love and affection to anyone and everyone who needed it. Her mum had never been that way. She'd been quiet. Reserved. Stevie had never doubted that she was loved, but it didn't come with displays of affection or gushing compliments. Sometimes, in moments of self-reflection, she wondered if that was why she was still single at thirty-three. Mum had been such a solitary, sensible person. Maybe some of that had rubbed off.

'What can I do to help?' Gilda asked, when she finally released her.

'I was just about to ask the same thing,' Caleb said, coming in with more boxes, which he dropped on top of the pile that Keli had left near the door.

Stevie took the teabags, sugar and cups from cupboards as she spoke. 'Let's have a cuppa first, and then I thought we'd make a start upstairs today and clear out the bedrooms. I think clearing Mum's room will be the toughest so I'm grateful you're all here for that one. My room is still exactly as it was when I moved out. If anyone wants a One Direction poster, they're welcome to it.'

'That's my birthday present sorted,' Caleb joked.

'It's yours. And then maybe next week I'll do downstairs. It's not going on the market for a month or so, and I've got another two weeks off work, so I'm not in a rush. I've got plenty of time – and much as I want it over with, I don't need to do it all at once.'

'I can try to come back—' Caleb began. He planned to go home tomorrow, taking Keli and Gilda with him.

'Thank you, but honestly, I'm fine. You've already been here with me for three weeks and I'll never be able to thank you...' That was so true. 'But I can manage this by myself.' She'd already contacted a couple of local refuges that were willing to take all the furniture, and everything else would go to the charity shop in Galway that supported the nursing home her mum worked in, so it really was just the personal stuff she wanted to keep that she would pack into Mum's car and drive back to Glasgow.

The pot of tea she'd just brewed went in the middle of the table, next to the biscuit barrel, milk and sugar, then Stevie dished out the mugs. There was a comfortable silence while everyone sorted their drinks. She was about to take a seat, when she spotted the box on top of the sideboard on the opposite wall and felt her chest tighten.

Two gardaí had brought it round the day she'd arrived, when they'd met her here to give her the details of the accident. It contained Mum's personal effects that she'd been carrying when she died. In Stevie's grief, she'd put it there and then got distracted by everything else. She considered leaving it a bit longer, but then changed her mind. If she was going to open that box, she wanted to do it when she was surrounded by the people she loved who were here to support her.

Retrieving the box from the sideboard, she placed it on the table then sat in front of it, before using the end of a teaspoon to slice open the gaffer tape that held the flaps together. 'My mum's things. The stuff she had with her on the day of the accident,' she explained.

'Oh, Stevie, are you sure you want to do this right now?' Gilda asked, and Stevie appreciated the care and concern that was written in every line and curve of this lovely woman's face.

'I do. Is that okay? I mean, I don't want to make anyone uncomfortable.'

Keli put her hand on Stevie's. 'Do whatever you need to do. That's what we're here for.'

Stevie opened the box, and stared at the bag inside, recognising it immediately. It was a Coach tote that she'd brought back as a gift for her mum from her holiday to New York last year. It was another difference between them. Stevie loved to travel. Her mum liked to stay home. Lisa hadn't had an adventurous bone in her body. If Stevie had to describe her, she'd say her mum was a homebody, who was averse to taking risks, overprotective, anxious, yet emotionally cool and strangely distant. It was an odd combination of traits that Stevie had always struggled to navigate, both as a child who felt curtailed and as an adult who struggled to connect in any kind of deep way to the woman who'd given birth to her.

Removing the bag from the box, she hesitated. 'It feels wrong to look inside. Like somehow I'm invading her privacy.'

This time it was Gilda who reassured her. 'But you're not, sweetheart. You're just taking care of business. There might be something in there that your mum wanted you to have. Much as it hurts, you need to look at everything.'

Stevie knew she was right. With hands that were suddenly trembling, she opened the bag and began to remove the bigger items. Her mum's purse. Her iPhone – with a blank screen because it was obviously out of charge.

There was a small make-up bag with lipstick and a compact in it. A hairbrush. And the next thing she pulled out was an electricity bill. 'That explains the trip to the post office,' Stevie said aloud. 'She was such a technophobe. Refused to have a computer at home. She hated paying bills online. Always took them to the post office. Although, she might have been killing two birds with one stone...'

In her hand now were the last two things from the bag – two letters. Stevie checked the front of the envelopes. One was addressed to her mum, and open. The other was addressed to someone called Moira Chiles, at an address in Scotland, and it was still sealed. Two lines formed between Stevie's eyebrows as she frowned. The writing on the front of that envelope was unmistakably her mum's, but she didn't recognise the name.

She held it up to show the others. 'Moira Chiles,' she murmured. 'I've no idea who that is.'

This time it was Gilda who was first to speak. 'Unusual name, though. The only other person I've ever heard of with that surname is Ollie Chiles – the actor from that *Clansman* show. If you laid that man down you could use his abdominal muscles as a toast rack. Not that I pay close attention.'

'Mother!' Keli exclaimed. 'That's so inappropriate.'

'You're right, I'm sorry,' Gilda said, flushing. 'I'll close my eyes next time I see him on screen. And I'm gluten free, so I'm not interested in toast anyway.'

Stevie had zoned the conversation out, too busy concentrating on the letters. Her fingers hovered over the open one for a few seconds, before she reminded herself once again that she wasn't invading her mother's privacy.

Slowly, gently, she pulled out the letter inside.

'What does it say?' Caleb was leaning forward expectantly.

Stevie took a breath as she checked out the bottom of the page first. 'It's signed by someone called Moira. Must be the same person Mum was replying to in the other letter.' She went back to the top. 'It says... *Dear Lisa and Carina*... I've no idea who Carina is.'

'Keep going,' Keli encouraged her.

Stevie focused back on the paper, as she continued to read the words, her voice oozing puzzlement until she got halfway down the page, when there was mention of someone called '"my Ollie".' Gilda's eyes widened as she exclaimed, 'No, it can't be? Mr Toast Rack? Surely not. What does it say next, Stevie?'

Stevie carried on, until she got to the line that stunned her into silence.

'"*Chums, do you realise that this summer, it will be exactly thirty-five years since we met in Hong Kong? July 1990. Oh my, what a time to be alive that was.*"'

'There must be some mistake,' she whispered, more to herself than her friends.

Keli bit first. 'Why do you think that?'

'Because my mother was never in Hong Kong. At least, not that she ever mentioned, and surely that's something I would know.'

She carried on reading, the confusion turning to astonishment when the writer got to the bit about a reunion. '"*So here's my plan... The Harbour Lights Hotel. 1 July...*"' That was the day after tomorrow. None of this was making sense. Although, the one thing Stevie knew for sure was that there was no way her mother, Lisa Dixon, would galivant off to Hong Kong. All Stevie's life, it had been a struggle to get her mother to leave the village.

'This definitely has to be a mistake...' She repeated as she got to the end of the letter and the P.S. that was there. 'Oh wait, hang on. It says there's a photo.'

She delved back into the envelope and picked out a slightly grainy photograph of three women and a man, in what looked like a bit of a shabby room. The guy was behind what appeared to be a reception desk, so maybe the lobby of a hotel?

'Definitely a mistake,' she said, feeling a tad relieved. 'My mother isn't in the photo.'

She put both the letter and the photo down on the table, and Caleb picked up the image, studying it. 'Wow. That's like total nineties fashion right there and...' He paused. Looked closer. 'Erm, Stevie, are you sure she's not there?'

He turned the photo around so that she could see it. 'That woman there...' he pointed to the female on the right of the picture, a rock chick in Doc Martin boots, with long shaggy blonde hair, her fringe coming down low over her eyebrows.

Stevie peered closer. The woman must have been early twenties or so and she was holding a cigarette in one hand...

Her mum didn't smoke.

And a bottle of beer in the other.

Her mum didn't drink.

And she was wearing what looked like denim hot pants and a tiny vest top.

Her mother definitely didn't dress like that.

But the face... She froze, her gaze fixated on the woman from the shoulders up.

'She looks like you,' Caleb said softly, and Stevie felt goosebumps pop up as the realisation dawned.

'Oh. My. Holy. Crap. That's my mum.'

For what felt like hours, she just stared, unable to process or make sense of this. It still had to be a mistake. Yes. Had to be. Didn't it?

The other letter on the table, the one addressed to Moira Chiles, written in her mum's handwriting, began calling out to her. That might have the answer.

Stevie snatched it up and hurriedly opened it, before unfolding the single sheet of paper inside.

Dear Moira,

I've missed you too, pal. And you're right – my first instinct was that this wasn't a good idea. But sod it, maybe it's time I made a couple of bad decisions. I'll see you there.

Love, Lisa x

If her mother rang the doorbell right now, Stevie wouldn't have been more astonished than she felt in this moment.

According to these letters, her mum once lived in Hong Kong. She had friends there. She was planning to visit them in a couple of days. And they knew her when she was a smoking, drinking, sexy rock chick. Who the hell was this Lisa? Because she bore no resemblance to the restrained, reserved, loner, low-key mother who had brought her up. Her mind was spinning, running back and forward across the letters, the photo, the shock of it all.

'This is crazy,' Caleb exclaimed, picking up the photo again.

'I mean, I can see that's your mum there, but who are these women? What's the story here?'

Stevie didn't answer for the longest time, until one thought bubbled to the surface of her mind, then came out of her mouth before she could stop it.

'I've no idea. But is it bonkers that I kind of want to go to Hong Kong and find out?'

5

AUGUST 1990 – HONG KONG

Carina

'This wretched wig is killing me,' Carina moaned, adjusting her hairline before picking up the glass that the bartender had just slid across the bar and taking a sip. 'Excellent crowd tonight, though.' It was fifteen minutes until showtime for the first set – Carina and Lisa playing Christine McVie and Stevie Nicks in Fleetwood Mac – and every single table in the bar and restaurant of the Harbour Lights Hotel was taken for the third week in a row.

'That's because we're superstars, Posh Pal,' Moira joked, giving her a nudge with her elbow. 'And you either need to get used to the blonde wig or send Christine McVie a wee box of Nice N Easy, walnut brown.'

Carina felt the corners of her mouth turn up. Meeting Moira had been an education, not least in expanding her vocabulary. The Glaswegian vocal powerhouse with the gravelly voice had added several new expressions to her vernacular, most of them sweary, as well as giving her a new nickname. Posh Pal. Actually, it was the first nickname Carina had ever had, but surprisingly, she didn't mind it in the least. Moira made her laugh too much to get offended by anything that came out of her mouth.

They'd only met a month ago, but already – clichéd as it was – it felt like they'd known each other for ever. They lived together, worked together, partied together, and Moira had slotted right into the friendship that Carina already had with Lisa. On paper, the three of them had nothing in common. Carina had grown up in Chelsea, with a father who'd ran his family's hedge fund, and a mother who treated socialising, fundraising and philanthropy as her life's vocation. Moira had been perfectly blasé about the fact that she'd been raised in a rough housing scheme, in a dodgy area of Glasgow, to parents who both worked in a local factory. Lisa came from a village near Galway, but every time Carina had asked her about her family or childhood, she'd shrugged the conversation off and changed the subject, so that was all she knew. Meanwhile, Carina had a private piano tutor from the age of five. Had gone to boarding school from the age of twelve. And had gained her degree at the prestigious Royal Academy of Music. Moira had left high school after her O levels, and her mother had worked extra shifts to send her to a theatre school, where her vocal talents had been developed. Carina dreamt of playing the piano on concert stages. Moira dreamt of singing in a Broadway show. Lisa just wanted to live life on her own terms with no rules or boundaries. And that's where the things they had in common came into play. They all adored performing. They all had dreams. They all had a weirdly similar sense of humour. And maybe they were not quite superstars, but they were all pretty good at what they did, as evidenced by the full capacity in here for the third week in a row.

Oh, and when it came to Carina and Moira, they were both

not quite being honest with their mothers about their lives here. Moira had called home once a week and assured her mum that their accommodation was just lovely, and that she went home every night straight after work. It wasn't and they didn't.

And for the last six months, Carina had been assuring her mother that she was here to have a cultural experience, living in a respectable English boarding house while teaching piano to the children of expats to cover her expenses. That had been true for about a month, before she'd decided that the kids were all spoiled little shits, and she'd stumbled across Lisa's Stevie Nicks tribute act at this hotel and managed to get signed by the same agency to play Christine McVie.

Now she had two gigs every night. She was the Christine McVie in Fleetwood Mac for the first set, and then she tossed the wig and played piano and percussion for Moira's act, singing hit songs from musicals on a Wednesday, Friday and Sunday, and doing covers of Madonna, Whitney Houston, Celine Dion and a rake of other female stars on a Tuesday, Thursday and Saturday. It was going down a storm with both the expat community that loved a bit of international entertainment and locals who loved the fact that Carina played a mean tune on the ivories and Lisa and Moira were great singers. Although, tonight, the act might be missing a very vital component.

'You won't be laughing at me when you're squeezing yourself into a wig and singing Stevie Nicks' lines if Lisa doesn't hurry up and show,' Carina muttered. 'Where the hell is she?'

They both automatically glanced over at the door in the hope that their wayward friend would be strutting in right about now, but no. No sign of her.

Moira shook her head. 'No idea. She was hanging out with Nate at reception when I left. Still think he's Michael Hutchence's secret twin. Anyway, you know what she's like.

She'll be here and then we'll look like tits for worrying. Oh, and she'll be half cut...'

Another lesson in Glaswegian that Carina had picked up. *Half cut: Adjective. Meaning having imbibed alcohol to a point of obvious inebriation, but not to a level that renders the subject incapable of functioning.*

'Yet, she'll still go up there and blast every one of us out of the water,' Moira added.

Right on cue, something – or rather, someone, caught Carina's peripheral vision and her gaze went back to the direction of the door. Moira was right. With five minutes to showtime, Lisa was strutting towards them, her mass of shaggy blonde hair as wild as ever, her upper body squeezed into a tight black corset, her lower body in a long black mesh skirt, and a flowery shawl draped across her shoulders. Stevie Nicks was in the building and damn, she was stunning. No wonder every pair of eyes in the room fixed on her as she passed. As she got closer, though, Carina could see Moira hadn't been wrong. The walk was always the giveaway. When Lisa was sober, she would have her head down, like she wanted to blend into the background, but when she was, as Moira put it, 'half cut', she came with a swagger of confidence that made her mesmerising. She hugged them both in turn. 'All right, chicas?' Carina wasn't sure when that had become a collective name for their gang of three, but hearing it in Lisa's Irish accent always made her laugh. 'Are we ready to go?'

'Thank God you're here.' Moira told her. 'Carina was about to put me in a blonde wig and force me on stage.'

Lisa raised one eyebrow as she chuckled. 'Never miss a show. Might not remember all of them, but never miss them.'

Carina shook her head and channelled her inner school prefect. 'I did fifteen years of classical training for this shit.' She slipped her hand into Lisa's and tugged her in the direction of the stage. 'Right, come on then, you car crash of a human being. Let's go.'

The musicians that worked the stage with them in the tribute band were a ramshackle bunch. A Canadian guy who looked about 106 took the part of Mick Fleetwood. And a curly haired English bloke with more of a resemblance to Art Garfunkel played Lindsey Buckingham. The Japanese student who'd stood in as John McVie had packed up and gone home a couple of months ago, and they didn't have a replacement yet. But none of that mattered, because the minute Carina got behind the keyboard and played the opening bars of 'Rhiannon', the place broke into a roar of cheers. And when Lisa opened her mouth, the whole room fell silent, captivated by the voice, the actions, the absolute star power of the lead singer.

Carina winked over at Moira, who was, as always, watching them in the Fleetwood set before getting on stage for her own act, and she returned the smile. Yep, Lisa was blowing them all out of the water, just as predicted. For the next hour, Carina lost herself in the music, in the performance, in the rowdy appreciation of the crowd, only realising how much time had passed when Lisa closed out the last bars of 'You Make Loving Fun', to thunderous applause, and then announced that Moira would be on after the break.

Carina came out from behind the keyboard, and took Lisa's hand, murmuring, 'Come on, my darling, I'm dying for a cigarette,' into her mane of hair.

'Me too. With a side order of Jack Daniels.'

Carina tried really hard not to judge. Lisa was a grown woman – what she did with her body and her blood alcohol levels was up to her.

They fought their way through the crowd to the spot at the

bar where they'd left Moira. At first, Carina thought she wasn't there, but then she realised that someone was standing in front of her, chatting to her and blocking the view. All she could tell from behind was that it was a woman. Slim. Glossy dark hair pulled back in a low bun.

Still holding her hand, Lisa reached them first and Carina heard her say, 'Move yer arse, Moira, we're in need of alcohol and nicotine.'

'Preferably both at the same time,' Carina added, laughing, until the smile was well and truly wiped off her face when the stranger in conversation with Moira turned around.

'Really, darling? Spending all that money you earn as a piano teacher?'

She wasn't usually the sweariest of the three friends, but— Oh. Holy. Fuck.

'Carina, you didn't tell me your mum was in town!' Moira exclaimed, clearly not reading the dynamics of this situation.

'That might be because I didn't know,' Carina answered tersely, panicking inside. If it were possible for a heart to thud louder than the drum kit on that stage, that's exactly what was going on inside her chest right now. This was bad. Worse than the time she got caught with three bottles of Pimms under her bed at boarding school. Worse than the time her mother saw her snogging the face off one of the students who'd joined the landscaping crew at their Chelsea home for the summer. Worse, even, than when she'd told her parents that instead of auditioning for the London Philharmonic, which had always been the post-university plan, she'd decided to bugger off to Hong Kong for a year. Her mother had almost burst her pearls that day.

Yep, this was worse.

'Ah, I thought I'd surprise you, darling,' her mother said,

deploying the smile that assassins used right before they stuck a knife in your neck. Felicity Bateman would rather eat her favourite Jimmy Choo pumps than cause a public scene. They didn't do that in her family. They did polite sabotage and muted, elegant fury. 'I've had a lovely chat with your... *friend* here.'

Carina could see from Moira's expression that she was completely oblivious to the undercurrent of disapproval, and Lisa, meanwhile, didn't help when she said, 'Good to meet you, Carina's mam. Joe—!' Lisa shouted to the barman. 'Can we have the usual Jack and Cokes and an extra one for Carina's mammy,' before pulling a packet of cigarettes from her pocket, pointing them in the direction of her mother, saying, 'Cig?'

Carina thought her mother was about to combust.

'Mummy, can I have a chat with you outside, please?'

'Certainly, darling. Lovely to meet you, girls,' her mother said to Moira and Lisa, as if she were addressing the local chapter of the Girl Bloody Guides. Even in times of chaos and rage, Felicity Bateman never lost her manners.

They'd barely got outside the front door, when her mother rounded on her, eyes blazing, speaking through clenched teeth. 'What the hell are you doing? This is your life? This is your "year out to teach and experience another culture?"'

Carina felt her own blood pressure rise. 'I'm definitely experiencing other cultures,' she bit back, utterly aware that it wouldn't get her anywhere. 'How did you find me?'

'Well, darling, the little flaw in your plan is that Daddy gets your credit card statements since we're still covering your costs...'

Ah, damn. Once her paltry wages were gone, she used her dad's card for essentials like food, water and drinks at the bar here.

'And on that itemised statement, this little slice of heaven seemed to show up on a nightly basis.'

Carina didn't have time to comment on the sarcasm, because her mother was on a roll and was now sneering as she looked her up and down. 'What the hell are you wearing? And since when did you drink or smoke?'

Again, she didn't stop for breath or for an answer.

'It's disgusting. You gave up an audition with the Philharmonic for this? Not to mention the tens of thousands of pounds we clearly wasted on your education.'

Carina finally squeezed in a retort. 'It wasn't wasted. Look, Mum, this is harmless. It's just some fun.'

If it were possible for a head to spin around then take flight, Carina was pretty sure it was about to happen.

'Harmless fun? You lied to your family.'

Carina threw up her arms. 'Because I knew you'd react like this. My whole life, I've never been allowed to make my own decisions. I was at boarding school, then university, and you and Daddy decided on the career I should have—'

'The career you wanted!'

'I don't know what I want. That's the point. I just want to try new things. Work it out by myself.'

'Pfft. Work it out by yourself? You've never done a damn thing by yourself. Everything has been given to you. Everything except this hideous job and those awful friends. Is this it, Carina? Is this really what happens when you make your own decisions? This is where you end up and those are the kind of people you choose to associate with?'

Carina felt the arrow of that judgement pierce right through her soul, swiftly followed by a second arrow delivering a cool seethe of rage. There was nothing wrong with her friends. And this job was the most fun she'd had in her life. Before she could plead the case, though, her mother took charge.

'I'm not going to stand in the street arguing with you, Carina. Come on, let's go. You're coming back to the Mandarin Oriental with me and then we'll fly back to London tomorrow.'

'I'm not, Mum.'

'You damn well are.' They both knew that Felicity Bateman wasn't someone that people ever said 'no' to. Until now.

'Unless you're going to drag me down that street, I'm not coming.' Shots fired. Carina knew, though, that her mother's unfailing decorum would prevent Felicity from escalating to physical force or delivering a shouty barrage of demands. This whole conversation had been conducted in the kind of hushed tones that would befit afternoon tea at a five-star hotel.

'I promise you, Carina, staying here is going to be the biggest mistake you'll ever make.'

Carina took one step backwards. 'Then like I said... I guess I'm going to have to work that out by myself.'

With that, she turned around and walked back inside, praying that her mother was wrong.

And praying that she wasn't going to follow Carina back in and have her dragged out by security.

6
TUESDAY, 1 JULY, 2025 – HONG KONG

Moira

Thirty-four years after leaving Hong Kong, Moira was back, and she already had one crucial question. How, in the name of the bushy coiffure, had she managed to forget the humidity here? Was it like pregnancy? The minute it was over, you forgot the woes and that's why you did it all over again? Because yes, just like that day back in 1990, Moira knew that the second she stepped outside, her hair was going to frizz to the size of a beach ball.

Only this time, she couldn't care less, because... she was here again. She was different. The times were different. The government of the island was different, now that it had reverted to Chinese rule. Even the airport was different – she'd flown into Chek Lap Kok, the modern airport in the New Territories that had replaced the hair-raising descent over Victoria Harbour to touch down at Kai Tak. However, as she looked out of the car window at the packed streets of Wanchai, nothing obviously different was sticking out. Still the crowded pavements. The eclectic, haphazard mix of old and new, of traditional and modern, of Chinese and European influences. Excitement was swirling in her gut, like a tumble dryer on high speed. She was here. And she felt just as thrilled as she'd been over three decades ago.

Her plan had been to just jump in a taxi at the airport, but when she'd come through the arrivals terminal, there had been a capped gentleman there holding a sign with her name on it. It was the second surprise of the last twenty-four hours. The first was when she'd got to Glasgow Airport and was informed that she'd been upgraded to business class for both the flight to Heathrow and then the onward journey to Hong Kong. At first, she'd thought it was a mistake, but then the realisation had dawned. It wasn't a random stroke of luck. Thirteen and a half hours of airborne luxury with a seat that slid down to a flat bed, allowing her to kick off her sparkly sandals and put her feet up, while watching four movies, reading fifty pages of an old Judith Krantz bonkbuster, and eating meals with real cutlery, all thanks to one very special person.

Now, as her car edged through the packed afternoon traffic, she took out her mobile and pressed her most frequently used number. Ollie answered on the first ring.

'Hey, Ma, arrived safely?' She'd known he would pick up. It would be around 10 p.m. on his first night back in LA, so he'd probably be in his apartment on Sunset Boulevard. She could picture him on the sofa, the lights of Los Angeles twinkling in his floor to ceiling windows.

'Arrived safely, son,' she replied, her smile automatic. 'However, there seemed to have been a couple of mistakes along the way.'

'Oh, really? What's that then?'

She could hear the amusement in his voice.

'Well, first of all,' she went on, 'Some mysterious benefactor upgraded my flight from economy to business class.'

'Wow, that was a lucky break,' he piped up, still going with it.

'And then someone appears to have very kindly ordered me a chauffeur driven ride in a swanky car from the airport to my hotel.'

'Someone is clearly trying to make you feel loved and appreciated, Ma. I'd definitely hang on to that person. Must be a really nice guy.'

That made her chortle and drop the game. 'Ollie Chiles, what have I told you?' She was trying and failing to sound stern. 'I don't want you buying me things. I'm perfectly capable of taking care of my own life, thank you very much.' She'd told him that a hundred times over the years. When he'd first made it big and started banking huge pay cheques, he'd offered to buy her a house back in Glasgow and make her financially comfortable for the rest of her life, but she'd refused.

'But Ma, you supported me my whole life. It's my turn,' he'd argued.

'No, it isn't, and I don't want to hear that again from you. As long as I'm capable of earning a living, I'll make my own money. And if I'm not, I've told Jacinta to sell my worldly goods on eBay. My Tom Jones album collection will make enough to keep us in prosecco for a while.' She was joking, but the point was made. He'd never offered her charity again. Her new job at the Academy came with a good salary, but no more than she'd earn anywhere else, given her talent and experience.

That's why, since she'd returned from her life at sea, he'd taken to doing little sneaky things like this. Upgrades on flights. Expensive Christmas presents. Trips with him to Los Angeles, or wherever he was filming. It was never his success that made her swell with pride – it was the fact that she'd raised a genuinely good man, who'd somehow managed to remain grounded despite the whole fame and fortune thing, and who was happy to spend time hanging out with her. As a mum, she couldn't ask for anything more.

'Message received, Ma. But do me a favour – if there's a slight change in your hotel room, don't make a fuss. Like I said, you deserve it.'

'Oh, dear God. Ollie, if you've changed me to a flash, expensive room, I'll be mortified. I won't be able to put my Primark pyjamas in the laundry. And I'll need to put my posh voice on the whole time I'm there.'

That made him laugh. 'Yeah, well, it'll be worth it. Have you heard from your old friends yet? Are they going to make it?'

'Not a word.' She tried to ignore the sucker punch of disappointment that answer caused. No response from either Carina or Lisa. She understood. Thirty-odd years was a long time to try to maintain a friendship without seeing each other, but she thought they'd done a decent job of it. Birthday and Christmas cards every year. An occasional letter or postcards from their travels. She'd once suggested one of those Zoom calls, but Lisa had put the kibosh on that one, saying that she wasn't one for modern technology and she had no interest in learning. Moira hadn't been offended. Lisa had always been the maverick in their group, and she couldn't imagine that had changed in the last three and a half decades.

She held onto the door handle, as the car took a sharp turn into a street she recognised only too well. The Harbour Lights Hotel was only a few minutes away now. 'Anyway, I'm not going to overthink it or let it spoil the trip. If they show up, I'll be delighted, but if not, I'm perfectly happy to go down memory lane on my own.' That was true but she didn't add that this next week was so much more than that. It was the end of a chapter, one of grafting to earn a living, working away from home, being told where to be and what to do every day and the start of a new one, back in Glasgow, in a job she was going to love, with so much more freedom to dictate her own life and make her own choices. She just hoped that being here with the ghost of twenty-three-year-old Moira, would inspire her to start writing the story of what came next. Remind her what made her happy. Help her to find joy in her newfound freedom. Oh, welp, she was sounding like one of those navel-gazing self help audio books that Jacinta listened to in the sauna. They were always banging on about finding purpose and fulfilment and inner joy. Moira would settle for some outer joy and a half-baked plan to get her mojo back.

'Anyway, son, that's me at the hotel, so I need to go. I'll call you tomorrow and thanks again for the lovely surprises. You made a knackered old boot very happy.'

They exchanged goodbyes and she hung up just in time to see the hotel come into view. The Harbour Lights Hotel – the same one where they'd sang for their supper six nights a week back in 1990, during one of the very best times of her life. Sure, she'd been skint, sleep deprived and living in a hovel, but none of that had mattered. She'd made friends that she dearly hoped would show up today. She'd laughed until her cheeks hurt and partied until she couldn't feel her feet. She'd made great decisions and reckless ones. She'd been young and vibrant, her joints hadn't ached after dancing all night and she didn't need specs to read a menu. She'd even fallen in love. She'd broken someone's heart. And her own. Back then, she'd been convinced that it was only the start of a glamorous, illustrious life. And if anyone were to ask twenty-three-year-old Moira how her dream life would look, she'd say that she would be swept off her feet, marry someone wonderful and live a life of comfortable wealth, while treading the boards of London's West End and New York's Broadway.

If she'd have known what was ahead of her, would she have left? Barely two years later, her dreams had been abandoned and she was dealing with an unplanned pregnancy. Then came single parenthood. Living with her ailing parents for over a decade. A life of graft, and financial struggle, supporting her son, and her mum and dad until they passed. Nope, not the future she'd expected back then.

But... this was her reset. And she was going to make the most of every second, even if she had to do it alone.

The car drew to a halt under the *porte-cochère* outside the hotel entrance and the driver immediately jumped out to get her suitcases, while a bellman from the hotel rushed forward with a luggage cart. 'Good afternoon,' he greeted her. 'Welcome to the Harbour Lights Hotel and Spa. If you'd like to proceed directly to reception, I'll bring your luggage up to your room.'

Moira had a fleeting thought that when she'd bought her suitcases in the Argos sale, she hadn't envisaged them being carted around a five-star hotel. Maybe she should have gone with something a little classier than screaming pink, with large purple pansies imprinted on the front. Not exactly Louis Vuitton.

Moira fished in her purse for two hundred-dollar bills and tucked the tip into the driver's hand, re-running the maths of the currency exchange rate in her head several times to make sure that she didn't make a mistake. No, she was fine. Two hundred HK dollars was definitely around twenty quid. Higher than the tip she'd give a taxi driver at home, but less than the average punter probably tipped in a place like this.

Another surge of excitement gripped her as she walked along the carpet to a huge glass door that was opened by a uniformed doorman. 'Good afternoon, and welcome...' He went on, repeating the same message as the lovely chap who was currently loading Argos' finest luggage onto his cart.

The lobby and reception area looked the same, yet different. The desks were in the same place, the glass lifts at the back of the atrium were still taking guests up and down, and the coffee bar was still there, over in the corner. But that was where the familiarity ended. The whole area had undergone a stunning makeover: the shiny tile floors replaced by marble, the brown walls now a contemporary mix of granite and wood accents. Gone were the old wooden reception desks, and in their place, a row of gleaming stone podiums, each of them with a uniformed member of staff behind them. There was no queue, so Moira walked towards the first receptionist who made eye contact. 'Hello, I'd like to check in, please. Moira Chiles. You should have my reservation.' Yep, the posh voice was on. She couldn't help herself. Ollie would be teasing her mercilessly if he were here, because she was all too aware that her posh voice was a startling cross between the late, great Dame Maggie Smith in *Downton Abbey* and Princess Anne.

'Certainly, Ms Chiles. Can I have your passport, please?'

She handed it over, and watched as he began tapping away, before raising his gaze.

'Ms Chiles, you've been upgraded to the penthouse suite.'

Her face went straight to flushed. The accent was going to have to stay on all week. That son of hers was going to get another stern talking to. And maybe a big hug too.

The receptionist finished the check-in, then slid her passport back to her, then followed it with a room key that looked like a gold credit card. 'Ms Chiles, your penthouse is on the eighteenth floor, and if you wouldn't mind having a seat for a moment, I'll call our Guest Services Manager, who will show you to your room and explain the features of your suite.'

'Thank you so much,' Princess Anne replied, with a grateful nod. She was about to step away when she paused.

'I don't suppose there have been any messages left for me? There's a possibility that a couple of friends will join me.'

He checked his screen again. 'I'm afraid not.'

'Okay, thank you.' Dame Maggie Smith this time.

She hadn't even turned away from the desk when she heard a voice behind her.

'I think perhaps that message you're looking for might be from me?'

Moira spun around and threw open her arms, as she recognised the very genuine, dulcet tones of the poshest pal she'd ever known.

7
CARINA

The wait had been interminable. Carina had been sitting on an armchair in the lobby for an hour, watching the door, replaying every detail of the last twenty-four hours since she'd seen her husband saunter out of the bathroom at their thirty-fourth wedding anniversary celebrations, having just had sex with their thirty-year-old daughter's best friend.

The utter bastard.

Carina still couldn't quite take it in, and it didn't help that what happened next was still a bit of a hazy blur. There had been no crying. In fact, not a single tear had been shed since that moment. Maybe it was the shock. Or devastation. Or perhaps it was the fact that she was so fucking furious she could barely breathe.

Of course, dramatics and hysterics had been out of the question. Her late mother, the formidable Felicity Bateman, had passed away a couple of years ago, but she would have whipped herself into a very elegant spin in her grave at the merest hint of an emotional outburst at a public gathering. Instead, Carina had stayed in her room for a few minutes, pain ricocheting around her mind. That's when she'd spotted the letter, the one from Moira, tucked into the book on her nightstand, where it had been since the day it arrived and she'd immediately, intuitively, decided what she needed to do. But first, she had to work out the details. Like Emma Thompson in that heart-wrenching scene in *Love Actually*, she'd straightened her dress, composed herself and then gone back downstairs. Spencer was back in his seat at the end of the table, with the senators on one side of him, and Imogen and Ara— Ara— she couldn't even say the name in her head. *That woman*. Yes, *that woman* on his other side, all flirty hair flicks and smiles.

Her initial thought was to go and speak to Imogen, but she dismissed that almost immediately. No. The horror of this wasn't going to be put on to her daughter. Imogen had been betrayed in all this too and Carina couldn't even imagine how her daughter would feel when she found out her best friend was having sex with her father, but Carina wasn't going to do Spencer's dirty work this time. He could tell his daughter what he'd done and he could navigate the devastation that would cause with the young woman who'd hero worshipped him her whole life.

Instead, she'd slipped back into her seat, next to Ben who'd been nursing a brandy while chatting to one of their neighbours on the other side of him. The neighbour took advantage of her arrival by going off to join his wife on the dance floor.

Ben had turned to her and immediately reacted to her appearance. 'Are you okay? You look like... actually, I don't know how to describe it.'

'Like someone who just heard her husband having sex with someone else in the bathroom?'

Naturally Ben thought she was joking and began to laugh. 'Yes, exactly like... Oh hell, you're not joking.'

'Not joking,' she'd confirmed, still stunned with disbelief at the words she was being forced to speak.

'Carina, I'm so sorry. Christ, he's an idiot.'

Something had struck her. 'You don't look surprised,' she'd said, fear building again. Her brother-in-law said nothing, so she pressed on. 'Ben, has he done this before?'

'I honestly don't know, but I've suspected.'

Carina had taken her glass of wine from the table and knocked it back before asking another question she didn't want to hear the answer to. 'Why didn't you tell me?'

'Because I didn't know for sure. It was only suspicions, Cary.'

Carina had fought the urge to misdirect her anger. This wasn't Ben's fault. The only one who'd done something wrong here was her husband. And Arabella, too, but not for the obvious reasons. She couldn't blame Arabella for being swept up in the attentions of a wealthy, handsome, successful man who could pour out the charm on tap, but to go near your best friend's father broke every 'woman code' in the book. They'd welcomed Imogen's friend into their house for years and this is how she'd repaid them? That said, Arabella wasn't the one who'd just broken a promise to be faithful. That was Spencer. Right then, all her rage went in his direction.

She'd inhaled, exhaled, tried to calm her racing heart, before turning back to Ben.

'When are you going back to Hong Kong?'

He'd checked his watch. 'The Emirates flight leaves at 3.30 a.m. Crazy time, but I need to get back for an afternoon meeting tomorrow, so it works. I was planning to head to the airport in an hour or so.'

It hadn't escaped her that the DJ had just changed the tune, and 'I Will Survive' had become the soundtrack to the conversation.

'Can you book a seat for me, please?'

Ben hadn't looked convinced. 'Cary, are you sure? You don't want to stay here, try to work this out?'

'There's every chance I'll remove his genitals,' she'd said, her voice low and leaving no doubt that she meant it. As that moment, she definitely had.

'I'll do it now,' he'd agreed hurriedly, fishing his phone out of his inside pocket. She'd watched as he clicked on to the Emirates app and made the booking, then she'd excused herself. 'I'm just going to quickly pack a bag and then I'll come back.'

Upstairs, she'd tossed some things into one of the Louis Vuitton cases Spencer had bought her for a previous anniversary and grabbed her favourite jewellery from the safe – not only the expensive stuff, but the sentimental treasures too. There was no way in hell she was leaving the ring the girls had bought her one Christmas when they were about ten and eleven and they'd pooled their allowance. Organising for a trip was in her muscle memory, so, almost on automatic, she'd collected everything she needed. Her passport had gone into her handbag, where it sat next to a purse containing all her credit cards and the book that had been on her nightstand, with Moira's letter tucked inside. There were some HK dollars in the safe, so she'd taken them, too, then checked her watch. Spencer would probably be looking for her, wondering where she was. Or perhaps he'd just assume that she was flitting around, checking that all was running smoothly as usual, while he got to sit there and be king of his adulterous bloody castle.

She'd felt the knot in her chest begin to tighten again as she'd strapped her handbag onto the handle of her trolley case. Time to go. She'd called down to her house manager and asked him to arrange a car at the door to take Ben back to the airport in ten minutes. She didn't mention that she'd be going with him, or ask him to come up for the case. Instead, she had pulled it to the lift at the end of the corridor and taken it downstairs herself, then wheeled it over to the front door.

Her house manager was already there. 'The car is outside, Mrs Lloyd,' he'd informed her and if he was confused by her sudden departure, he didn't say. Discretion was part of his very well-paid job. 'Thank you. Can you put my bags in it, please?'

He'd nodded. 'Of course.'

Ben had come out at that moment and seen that she was there. 'Ready?'

'Just one more thing to do. I'll be back in two seconds.'

Deep breath. Then another. Then she'd pulled her shoulders back, lifted her head high, and walked back into the terrace, where, yes indeed, Spencer had been sipping on his eye wateringly expensive Hennessy Paradis cognac, the bottle sitting in front of him on the table. It was his favourite after-dinner talking point and he liked to show off the $5,000 bottle so that his guests would be suitably impressed. Imogen was nowhere to be seen, but he was still holding court with the senators and Arabella.

The DJ had switched vibes, and a slow, quieter song was playing now – Madonna's 'Crazy For You' – one of their favourites when they'd been dating. She'd forgotten that she'd added that to his playlist.

Spencer had spotted her approaching and his handsome face had broken into a grin as he'd opened his arms. 'Darling! I just sent Imogen to search for you.'

Returning his smile, she'd taken him off guard as she'd moved close to him. Perhaps that was why he hadn't been prepared for her to elegantly reach over and tip the bottle of cognac forward, so that the ludicrously expensive nectar gushed across the table and into his lap, only stopping when he'd snatched the bottle up. Or why he'd been stunned into silence when she'd purred, 'Oh, darling, I'm so sorry. I'm getting clumsy in my old age and now look – your crotch is damp. Perhaps you should go to the bathroom and sort that out. I'm sure Arabella will be able to help you.'

With that, she'd turned and walked out, leaving four astonished faces to watch her go.

Spencer had blown up her phone all the way to the airport and Carina had declined every call. It was only when Imogen had messaged to ask where she was, that she'd replied with a text.

> Sweetheart, I'm fine and so sorry to leave so abruptly. Ask Dad to explain. Taking a trip, and I'll be on a flight for the next few hours. If you want to join me, just let me know and I'll make the arrangements. Love you x

She'd deliberately left the message opaque, because she wasn't sure what her daughter knew, and hadn't wanted to put Imogen on the spot by revealing the truth about what had happened. Her daughter had always been a daddy's girl through and through, and the reality was that his opinion and thoughts were the ones that had always mattered most to their daughter, even more so now that they worked together. The fact that a friend had betrayed her would also be devastating for Imogen, so Carina knew it was best to leave Spencer to handle that situation. Imogen would undoubtedly forgive her father because she adored him, and for once, Carina wasn't going to put her own feelings to one side in order to smooth over Spencer's behaviour. That had been the story of their lives. Every birthday he missed due to business, every time their lives were uprooted with a move to a new country, every time Spencer missed a significant event in their world, Carina would be the one trying to make it better while taking the brunt of her children's pain. Not this time. He could handle the fallout of this one all by himself. Carina had pushed that thought from her mind, as she'd switched off her phone and thrown it in her handbag, resolving not to switch it back on until she was ready to talk about what had just happened. And it had struck Carina that the only person she wanted to speak to about this was a friend she hadn't seen for thirty-odd years.

Perhaps that was why now, standing in the reception of the Harbour Lights Hotel, with Moira's arms wrapped around her, she finally felt her shoulders begin to shake and tears pooling in her lower eyelids. She blinked them back. This wasn't the time. Again, her mother's aversion to public dramatics, drummed into her for decades, was calling the shots. Although, many times over the years, she'd hoped that was the only attribute she'd inherited from the condescending snob that was Felicity Bateman.

'Oh, you sentimental old thing, I'm so happy to see you too,' Moira said, misunderstanding the emotion in the hug. Under normal circumstances it would indeed come from a place of joy.

'Come on, let's park here and have a drink to celebrate this bloody marvellous occasion.' Moira chirped, before turning back to the receptionist. 'Can we hold off on the room tour please? I'm just going to have a drink with my friend before I go upstairs. In fact, I'll just go on up by myself when we're ready.'

'Of course, Ms Chiles,' the receptionist replied, before giving Moira directions to the room.

Carina had barely sat back down in her chair, when a brick fell out of the dam that had been holding back her reaction to everything that had happened in the last twenty-four hours.

'I caught Spencer having sex in a bathroom with a thirty-year-old last night.' She blurted it out before she could stop herself. Maybe her mother's 'privacy and discretion' genes weren't so strong after all. Moira's eyes widened but she barely missed a beat.

'Okay,' she said softly, seriously. 'So let's have a drink and plan what we're going to do about that. I'm so sorry, Carina.'

Carina felt an instant pang of remorse. 'No, I'm sorry. I'm sure this wasn't how you expected to begin this trip. I just needed to tell you that first because... because...' She bit her lip, as a single tear ran down her cheek. 'Because I'm not okay.'

'You don't need to be,' Moira told her, putting her hand on Carina's. 'Let's forget the drink here and go upstairs to have this conversation. What is it that the young ones say? I've got you, pal. And I have. If all we do this week is handle drama and put each other back together again, that's just fine. It'll be exactly like the way it used to be. Good times and bad.'

'Good times and bad,' Carina repeated, a sad smile of gratitude pushing her tears back down, as they both picked up their handbags. On the flight, she'd told Ben about Moira's letter, and plans for a reunion, and then used his laptop to book a room here. The hotel was almost fully booked, so she was in a tiny, basic double room on the second floor – no guest services manager offering to show her to her room – but she didn't give a damn. Right now, she'd sleep in the cleaning cupboard if it meant she got to be here.

Standing up, she pulled her bag onto her shoulder, and lifted her chin, determined not to let another brick fall out of the dam until they got upstairs.

'Let's go,' Moira said, but then, strangely, stopped so abruptly that Carina almost crashed into the back of her. She didn't understand what was going on.

'Moira! Did you drop something?' she asked, beginning to scan the floor in case there was something obvious.

Moira took a few seconds to answer. 'No. But...'

Eyes raised, Carina could see now that Moira was staring at something to their right. Before she could catch up, Moira nudged her, her gaze never leaving its target. 'Carina, can you look over there and tell me if you're seeing what I'm seeing or was there something dodgy in the gin I drank on the plane?'

Carina turned around, squinted, blinked. Then blinked again. No, she wasn't imagining it.

Walking towards reception, was a petite blonde woman, her hair a shaggy tangle of waves, her fringe dropping over her eyebrows, her face perfect. She was wearing black trousers and a flowery kaftan over a black vest top.

'It can't be,' Carina gasped. 'But yet it is.'

Heading straight for them was the third person in their trio. Yet it didn't make sense, because yes, it was Lisa... but it was the one from 1990.

8

STEVIE

Wow. The foyer of this hotel was like nothing Stevie had ever seen before. She tried to take in every detail so she could recount it all to Caleb, Keli and Gilda when she got back to Glasgow. Or Ireland. Or wherever she went after this. To be honest, she hadn't even considered what happened next. The last couple of days had been such a whirlwind, that it was hard to grasp where she was now.

The first thing she'd done after she'd found the letters and discussed them with her friends, was to charge up her mum's laptop. It was Stevie's old one from university, because Lisa hated technology and rarely used it for anything except playing music and the very occasional essential email. Even then, Stevie had got used to getting a reply from her mother in 6 – 10 business days, because Lisa never checked it.

'Who would be emailing me?' was her familiar objection. 'Only someone who wants to scam me or sell something to me and I've got no interest in either.' There was no point in pressing the matter. Her mum had always marched to the beat of her own drum and Stevie had long since stopped trying to change her.

Unsurprisingly, the password was still the same one Stevie had used when the laptop belonged to her. As soon as she got into it, she checked her mum's emails, while Caleb, Keli and Gilda waited with bated breath, transfixed by the whole situation.

'Holy shit, she was really doing it,' Stevie blurted. 'The confirmation email is here. Air Lingus. Tomorrow. Direct flight from Dublin to Hong Kong.'

'And what about the hotel?' Caleb had asked.

Stevie had scanned the rest of the inbox. 'Yep, it's here too. The Harbour Lights Hotel. Reservation for Lisa Dixon. She never said a word about this to me.'

A whole explosion of emotions was churning up her stomach. The grief was still there. But now there was also confusion. Shock. Dread. Sorrow that her mum had never shared this with her. Astonishment that there was clearly a whole side to her mother that she never knew. And a sickening realisation that it was now too late to ask.

'I can't believe she never told me.'

'I'm sure she was planning to. Look there,' Caleb said, pointing to the screen. 'The confirmation emails were sent the day before she died. I'm sure she'd have told you the next time you spoke.'

Perhaps he was right. They had a weekly phone call every Sunday and rarely spoke in between. Stevie had to believe her mum would have shared this little nugget of information before she went tearing off to the other side of the world.

Sitting back in her chair, deflation had been added to the emotional cauldron. 'I don't know what to do with this.'

'Yes, you do,' Gilda had said softly, as always in tune with Stevie's feelings. Probably more than she herself was.

Closing her eyes, she'd thought about it for a moment. The others were only going to be there for another day, then they were all heading back to Glasgow. She'd planned to stay here just as long as it took to clear the house, but the reality was that she had plenty of time. And she had loads of holiday days stored up at work because they were always too short staffed for anyone to take a decent break. She could add a week or two to her compassionate leave to give her more time off to... to... She couldn't believe she was even considering this... to take the trip that her mother had been planning.

She'd decided to leave it up to the universe to make the decision. There was no way she had the funds to jet off to Hong Kong, but her mum had already paid for the flight, so if the airline's website allowed her to change the name on the booking...

Her fingers had flown across the keyboard as she'd given it a try. She'd used her mother's usual password – Fleetwood1 – to sign in and yep, that worked. Next, she'd gone into the section to manage the booking, clicked 'name change', filled in the required details and then waited as the spinny disc on the screen had told her that the computer was considering her request, despite it being made over a shite Wi-Fi signal.

It had crossed her mind to wonder if what she'd been doing could be considered fraud, but then she'd dismissed the thought. She was her mum's only living relative, so everything, including airline bookings for sneaky, secret life holidays, must surely now be passed to her? Stevie had never done anything dodgy or illegal in her life, but it was amazing how someone could justify an action when they were desperate.

A message had popped up. Forty Euros to change the booking. Her fingers moved like lightning to click 'accept' before the website changed its mind. She knew her credit card number off by heart, so she'd input the details, and then she'd waited. And waited. And waited.

Ping.

Your booking has successfully been changed.

Possibly the most terrifying sentence she'd ever read.

'Babe, do you want me to come with you for moral support?' Caleb had asked. 'I have no holidays left, but I can ask for unpaid leave.'

Stevie had felt a swell of gratitude, but she'd instinctively known the answer. 'Thank you, hon.' She'd reached over and hugged him. 'But you've done enough for me over the last three weeks. I think this is something I need to do on my own.'

Was she really doing it? Yes, she was. It was insane. Rash. Spontaneous. Her poor mum had only died three weeks ago. Her funeral had been less than twenty-four hours ago. And now Stevie had just hijacked a holiday booking to a place she hadn't even known was in her mother's past.

It was the most ridiculous thing she'd ever done and it had all led to this moment, walking into a hotel so flash, someone at the NHS was probably checking that she wasn't selling paper towels and toilet rolls out the back door of the hospital to pay for it. Which would be just as outlandish as the fact that her mum, the woman who rarely splurged on anything more than a new tube of Nivea from ASDA, had booked and paid for a hotel as swanky as this one. Thankfully, the name change on the accommodation reservation had been as straightforward as the flight, which was just as well, because it was non-refundable, so her mum's money would have been wasted.

However, she was still sweating slightly when she got to reception.

'Hi, I have a room booked. The name is Dixon. Stevie Dixon.'

The very smiley receptionist, a stunning girl with a sheath of glossy black hair tied back in a low ponytail, asked for her passport, then got to work on her computer. Stevie had seen scenes like this in movies. The receptionist was stalling her, so she could alert the authorities that a fraud was taking place. She could see the headlines. *'Nurse takes dead mother's holiday.'* She'd never be able to show her face at the hospital again.

'There we go, Ms Dixon,' the smiley receptionist said, handing her passport back, together with a room keycard, before giving her directions to the lift. 'Do you have luggage?'

Stevie nodded, relief oozing from her pores. 'The gentleman at the door took it.'

'No problem. I'll let them know and have it sent straight up to your room.'

'Thank you.' Stevie put her passport and the room keycard into her bag. 'One more thing. Can I leave a message for another guest, please? A lady called Moira Chiles. I believe she's staying here.'

'Certainly.' Stevie noticed the receptionist didn't confirm or deny that someone of that name was in residence. Probably a security thing. Or maybe... Maybe the plans had changed. Perhaps this other woman wasn't even going to be here, and Stevie had come all this way for nothing. At least a dozen times between deciding to come and getting on the flight, she'd contemplated how she could have just stayed at home and written to the woman and asked her to meet when she got back to Scotland. Yes, that would have been a far more sensible thing to do. But somehow, it didn't feel like it was enough. Stevie wanted to see this past life of her mum's with her own eyes. Wanted to share the experience. Right now, it felt like the only connection she had left.

'Excuse me...'

Stevie vaguely registered the voice behind her, but she ignored it, fully aware that it couldn't be directed at her. She knew no one here and no one knew her.

'Excuse me!' Louder, more urgent this time. Instinctively, Stevie turned around to see if she could help. There were two women standing a couple of metres away, both of them wearing really strange expressions, their eyes trained on her. Bugger. Maybe the receptionist had called the authorities after all. Although, these women didn't exactly scream Fraud Squad. Or Interpol. Or whatever the police agency was here. One of them was carrying a Chanel bag.

'Yes?' she asked, heart beginning to thud.

The one without the Chanel bag spoke first. 'I think I just heard you asking for Moira Chiles?'

The Glaswegian accent seemed out of place so far from home. 'Yes, that's right.' The thudding inside her chest was getting louder now.

'I'm Moira.'

'Oh.' Stevie wasn't sure what to say next. In hindsight, she should have thought this through, come up with a plan to break the news gently to these ladies, who'd apparently been her mum's friends at some point.

'Hello, Moira, my name is Stevie—'

'Lisa's girl. You couldn't be anyone else.' Moira's face broke into the widest of grins and the strained face of the woman next to her beamed too. This. Was. Crazy. How did these ladies know who she was? And why had her mum hidden all of this? It was just bonkers.

She nodded, trying to return their smiles. 'I am.'

'Oh my word, this is wonderful. When I didn't hear back from your mum, I assumed she'd cancelled on us. Wouldn't be the first time. But... you're here! So lovely of you to come all this way with her.'

Stevie felt dread rising as she caught up with their assumption, but Moira was going full steam ahead and Stevie didn't know how to stop the train.

'Where is she?' Moira asked, looking around. 'Or did she get a different flight?'

There was nothing else for this, she was just going to have to blurt it out, say it straight. She saw that a cluster of four chairs around a mahogany coffee table was free right behind them. 'Erm, no. I'm afraid Mum isn't here. I wonder if we could take a seat so that I can explain,' she began weakly, and then watched as the women went from elated to confused to suspicious that something was wrong. Still, they did as she asked, and only when they were all seated did they both eye her expectantly. Shit. She had to do this. Had to say it out loud. With a sinking heart, she realised this was the first time she'd had to tell someone from her mum's life. Or at least, from a past life.

'I wanted to come and meet you here today because I read the letter you wrote to Mum. She actually wrote a reply to say that she was coming.'

'I didn't get it,' Moira said. 'Honestly, the post round our way can be a bit hit or miss.'

'No, she didn't get to post it. I'm so sorry to tell you this, but before she could send it—' The next words got stuck in her throat and she had to force them out. 'Mum was in an accident. She was knocked down while crossing a road.'

'Nooooo!' That came from the other woman. 'Oh, you poor thing, that must have been awful for you both. Is she okay? Is she hurt?'

Stevie was still forcing out the words. 'I'm so sorry – she's not okay. She was killed instantly.'

Both of them gasped at exactly the same time, but handled the news very differently. Moira was still staring at her, disbelieving, as if she expected a punchline, or to be told that it was all a big joke or a mistake. The other lady's hand was over her mouth, two tears rolling down her cheeks.

'I'm so sorry,' she said again.

'Lisa is dead?' Moira whispered, as if checking what she'd just heard.

'Yes. She passed away at the scene.'

Stevie had spent almost fifteen years in the health service, she'd seen many tragic things and desperately sad situations and she'd been trained to manage her emotions, to put them to one side and focus on the situation. And right now, seeing the devastation on these ladies' faces, that training was the only thing stopping her from crumbling into a heap.

After a pause that felt like forever, Moira found her words first, her voice cracking as she said, 'My heart is broken for you, pet. I can't even begin to tell you how sorry I am and I'm so grateful that you came all this way to tell us.'

Stevie nodded, getting ready to share an uncomfortable truth. 'The thing is, I wanted you to know, but I need to confess to having an ulterior motive too. You see, my mum never mentioned ever being in Hong Kong.'

'Never?' Moira was incredulous.

'No. And please don't be offended, but she never mentioned either of you either.'

The two stricken women turned to each other, locked tear-filled eyes, both clearly bewildered by this revelation.

'So while I wanted to tell you what had happened, I also wanted to ask you some questions. So many questions, actually.'

Moira nodded solemnly. 'In that case, we were just about to move upstairs to my room, so that we could chat in private. If you'd like to come with us, we'll tell you everything you want to know.'

For a second, Stevie hesitated. Did she really want to do this? Her mum must have kept it all a secret for a reason. Maybe the truth would be difficult, or uncomfortable, or heartbreaking. Maybe she should stop, think about it, make sure she was ready to hear things that were never meant for her ears.

Or...

She stood up and pulled her bag onto her shoulder. 'Thank you. I'm ready when you are.'

9

SEPTEMBER 1990 – HONG KONG

Lisa

Lisa woke up and performed the same morning ritual as she did every day. First of all, check if she's alone. Without opening her eyes, she did a quick pat of the mattress and established that there was no one next to her, so that was a good start. One morning last week, she'd woken to find a bloke from Denmark in bed next to her, who'd told her in broken English that after their conversation the night before, he felt they had a deep, spiritual connection. Since she spoke no Danish, and he clearly spoke very little English, she highly doubted his claims.

She held her breath, listening for any sounds in the bathroom. None. More good news.

Still without exposing her eyes to daylight, she felt along the top of the chest of drawers next to her bed, located her packet of Marlboro Reds, took a cigarette out using one hand, popped it in her dry mouth, then lit it with the lighter that sat next to the packet. Only after her second or third inhalation did she squint open her eyes and saw that the room was bathed in bright sunlight. She'd obviously forgotten to close the curtains again last night. In fact – she tried to rewind her mind, but nothing was coming – she'd obviously forgotten pretty much everything about last night. Not exactly an unusual occurrence, but still... damn, this had to stop. Two paracetamol next for the hangover, washed down with whatever liquid she could find. Yesterday, it had been a bottle of Tia Maria, but thankfully, there was a bottle of water on the floor next to the bed today. She knocked it back with the tablets, then pulled on the oversize white T-shirt that had been lying on the floor next to the water. She really had to clean this place up. Later. She'd do it later. First, though... She leaned back over to the bedside table, to the cassette tape machine that had sat there since she'd moved in, and as with every morning, she pressed play.

'Hello,' the voice of an elderly Irish lady came from the speakers, the same one, saying the same thing that she listened to every morning. An old voicemail message that she'd recorded years ago. *'This is Netta Dixon. Don't leave a message because I don't know what to be doing with this damn contraption anyways. There. Are ya happy now, Lisa?'*

Lisa felt the warmth of her grandmother's voice wrap around her and heat her insides like a slug of Jack Daniels. In the background, Lisa heard a young eighteen-year-old woman laughing. 'Aye, Gran, ecstatic. Welcome to the technology of 1985.' Usually, she'd switched the machine off before she got to the bit where she heard her own voice. That Lisa, 1985 Lisa, was someone that she didn't recognise, like a long-lost cousin that you only saw at funerals. That Lisa was the one who still had someone to call family.

'I thought I heard you speaking to someone there.' The voice from the doorway to the bathroom made her jump. A guy was standing there, tall, butt naked, long dark hair, familiar face... It took her a few seconds. He was one of the barmen at the Harbour Lights. No one ever stuck around there for very long, because they were usually backpackers who were working their way around Asia, just grafting for a few weeks in one place to get enough money to move on to the next. This one was Australian, by the sound of it. Or maybe a Kiwi. Her brain began filling in the blanks. After her set last night, she'd waited at the bar to watch Moira and Carina's gig as she did most nights. At some point she'd got talking to the new guy behind the bar, he'd slipped her a Jack and Coke, then another, then another, and... vague recollection of being naked and rolling around this bed. Damn it.

A bang at the door saved her from having to explain, because it immediately swung open and Carina and Moira charged in. She really had to take the spare key off Carina, but her friend had insisted on it a few weeks ago when they'd been unable to wake Lisa because she'd had one too many drinks the night before and blacked out. Nate at reception couldn't find the master key, so Moira had kicked the lock out of the door, and they'd barged in to find her sound asleep in the bath. Lisa still had no idea how she'd got there.

'Right, that's it!' Carina had demanded that morning. 'You have to give us a spare key for your room because every time this happens, I think you're dead and I'm going to have to identify the body. I can't stand the stress. I swear it's giving me wrinkles before my time.'

'I don't need a fecking babysitter,' Lisa had pushed back.

Carina's right eyebrow had raised, and her hands had gone to her hips. 'Oh really? So far this month, you've gone missing twice, thrown up in that plant pot, fallen asleep in the bath—'

'It was empty. It's not like I was going to drown.'

Carina had ignored her. 'And brought home at least one guy

that I'm sure I saw on *Crimewatch* last year. Come on, darling, you can't keep doing this.'

'And we're only saying this because we're your pals,' Moira had interjected. 'And because I can't ruin another pair of shoes kicking in your door.'

The warmth in Moira's voice had been the thing that had swayed her. The new chick from Glasgow had only been here a couple of months, but she had one of those personalities that just made you feel okay when she was around. And it was a long time since Lisa had felt okay. Grudgingly, she'd had Nate at reception cut them a spare key and handed it over, a decision she was already regretting.

Now that her room had been invaded for a second time, all she could do was roll her eyes as Carina gave her new friend his marching orders. 'Sorry to interrupt your little rendezvous, but we're Lisa's lesbian lovers and we're the jealous types so it's time to go,' she said, in a voice that left absolutely no doubt that she wasn't to be argued with. Lisa just shook her head. This was better than the time she said they were religious evangelists, recruiting single men to their mission. Or CID looking for drugs. The poor bloke who'd been with her that morning had almost fled out the window.

What Moira had in warmth and humour, Carina had in no-nonsense authority. Just about everyone who met her thought she was mildly terrifying, but Lisa knew she was all posh bark and no bite.

Stretching down from the bed, Lisa picked up his jeans and T-shirt from the floor and tossed them to him. He disappeared into the bathroom and emerged a minute later, pulling on his second trainer as he hopped towards the door. At the threshold, he paused. 'I'll erm, see you at the bar, I guess,' he said to Lisa, giving her what he probably thought was a sexy wink, and saying, 'By the way, last night was—'

Moira cut him off. 'I will kill you stone dead if you finish that sentence in front of us.' He left, unwilling to test the threat.

Carina closed the door behind him and then rounded on Lisa. 'You officially have the worst taste in men. I beg you – please pick them when you're sober.'

Lisa was in the process of lighting another cigarette, so she didn't answer until the tip flamed red. 'You two are like fecking storm troopers, you know that? I'm sure that there's a planet somewhere that needs you to defend it.'

Moira plumped down on the end of the bed. 'Ignore her, Lisa. She's just jealous because she hasn't had sex for a month and her mother has cut off her allowance.'

Carina rolled her eyes. 'I'm trying to pretend I don't care that I'm skint. Makes me seem more badass. But my Clarins Flash Balm is almost done, and I can't afford to replace it.'

'Bob Geldof needs to hear about that,' Moira said, straight-faced. 'He'll have a whip round going in no time.'

Despite the fact that the paracetamol hadn't kicked in on her headache yet, that made Lisa laugh. And threw up a memory too. Her and her gran, watching *Live Aid* on TV. 'Lisa, love, go phone that number and pledge them a tenner. If they don't send it to those poor kids, then maybe that Geldof lad can use it for a haircut and a shave.'

'What about your parents? Are we going to get a visit from them?' Moira asked. 'Can't go any worse than Carina's mum.'

Lisa flicked her ash into the ashtray on her bedside table. 'My mum died when I was a kid. No idea about my dad. I was brought up by my gran. She was more than enough to replace them.'

Lisa watched Moira's face crease in sympathy. This was

exactly why she didn't tell people about her life. She'd known Carina for months before she'd shared her story and even then, she'd made it clear she never wanted to discuss it again. Obviously Carina hadn't shared the information with Moira, though.

'I'm glad you've got your gran,' Moira said, emotion oozing from her words. Lisa almost couldn't bear to say the next bit but there was no point in holding it back. It would come out at some point.

'*Had*,' she said. '*Had* my gran. She died almost five years ago.'

'Oh no, Lisa, I'm so sorry.'

Lisa stubbed her cigarette out, as Moira went on, 'You don't want to talk about this, do you?'

'Not even a bit,' she replied honestly.

Moira nodded, instinctively understanding. 'Okay, well, we love you. And that's why we're asking you to stop bringing home random guys just in case one of them really is the bloke that was robbing post offices on *Crimewatch*.'

'Point taken,' Lisa promised. 'Okay, I'm just going to shower, then I'll be ready. Where are we having breakfast?'

She watched Carina and Moira make some kind of weird eye contact.

'What? What did I say?'

Carina broke the news. 'It's 4 p.m. That's why we came to get you. It's almost time to go to work.'

Lisa groaned. This was the fourth or fifth missing day this month. 'Well, dinner then,' she shrugged, trying to act like that wasn't freaking her out. 'You guys decide. I'll be back in a minute.'

She made her way into the en suite, turned the water in the shower to hot and stood under it, leaning forward, her hands splayed against the tiled wall.

God, her head hurt. If her gran could see her now, she'd be

horrified. Netta had been so worried that Lisa would go the same way as her mum – alcohol, drugs, overdose, dead at twenty-five – that she hated to see her drink any more than two glasses of Babycham at Christmas.

This had to stop, she knew that, but it didn't help that the only time she felt good, the only time she didn't hurt, was when she was too drunk to feel the pain. That couldn't be an excuse any more though. The booze had to go. The men too. She had to clean up her act and she had to start now before she got herself into something she couldn't get out of.

Out of the shower, she dried off, brushed out her wild mane of hair and tucked a towel around her, before going back into the bedroom to get dressed. Carina and Moira had cleared the place up a bit, emptied her ashtray, folded the clothes that were on the floor, and they were now sitting on her bed, their backs leaning on the wall, working out a new harmony to Cher's 'If I Could Turn Back Time.' Tonight, they were doing a Cher tribute night at the hotel, so Moira had been working on Cher's greatest hits for the last week.

Lisa left them to it while she went into her wardrobe and selected one of her stage outfits. Long. Flowing. Usually black. Sometimes white or flowery. If Stevie Nicks ever changed her style, Lisa was going to have to buy a whole new wardrobe.

When she was dressed, they headed to a shabby but clean and cheap street joint that did amazing dim sum a few minutes away from the Star Ferry terminal. They were on their second round of the little pork dumplings, when Moira nudged her.

'Sorry if I upset you earlier by talking about... you know...'

Lisa shook her head. 'You didn't. It's just the way it is. Nothing I can do about it.'

The old familiar curl of loneliness began to tighten around her heart, and she pushed it away. She wasn't alone. She had these two friends. She had her career. She had her music. And she also had a tiny voice in her head telling her that she was going to lose it all if she didn't sort herself out. Her vows from earlier started replaying in her mind. It had to stop. She had to clean up her act. No more booze. No more blackouts. No more one-night stands. She could do this, she decided. Cold turkey. Starting today.

When they'd been fed, they took the Star Ferry across the harbour. As always, Lisa sat at the end of one of the wooden bench seats closest to the open windows, to try to catch a breeze in the 90-degree heat. A ten-minute walk at the other end got them to the hotel, and she was feeling hot, sweaty, but more positive than she had in a long time. Even the presence of the bloke from last night behind the bar couldn't burst her new bubble of optimism. It was going to be okay. She skipped her usual pre-set double Jack and Coke, then, for once, filled the bottle she always took on stage with water instead of booze. Doing this sober felt weird and scary, but it had to be done.

Her new attitude of positivity and resolve lasted all the way through her set and the audience obviously felt it because they were all in: singing, responding to her energy, riotous applause after every song. The harmonies were clearer than ever and even Carina, over on keyboards, gave her a huge grin and looked impressed. By the time they came off stage, she was drenched in sweat and high on nothing more than life.

Carina went straight off to the loos to lose the Christine McVie wig and prepare for Moira's set, but Lisa went to their usual viewing spot at the end of the bar. Moira was already there and in her 'Turn Back Time' costume – black thigh-high boots, fishnets, and black G-string body suit under a faux-leather bomber jacket that squeaked when Moira threw her arms around her. 'You killed it, doll. Fricking incredible tonight. You even managed to take my mind off the fact that this G-string is giving me a friction rash in a place you don't want to know about.'

Laughing, Lisa felt her face flush, but took the compliment. When Carina came back from the toilets, brunette again, the two of them hit the stage, Carina on piano and Moira opening with the number they'd been practising earlier. If Cher had been in the audience, she'd have taken her big sparkly head-dress off in appreciation of the vocals Moira was throwing down right now. She was fecking spectacular.

'Hey, gorgeous,' last night's mistake drawled, leaning over the bar to get closer to her. 'Usual?'

'Nope. Just a coke.' He didn't even try to hide his surprise, but she didn't care. In the cold light of day and sobriety, she'd already decided there would be no second dance with this one.

He slid the drink over to her and leaned forward again. 'So I was thinking... How about I make the thirteenth lucky for you later tonight?'

She didn't understand. 'What do you mean? I don't get it.'

'You know, lucky for some,' he answered, weakly now. He'd probably been practising that line for the last hour, and he looked crushed as he realised it had fallen flat. He gestured to the poster behind him, stuck with tape to the bar mirror.

Cher Tribute Night. 13 September.

'Today's the thirteenth,' he said, 'so—'

She didn't listen to the rest, because the curl of her demons was back, and it was squeezing the breath right out of her. Today was the 13 September.

The one day of the year that should be hers, should be special. But did something really exist when no one knew about it? Obviously not, because the black cloud that was suddenly enveloping her came with a reminder that not a single person on this earth either knew or cared that today was her birthday.

'I've changed my mind,' she told whatever his name was, sliding her glass of coke back towards him. 'Can you put a double Jack Daniels in there? And sure, I'm up for a bit of fun later.'

Fuck being on the wagon. Fuck being alone.

It was hard to care about your life when you had absolutely nothing to lose.

10

WEDNESDAY, 2 JULY, 2025 – HONG KONG

Moira

The ring of the room's doorbell woke Moira from a fitful sleep. She hadn't even made it to bed the previous evening and her bones ached from the discomfort of spending the night on the couch. Last thing she remembered after Carina and Stevie left the room last night, was showering, then sitting on the sofa, looking out over Victoria Harbour and the lights of Kowloon on the other side of the water, drowning in the memories of Lisa until sleep eventually came.

Their friend was dead. Not even out of her fifties and she was gone. And the irony that they were so close to seeing each other again would haunt Moira for ever. Lisa had been planning to meet them. She'd decided to come, booked it all and she was only three weeks away from being here when she was so tragically taken from them. How was that fair? More importantly, why had they waited this long? Sure, she was on the cruises, and Lisa was in Ireland, and Carina was all over the bloody place, but still, if they'd really tried, made it a priority, they'd have made it happen. Now it was too late. Now all they had was her poor daughter, coming all this way to tell them that her mother was gone. Stevie had stayed with them for a couple of hours, sharing the whole story of how her mum died, but by the time she'd explained everything, the poor lass's eyes were almost closed with tiredness, tears and jet lag. Moira had so many questions, so many things to say, especially when Stevie had shared that Lisa had never told her that she'd lived in Hong Kong or mentioned Moira and Carina to her, but last night hadn't been the time. It had been too emotional. Too shocking. Her heart had been broken for Lisa and for her poor lass, so both her and Carina had kept their thoughts to themselves and just let Stevie tell them what had happened, until she was wiped out.

'Stevie, love, why don't we call it a night and meet again in the morning? It's been such a long day for you. There will be plenty of time for talking this week. That's if you'd like to meet up with us again.'

Stevie had nodded, a sad smile on a face that Moira still couldn't get used to seeing on anyone other than her gorgeous pal from the early nineties. Stevie had hugged them both, then left for her room, leaving Moira and Carina to talk until Carina's eyes were closing too and she'd gone off to bed as well. They'd barely drunk the wine that had been a welcome gift from the hotel, hadn't opened the fruit basket or cookies either – that had all felt too celebratory for the saddest of conversations.

A second ring of the doorbell cut through her thoughts, and Moira pulled her hotel robe tighter around her and went to answer it, hearing the clink of the room service trolley before she got there. Another vague memory. Carina calling down last night and ordering breakfast for them to be served here this morning at 10 a.m.

Swinging open the door, she saw that the waiter was right on time. He wheeled the trolley in and left it where she requested, in front of the double doors out onto her own private roof terrace. One of her many thoughts last night was that Lisa would love this. The three of them should be out there right now having their morning coffee, revelling in how far they'd come and making plans for how they were going to spend one of the best weeks of their lives.

Instead...

Throat closing with grief, she blocked the thought as she signed the room service bill, adding a generous tip as always before the waiter toddled off happy, gently closing the door behind him. Generous tipping was second nature. Nothing outlandish, because she didn't have a penny in savings left to her name. Most of her earnings had gone to supporting her parents, then Ollie, until he got his big break ten years ago. Since then, she'd allowed herself some treats, but squirrelled most of her cash away before blowing it all on a down payment on a lovely little one bedroom, riverside flat in Weirbridge, a village just outside Glasgow, that she'd bought last month. The bank would only give her a ten-year mortgage due to her age, so she'd put down a hefty deposit so that her monthly payments were manageable. Ollie had wanted to buy it for her, but of course, she wouldn't let him. Her salary at the academy covered it, while leaving enough that a few decent tips wouldn't bankrupt her. She'd been in the hospitality industry, albeit behind a microphone, for decades and she knew how hard most of the people in that industry worked, and how much the extra tips meant to them. Besides, it was only money and she couldn't take it with her.

That thought brought her back to Lisa. She had so many questions, but there was one that had woken her up after a couple of hours on the couch, and then kept her awake until she'd finally dozed off again around dawn. One that she had to ask Stevie, yet she wasn't sure she'd have the courage to hear the answer. Before she could play it back in her mind, the doorbell rang again.

Moira opened it and Carina came in looking both ashen, and annoyingly stylish, in white palazzo trousers and a black T-shirt, accessorised with a little cream cross-body bag and huge sunglasses. Moira had always envied effortless class because it took her several hours, a lot of make-up, a couple of rash, unaffordable purchases on an online shop and a good clothes steamer to look like she'd just casually thrown herself together at the last minute.

Moira instinctively wrapped her arms around her friend. 'How are you doing, pal?'

Carina sniffed, and then wiped away tears under her glasses. 'Awful. You?'

'Same. I still can't believe it.' They both made their way over to the room service trolley, where Carina poured them coffees, while Moira took the cloche off the plates of Danish pastries and fruit. Not that she had any kind of appetite.

Carina held her mug in both hands. 'That poor girl. Broke my heart to listen to her.'

'Mine too. And I just... I just keep thinking this isn't right. Lisa should be here with us now. And then I don't understand how I can miss her more now. We hadn't seen each other for over thirty years and yet I'm feeling bereft today. Am I just being self-indulgent?'

Carina shook her head. 'No. Because for all those years we always knew we'd see each other again one day. It was like the light at the end of a long tunnel, and we were almost there, out in the daylight. That's what we've lost. We've lost the Lisa that we loved, and we've lost that promise of our happy ending.'

Moira groaned. 'I hate it when you talk sense. And Lisa would be rolling her eyes and reaching for a Jack Daniels about now. She always said you were the grown-up in the gang because you were always the sensible one.'

Carina shrugged. 'Maybe being grown-up is overrated.'

Moira was tempted to take her coffee out into the sunshine, but she knew her west of Scotland skin would frazzle in seconds, so instead, she took her cup and sat back down on the sofa.

'We didn't even get a chance to talk about you and Spencer last night. I'm sorry.'

Carina joined her. 'Don't be. Not a single part of me wants to discuss it. I'm going with denial for today. Maybe tomorrow too. I only switched my phone on for a few seconds to check if either of my girls had called or texted – they hadn't, so I'm guessing they don't know anything about it yet. Spencer must have explained my absence away to Imogen and that's fine. I'm not going to be the one to shatter her illusions about her father or her friend. I'll leave that up to them. I ignored all Spencer's calls and texts, so that means that the only person who knows where I am is his brother, Ben.'

'I remember Ben! Sexy? Thick dark hair?'

Carina gave a rueful shrug. 'All of it gone now and I don't know about sexy – I never looked at him that way.'

'Well, I did. Lisa too. Both of us had a soft spot for him. He and Lisa came close to having a fling but she said he was too nice for her so I don't think they ever got together. Don't quote me on that.'

Carina's eyes widened. 'How do I not know this?'

'Probably because you were so obsessed with Spencer that everything else was invisible to you.'

Carina picked up a piece of melon from the fruit plate. 'And look where that got me.'

'I'm sorry, love. But anyway, if you're going with denial, then I will too. Let's just park that to one side until you're ready to think about it, and in the meantime, see what we can do to help Stevie. Is it just me that loves that that's her name?'

'No, I love it too,' Carina said. 'Makes me think it was Lisa paying homage to our time here.'

A knock at the door interrupted them, and Moira felt her stomach lurch. She wasn't ready for this. Not when she was still fighting a tsunami of anxiety about the question in her mind.

'That'll be her now,' she said. 'And look at the state of me – still in my dressing gown. Can you get the door while I throw some clothes on?'

'Yes, ma'am.' Carina saluted her.

Moira bustled off into the bedroom and yanked open her suitcase. Somehow flowery frocks didn't seem right for today, so she went for a navy sundress, that would hopefully keep her cool while shielding her freckles from the sun.

After a two-minute shower, she brushed her teeth, washed her face, pulled her hair back into a bun and slapped on some deodorant and tinted moisturiser before checking her reflection in the mirror. Bugger. Her eyes were so swollen that no amount of cucumber face serum would fix them. Not that it mattered. Right now, the only important thing was taking care of that lass next door.

Feeling not quite stylish, but at least clean and presentable, she slipped her feet into a pair of pale blue espadrilles and went back into the lounge, where Stevie was now sitting on the sofa with Carina, coffee mug in hand.

'Good morning, pet. How are you today? And aye, I know that's a daft question.'

Stevie gave her a warm smile. 'It's strange, and I know this is going to sound crazy, but I woke up this morning with an odd feeling of lightness. I mean, I'm still confused about why my mum kept all this from me, and more than a bit gobsmacked about it all, but weirdly I feel like I'm supposed to be here. Like I was supposed to meet you both. If my mum had got knocked down at any other time in the last thirty years, I'd never have learned about all this. Does that sound crazy?'

'No,' Moira said honestly. 'In a strange way, I feel like maybe we were supposed to be here for you too. Unless...'

'Unless what?' Carina asked her.

Moira's felt her anxiety rise to the surface again, heard the question that had been revolving in her head all night, and then realised that there was no way she was going to be able to keep it in a moment longer.

'Stevie, I need to ask you something that's been playing on my mind, and I need you to promise you'll be honest with me. No matter what, I won't hold it against you, because it'll be nothing that I haven't thought myself.'

Moira watched as Carina's expression turned to puzzlement, while Stevie leaned forward, put her mug down on the coffee table, and fixed her gaze on Moira. 'Okay, I promise.'

Moira took a deep breath, then blurted it all out.

'I keep coming back to what you said about your mum crossing the road to the post office, and that she had a letter addressed to me in her bag. Well...' Moira paused, struggling to put her thoughts into words. 'The thing is, if I hadn't sent her the invitation to come here, she wouldn't have written a reply. And if she hadn't written a reply, then she wouldn't be going to the post office. And if she hadn't been going to the post office, she wouldn't have been crossing that road and she wouldn't have been knocked down by a minibus driver with the sun in his eyes.'

Joining the dots, that train of thought made perfect sense to her. But if she was going to blame herself, then she had to know if Stevie blamed her too. And if so, what could she ever do to even begin to make up for it?

'So I need to ask you... Do you think it's my fault that your mum died?'

11

CARINA

Oh. Dear. Lord.

Carina's jaw almost hit the floor when she realised what Moira was asking. It wasn't even a possibility that had occurred to Carina, but now she could see where Moira was coming from, and if it were true, well, how would her friend ever live with the sadness of knowing that something she'd done had resulted, so tragically and accidentally, in the death of their friend?

'Oh, Moira, no,' Stevie blurted, 'Absolutely not. I'm so sorry that thought even came into your head.'

All the colour had drained from Moira's face and she just looked utterly devastated. 'But I'd understand if you did blame me. To be honest, it's hard to see it any other way.'

Carina watched as Stevie slowly rocked her head from side to side. 'No, no, no. That thought never crossed my mind, Moira, because the other thing in her bag was her electricity bill. She was going to the post office to pay it, as she always did, because she refused to do anything online.'

'But maybe it was to do both?'

'No. Because the other thing you need to know is that her

letter to you already had a stamp on it. She could have posted it in any of the other post boxes in the village. I promise, Moira, your invitation to come here wasn't the reason she was going to the post office that day.'

Moira took the biggest intake of breath and then blew out her cheeks as she exhaled. 'Thank you.' Carina saw her eyes well up, as the relief consumed her. 'I barely slept a wink for thinking about that.'

'I thought you were just always that attractive in the mornings,' Carina teased, desperate to dispel the tension and help Moira shake off the worry. Sarcasm and mild insults had always been their love language and the way to Moira's heart. This morning wasn't any different. Moira's pursed lips and roll of the eyes told Carina that she was going to be okay. Sad, but at least unburdened by guilt that any of this could be her fault.

Moira refilled all of their mugs from the large coffee pot on the room service tray. It was one of those insulated ones, so it was still piping hot. Carina felt her stomach begin to rumble, and reached for a croissant as she asked, 'So, Stevie, what are your plans while you're here?'

Before Stevie could answer, the landline in the suite rang and Moira reached for the phone sitting on the rosewood side table next to her. 'Hello?'

Carina was about to continue the conversation with Stevie, when Moira took the phone away from her ear and held it out to her. 'Carina, it's for you. Apparently, I'm your personal secretary now.'

Carina got up and took the phone with a dry, lofty, 'Thank you. But you're going to have to improve your attitude if you want me to keep you on my staff.'

She put the phone to her ear, while Moira swapped positions, taking the place she'd just vacated on the couch, next to Stevie. 'Hello?'

'Hey, it's me. Your travel buddy.'

'Oh, thank God, Ben. For a minute I thought Spencer had already tracked me down.' That wouldn't have surprised her at all. She'd only switched her phone on for a few moments and she'd ignored the missed calls from him, refused to listen to her voicemails, and had zero interest in reading his texts, but considering the staff would have told him that she left in a car to go to the airport with Ben, he'd possibly made an educated guess that she'd be in Hong Kong. Although, her hotel room downstairs had been put on Ben's credit card, so Spencer would have no idea where she was staying. For that matter... 'How did you know to ask for this room?'

'I asked reception to try yours first, but there was no answer. You said you were meeting Moira here, so she was my next try. Took me a minute to remember her surname, but it came to me. Used to be all over the posters in the Harbour Lights bar.'

The memory made Carina smile. 'Yes, it did.'

'Anyway, I won't keep you, but I just wanted to give you a heads up that Spencer suspected you came to Hong Kong, but he thought you were staying at my place.' Ben had a beautiful apartment in a brand-new high-rise right on the waterfront in Central, just a couple of miles away from where she was now. 'I put him right on that and told him I left you at Dubai Airport and have no idea where you were headed from there. Actually, I might have suggested that you mentioned going to Shanghai to see Erin. Or back to London to see your dad. I think it's probably bought you a bit of time, but I don't know how much.'

'Thanks, Ben. I just don't want to deal with him right now and I don't know when I will, so I appreciate your lies on my behalf.'

'Least I can do. I told him he was a daft prick and a disgrace for what he did, so I'm probably not up there with people he'd turn to now. That should keep him out of Hong Kong too.'

Despite the awfulness of the situation, she couldn't help but be amused by his defiance of his brother. The two of them had worked for the family business all their lives, but they were very different characters. Spencer was the one who brought the ambition and the big ideas that pushed the company forward. Ben was the cool head that implemented the plans and ran the financial side of the operation. Out of work, though, they reluctantly tolerated each other, their personalities too wildly different for them to be true friends as well as brothers. Spencer saw every man as a competitor, a rival to be the best, to be the winner. Ben had zero interest in the game, preferring to just enjoy his life on his terms. Once upon a time, Carina had been wildly attracted to Spencer's drive and the excitement that he brought into every room. She wasn't sure when that had dissipated, but if she were being honest with herself, it was well and truly gone by the time she caught him having sex with someone else in her newly decorated guest bathroom. Now, she was struggling to even care. In fact, if she hadn't discovered Spencer with Arabella, she'd be in London right now on an anniversary trip with a man who was screwing around, and Moira would be here dealing with the news about Lisa on her own. In that one, tiny way, her faithless, deplorable, excuse for a husband had done her a favour.

Last night, when she'd gone to bed, she would have expected to have spent her first night post-adultery fretting about her marriage, her future, the fact that her whole life had just imploded. Yet, every time she closed her eyes, all she saw was Lisa, on stage in the bar downstairs, her gravelly, exquisite voice singing the hell out of 'Don't Stop.' Or 'Rhiannon.' Or 'Silver Springs.'

It was like everything had been put in perspective and suddenly her problems seemed meaningless, next to the loss of the incredible Lisa Dixon.

'Okay, thank you. Keep him at bay for as long as you can. I've got no desire to see or speak to him.'

'Ever?'

Carina wasn't sure she knew the answer to that question. Was there a way to come back from this? And did she want to? She didn't even want to think about that right now.

'I don't know. I need time to think about it.'

'Take all the time you need. Look, I'm just about to head into a meeting, so I need to go. Call me if you need anything. And tell Moira and Lisa that I said hi. I'd love to see them both again, so let's try and tie up at some point.'

Damn. On the plane, she'd let him read the invitation, so he knew that the trip had been at Moira's instigation, and that Lisa had been invited too. He'd obviously assumed that they'd all made it. Now wasn't the time to explain why Lisa wasn't here, not with Stevie sitting across the room. She didn't want to add to the poor soul's sadness. Better to call him back later and tell him the whole story.

'I will do... and Ben... thank you.'

'Anytime. Always told you that you married the wrong brother.'

It was their inside joke, the one they'd repeated a million times over the decades, but today, for the first time, she wondered if there was some truth in there. Maybe she had.

She hung up and put the phone back on the base unit that sat on the beautiful table that matched the rosewood desk in the corner of the huge suite. The whole space was stunning. Floor to ceiling windows on two sides. A wrap around terrace. A separate bedroom with 1,000-thread-count sheets, no doubt. This was exactly the kind of room that she and Spencer would always stay in when they travelled. Ironic that the first time she travelled on her own, she was staying in a room so small she tripped over her own shoes this morning. And even more ironic that she really didn't care. Moira had offered to have her move her things into the suite and use the sofa bed in the living room, but she'd gratefully declined. Her own room was a welcome breathing space while she worked out what she was going to do with her life.

'Ben said hello, Moira,' she told her friend as she rejoined them on the corner sofa, pulling her legs up underneath her as she sat down. 'My brother-in-law,' she explained to Stevie. 'He lives in Hong Kong and was just calling to check on me.' She realised she hadn't told Stevie about the incident that had been the catalyst for coming here. What was the etiquette for telling your friend's adult daughter about a salacious incident in your life?

'That's kind of him. Did he know my mum too?' The question caught her off guard, but thankfully Moira stepped in with her usual frankness. 'He did. We were just talking earlier about how both your mum and I had a crush on him. Not that I stood a chance with your mum around. She was the most lusted-after woman on the island back then.'

Carina noticed that Stevie flinched. Maybe Moira's usual frankness was a bit too much today.

'Sorry,' Stevie said, shaking her head, 'but I just can't picture my mum being the young, carefree girl that you describe. It's such a world apart from the woman I knew.'

'In what way?' Carina asked, surprised and genuinely interested.

'My mum was cautious. Reserved. She didn't drink. She

didn't smoke. She divorced my dad when I was a kid, and never – as far as I know – met anyone else. She didn't socialise much, so she didn't really have many friends and definitely no close ones. She was just always… safe. Yep, that's the best word for her. Never took risks, never took chances. All she wanted was a quiet life, in her little village, with no drama, and…' she hesitated, and Carina could see she was struggling with how much she should divulge.

'To be honest with you, it caused a rift between us when I was a teenager because she didn't want me to go out, or party with friends, or have fun or do anything even remotely exciting. She just wanted to keep me wrapped in cotton wool, and she was permanently worried that something awful would happen to me. I ended up leaving home and going to university in Glasgow because I wanted to live my life. I always got the impression that she'd never done that. I thought she'd always just led a super-sheltered existence. And then when I saw the photo that you'd enclosed with the letter…'

She didn't have to say any more than that for Carina to know what she was thinking. The woman in the photo bore no resemblance to the mother she'd just described. And likewise, the woman Stevie was describing was not the Lisa they'd known.

Carina and Moira exchanged a glance of mutual astonishment, before Stevie went on. 'That's why I wanted to come and meet you both. Because I feel like there's a whole person there who I never knew and I'd like you to tell me about *her*.'

The last words caught in Stevie's throat and Carina ached for her. This woman was only a couple of years older than Imogen and Erin, and she couldn't even bear to think about them being in a situation like this. And if they were, if the tables were turned and they were sitting in front of Moira and Lisa, what would she want her friends to do?

She raised her eyes so that they met Moira's and despite more than three decades having passed since they'd last had a telepathic conversation, their facial expressions communicated in a way that they both knew what each other was thinking.

'You know, Stevie, when we were all together here we were twenty-three years old. We had a moment in time that was incredible and exciting and wild. But we weren't perfect people. We made so many mistakes and there were times when we didn't have our proudest moments. What if you don't like everything that you hear?'

Stevie pondered that for a minute and Carina could see what a lovely thoughtful woman she was. No matter what their relationship, Lisa had raised someone to be proud of.

'Then at least I'll truly know my mother. All of her. Not just the parts she trusted me enough to share.'

Ouch. It didn't take expert perception to see that there had been issues between Stevie and her mum. Carina wanted, with every part of her, to help.

Moira was the first to cave though, as she threw up her hands. 'Oh, love, that got me right in the heart. Carina, what time is it?'

Carina checked her watch. 'Almost twelve.'

Moira nodded. 'I think the young ones call that "day-drinking o'clock." You pour the prosecco and get on to room service for some chips and mayonnaise, and I'll go get my photograph albums. Time to let Stevie in on a few secrets.'

12

STEVIE

For a moment she'd thought that Carina and Moira were going to fob her off with sanitised niceties and refuse to share that part of their lives with her and she wouldn't have blamed them. But no. Carina had poured the sparkling wine, and Moira had come back with two photo albums. The chips and mayonnaise had been delivered, and Carina was taking advantage of this to tease Moira. 'Chips? I take it you've still never heard of an avocado then, Moira? Maybe a nice salad didn't tempt you?'

'Ignore her,' Moira said to Stevie. 'She was brought up without any appreciation of the humble chip. It's a shame really. Being that posh has deprived her of so much joy.'

Stevie was already coming to realise that these women had a relationship built on a basis of friendship and affectionately mocking each other for laughs. It reminded her of the easy banter and bond she'd always had with Caleb.

When she'd got back to her room last night, she'd received a text from Caleb saying:

> NO CONTACT FOR FIFTEEN HOURS. SEND PROOF OF LIFE IMMEDIATELY.

She'd given him a quick call to fill him in on everything that had happened since he'd dropped her at Dublin Airport, before carrying on with Gilda and Keli to the ferry. They'd got home safely and when she'd phoned him, Caleb was heading to work to start his evening shift. The time difference was taking a bit of getting used to. As was the fact that she was here. When she'd got the call about her mum and left the hospital that day, she would never have dreamt that just three weeks later she'd be in a flash hotel in Hong Kong with two strangers. 'You know, I keep thinking how much better mum's life would have been if these two women had been in it for the last thirty-odd years. Why did she choose solitude and a quiet life? None of this makes sense, Caleb.'

'Maybe that's because you don't know the whole story yet. Keep an open mind, hon. And if you need me, just holler. I've got a credit card and I'm not afraid to use it.'

She'd hung up, thinking that everyone should have a mate like that. And he was right. Here she was, her mind open, and ready to listen.

When they were organised and had chips in hand, Moira kicked off with, 'Where do you want us to start?'

'At the beginning, I guess,' Stevie said.

Carina had responded to that by explaining that her and mum had both been here for several months before Moira arrived, living in a run-down hotel on the other side of the harbour.

'And what were you doing here? Just working in bars or something?'

Both Moira and Carina had looked at her like she'd grown

another head. 'We were all performers, signed to a crappy agency that put us up in that hellish accommodation and paid us buttons, but we did it because we loved it and we were cool as anything. Of course, those were the days when I could get into size 12 leather trousers, and I still had full mobility in my hips.'

What???? Just when Stevie thought she had a handle on this story it took a sharp left turn. 'What do you mean, "performers"? Like, exotic dancers?'

Moira nearly spluttered her prosecco across the room. 'My hips weren't quite that bendy, I'm afraid.'

Carina took up the story. 'Moira was a singer, she had a nightly show in the bar downstairs – that's why we're staying here – and she used to pack them in. I was her piano player...'

'And what did my mum do?'

For the second time, she'd stunned the two of them into silence. She was beginning to feel like she was in some kind of parallel universe, where everyone knew what was going on except her. Which was, actually, a pretty accurate way to describe this.

'Stevie, how do you think you got your name?' Carina asked her, and Stevie could sense it was a loaded question, but she couldn't quite understand why.

'Because my mum's favourite song was "Landslide" by Stevie Nicks and she thought that was a cool name.'

'Oh Jesus, Carina, you'll need to take this one,' Moira said, fanning her face with her hand. 'I'm feeling a hot flush coming on and I was through the menopause years ago.'

Carina visibly took a sharp breath, before she began to speak.

'My other job – because I had two gigs, unlike this slacker here,' she gestured to Moira, 'Was that I played the role of Christine McVie in a Fleetwood Mac tribute act.'

'I bet my mum loved that,' Stevie interjected.

Carina was still speaking calmly but clearly, as if she were explaining a really difficult maths problem. Or nuclear physics.

'She did. But that's because your mum played the part of Stevie Nicks in the band. And every single night she went out on the stage and she was – excuse my language – fricking sensational.'

Now it was Stevie's turn to splutter. 'My mum was a singer?'

'You didn't know this?'

'No.' Scratch the earlier statement – this was far more complicated than nuclear physics.

'Wait... You never heard Lisa sing?' That came from Moira, who was now pulling at the neck of her navy sundress so that she could fan her chest.

'Only a few times late at night when I was in bed. I'd hear a record go on and then I'd hear her humming away or singing a few bars. I had no idea she'd ever done that professionally, never mind be... "fricking sensational".'

'She was more than that,' Moira said, wistfully. 'She commanded every stage she stepped on. No one could take their eyes off her because she had that thing that only the brilliant ones have. If she'd been starting out in the last ten years or so she'd have gone on *The X Factor* and she'd have won the whole damn thing. She was that good. I can't believe she gave it up.' That last statement was aimed at Carina, who looked just as astonished.

'I can't believe that's what she did in the first place,' Stevie replied, dumbfounded. She just wanted to sob. Her mum was a singer? When were the surprises going to stop? 'Do you have any photos of her on stage?'

Moira flicked through a couple of pages in the album and then turned it around. Stevie's breath got caught in her throat. It was like looking in a mirror. The face. The height. Even the style of clothes that she wore. Stevie loved to shop in vintage boutiques and she'd no idea she'd somehow been channelling her mother and her namesake in their younger days.

'You look so like her,' Moira said, her eyes welling up again. She started fanning her face again. 'Jesus, I'm a mess. I'm sorry. I promise I'm usually very calm and collected and in full control of my emotions. Except when I watch *Call The Midwife*, but that's only to be expected.'

Stevie was staring at the photo again. 'People have always said that we're alike and I could see the similarities, but there was such a big age difference that I never really understood.'

'Do you look like your dad too?' Carina asked.

'I don't think so, although I haven't seen him since I was really young. After he and mum got divorced, he went to Canada and built a whole new family there. I speak to him a couple of times a year on the phone – birthdays and Christmas – and I've thought about going over a couple of times, but he's never seemed particularly keen so it hasn't happened. He's pretty disinterested, to be honest, but that's never bothered me because it's just the way it's always been. Mum said we were far better off without him, just the two of us against the world.' That was all true. What she didn't say was that at the same time, her mum kept an emotional distance from her too. That there was an anxiety there that Stevie couldn't explain.

'He never mentioned that Mum was a singer, so maybe he didn't know either. Maybe she just kept this whole chapter of her life a secret from everyone. I can't believe she kept this hidden from me. All of it, but especially the singing. You know, the crazy thing is that when I was a kid, I wanted to be Britney Spears. Or one of the Spice Girls. I had a really good voice, always got the lead parts in the school shows, and I wanted to sing, but Mum wouldn't let me. She said it was a waste of time, and I should do something more useful. She pushed me into sport, running, nutrition – all the things that were good for me. And yet all that time there was this.' She pointed at the photo of her mum behind a microphone, her eyes alive, her mouth open, her hair drenched in sweat, her body curved as if she was belting out a high note. She looked like an absolute rock star. Her mum. Lisa Dixon. From their tiny little village in Ireland. A rock star. 'I don't think I'm ever going to understand this.'

Neither of them argued with her, and she suspected they felt the same.

They spent the rest of the afternoon looking through all the photos, the ladies taking it in turns to give some background, to tell her an anecdote or explain who was in the picture if there were other people there. Her mum on stage. Her mum on the Star Ferry (she'd read about that, but she hadn't ventured out to see it yet). Her mum at various places on the island. Her mum in bed. In a bar. Snogging some guy. Snogging another guy. Having drinks with her friends. Dancing on tables. Dancing in a nightclub. Dancing in the street. So much dancing, so much singing, so much laughing, so much drinking. It was almost as if she'd packed her whole life into one year and then become a totally different person. The medical professional inside her was beginning to wonder if Lisa had taken a bang to the head. Why give this up to return to her home town, get married, settle down and live an anonymous life? What happened to her to prompt such a change in direction? Why give up a good time for an existence of uneventful solitude? Definitely a bang to the head in there somewhere. Or had something awful happened? Something that made her return to Ireland and change her whole life?

Room service had made two more trips with sustenance by the time they'd turned the last leaf of the albums, and Stevie felt exhausted. She could see that the others did too. Moira suggested they get some fresh air, by taking their drinks out onto the roof terrace and Stevie went on out while Moira and Carina refilled their glasses.

The sun was beginning to go down over the harbour when they joined her just a few moments later, taking the two loungers to her left.

Carina inhaled the night air and stretched out her body. Stevie would bet a week's wages that she did yoga, Pilates and had a personal trainer. It was pretty obvious that she was very wealthy. It wasn't just the cut-glass accent. It was the Hermes sandals and the YSL sunglasses, while Moira had already shared that she'd bought her dress in the H&M sale.

Carina turned to face her. 'I just realised that I asked you earlier about your plans for this week and we got interrupted before you could answer.'

It was a great question, but one that she didn't have an answer to. 'I'm not really sure. I hadn't actually got past getting here and meeting you both, and finding out what my mum was up to. I think that was as much as my poor overloaded brain could handle this week. But now that I'm here, I think I'll perhaps explore the island. Maybe check out some of the places in those photos of Mum, just to share that with her. Does that sound crazy?'

'Not at all,' Moira said, with an understanding smile. 'The thing is, though, when I planned this week, it was all about a bit of nostalgia. I wanted to revisit my past and see if I could recreate those feelings that I had back then. That excitement and optimism that gets kicked out of you by life as you get older.'

'If this is supposed to be a motivational speech, you're doing a terrible job,' Carina cut in, deadpan. 'Don't ever do a Ted Talk.'

Once again, Moira handled the dig with pursed lips of amusement. Stevie loved the easy banter between them.

'Anywaaaay,' Moira said pointedly, with a bit of side-eye in her friend's direction, 'We were talking inside, and we wondered if you'd like to spend some time with us? We can show you what your mum's life here was like. Take you to those places she went to and share what happened there. We did some pretty cool things back then – be great to go back and do it all again.'

Stevie was incredibly touched, but she immediately realised she couldn't accept.

'Thank you so much for the offer, but I couldn't do that because it would be such an imposition on your holiday. I could tell by your letter how much you were looking forward to this week, Moira, and how much you wanted to share it with your friends. And the fact that it actually got my mum out of the house shows how much it meant to her too. I can't gatecrash that – it wouldn't be fair.'

This time it was Carina who stepped in with the Ted Talk, Part Two.

'Stevie, you wouldn't be gatecrashing because there are no expectations for us this week. It's not like we had some spiritual event planned. The truth is that we're here because Moira is having a mid-life crisis and a few nights ago, on my thirty-fourth wedding anniversary, I caught my husband having sex. And not with me. So trust me when I say you're not spoiling anything. We'd love to have you here with us.'

'Oh bloody hell – I'm so sorry about your husband.'

Carina sighed. 'Me too. But that's for another day. Tell us you'll come hang out with us and let us share endless stories about your lovely mum. To be honest, it would maybe help us to deal with what's happened too.'

'Are you sure?'

'We're absolutely sure.'

She thought about it, but only for a second because she was still desperate to know the answers to so many questions that were floating around in her mind.

What was her mum's life like here? Why did she leave? And what happened here that was so terrible she never talked about it again?

13

OCTOBER 1990 – HONG KONG

Moira

Moira was lying on the floor of her room, thinking that if anyone walked in right now they'd think she was indulging in some weird sexual fetish. Actually, she was just on her back, with a wire coat hanger attached to the slider on the zip of her jeans, because she was trying to pull the fricking thing up. She'd been here for ten minutes and it was still only halfway and threatening to burst at any second.

'Nate! NATE!!!!!' she yelled at the top of her lungs. There were too many crap things about her room to list them all, but two brilliant factors made up for them – the first was that she was between Carina and Lisa, which was mostly great, except for when Lisa was having loud sex with whatever random bloke she'd brought home from the bar or Carina was playing that classical stuff she loved to listen to at the crack of dawn. Moira had already demanded that at least one of them buy her earmuffs for Christmas. The second excellent thing was that the reception desk was just a few feet along the corridor, so if she shouted loud enough, Nate – their very own Michael Hutchence lookalike – could hear her. Or maybe not.

'Na—' she yelled again, but cut off mid word when her door flew open and there he was, looking more than a little wide-eyed and panic stricken, especially when he spotted her on the floor. 'Moira! Are you okay? What's happened? Aw, shit, I'm crap at First Aid.'

'I don't need First Aid, I need to lose the five pounds I've put on here because I'm eating too much fricking dim sum. Can you help me pull this up? I'm stuck. Urgh, this is mortifying,' she added, staring straight up at the ceiling. 'And don't you dare mention my bra – my mother made me buy it. I think she was trying to make sure I don't have sex until I'm fifty.' As if there wasn't enough indignity, today was washing day, all her sexy bras and knickers were in the machine, so she was wearing a massive cream bra with horrible clips down the front that should have been labelled 'contraception' in the shop because it was sure to kill any sexy notions stone dead.

Seconds passed and there was no sound, no movement, nothing. Had he buggered off and left her here in her moment of need? She strained her neck, chin forward, focused her gaze on the door and...

He was still there. But now there was a wide grin on that way too bloody handsome face of his.

'What?' she asked, exasperated. 'Are you stuck too?'

'Nope, just enjoying this too much to do anything about it,' he said, laughter punctuating every word.

'Noooo, don't make me laugh,' she begged, giggling, 'I'll do myself a permanent damage. Take pity on me. Please.'

He finally caved, still chuckling, and crossed the room to her. 'Okay, how do you want me to do this?'

Moira didn't want to say that she hadn't actually thought

through a plan, so she improvised. 'Put one foot on either side of my hips, then try to pull the two sides of the denim together and I'll yank the zip up. Squeeze, hold, pull.'

'If you ever give up singing there'll be a job for you on those dodgy sex chat lines. Although, you might want to work on your voice. No one ever understands that accent of yours.'

She gave him a playful punch on the calf, because it was the closest body part she could reach. 'Don't make me laugh. Don't make me laugh,' she pleaded again.

The thing was, he always made her laugh. That's why – after Carina and Lisa – he was her very favourite person here. It wasn't a crush, exactly. There were a couple of regulars who came into the bar that fell into the 'innocent crush but I would if they asked me' category. There was Zak, the only guy behind the bar who Lisa hadn't brought home with her yet. And a cute guy called Ben, who usually came in on a Friday night with all the guys from his office. Other than that, in the three months she'd been here there had been a few after-work snogs, and a brief fling with a Welsh guy who was on a short term posting to the British army barracks on the island, but she hadn't found anyone with the potential to sweep her off her feet yet.

'Right, I'm in position. Are you ready?' Nate asked.

Moira nodded. 'Ready.'

'Okay, go!' With that he pushed the sides of her hips inwards, she pulled the hanger and... The zip slid straight up to the top.

'Yasssss! Thank God. Okay, now you have to get me up, but I can't bend so it's going to be like dead lifting a 140lb weight. Just warning you.'

He was laughing again and Moira realised the contraceptive qualities of her giant bra only worked one way because she was absolutely definitely feeling stirrings of attraction and they were absolutely definitely taking her by surprise. There was no doubt he was gorgeous, sexy and kind – he'd carried Lisa up those stairs several times when she had passed out, and he always made sure they were up in time for work – but she'd firmly put him in the 'friends' zone' because unlike all the guys at the bar, he'd given absolutely no flirty vibes towards any of them. Not a single lingering stare, chat up line, or innuendo.

'Ah, you're killing me here,' he murmured, and Moira didn't understand. He hadn't even started to pull her up so he couldn't be feeling faint yet.

'Why? Did you put your back out?'

'No, I— Hang on.' He got up and took a few steps back towards the door.

'Tell me you're not about to leave me like this,' Moira said, panic setting in.

'Nope, but if I stay that close to you, I'll... I'll...'

'You'll what?'

He threw his hands up, apologetically. 'Moira, I want to kiss you, okay? There. I said it. I want to kiss you, and I know that's crazy, because we're mates, but that's how it is. And then I come in here and you... you're *like that*, and what's a bloke supposed to do?'

'Kiss me,' she blurted, in a voice that sounded so strange she had to rewind and check it was definitely hers.

He didn't move. 'Are you sure?'

'Seriously, Nate, my jeans are so tight I'm lying here like a plank, I can barely breathe and my internal organs are shutting down – if you don't kiss me now you might never get another chance.' It was so hard to laugh in these jeans, but she could definitely do the grin that was on her face right now, one that was only wiped off when he came back to her, crouched down and kissed her. Once. Twice.

'I think we're going to be here for a while,' he whispered, his fingers stroking the side of her face.

The grin was back, and her eyes were locked on his. 'I think I'm okay with that.'

This was like one of those movie scenes with fireworks and streamers and cheering crowds, only it was all going on inside her head. The only reason she hadn't allowed herself to be attracted to him was because she hadn't thought for a second that he was interested in her. Sure, they spent loads of time together. And yes, sometimes they'd sit up all night talking or playing cards or just listening to music on his CD player. And okay, he had started to come to their shows on his nights off. But Moira had just assumed he had a thing for Lisa, like every other male on the island.

Apparently not. Because he was kissing her again and oh, it felt good and now his fingers were trailing along her stomach and—

The door flew open and Carina and Lisa charged in.

'Eeeew, my eyes,' came a howl from Posh Pal.

Lisa was more supportive with, 'About time. He's been wanting to do that for months.'

'Really?' Moira asked him.

'Maybe.' Nate admitted sheepishly.

Lisa cut right in. 'It's all he talks about, he's fancied you for ages, but he swore me to secrecy so I couldn't tell you. Okay, that's you up to date. Jesus, what kind of bra is that? It's fecking huge.'

'Months?' Moira asked him, still stuck on that bit and trying to control a second round of fireworks in her head. He was now just grinning at her with a daft smile on his gorgeous face.

'Look, this is all very lovely, but it's going to have to wait because we need you,' Carina said, and for the first time, Moira noticed she was pacing the floor. Carina didn't do pacing.

Lisa echoed the demand. 'Yeah, we need you to come with us. Now. It's urgent.'

Why did this have to be now? Did the universe hate her?

It didn't matter. The bottom line was that pals came before blokes, so there was only one thing to do.

'Okay, but it's going to take at least two of you to get me up because I can't bend.'

Carina sighed and shook her head, but Lisa pitched in and between her and Nate they managed to pull her up.

'Can we take a raincheck on the whole kissing thing? I'll wear a better bra next time.'

Before he could answer, Carina firmly nudged him out of the room. 'We love you, Nate, but bye...'

As soon as the door closed behind him, Carina spun around. 'I'm late.'

'For what?' Moira asked. They weren't due at work until 6 p.m.

'No, *late* late. Period late.'

It was all starting to make horrible, terrifying sense. 'Oh no. No, no, no.'

'We bought a test,' Lisa interjected, pulling a brown paper bag from her backpack.

Moira grabbed a sweatshirt that was lying on her bed and pulled it on. 'Go do it now. Carina, it's going to be okay. Either way, we'll work it out.' Moira had no idea what she was saying, but she was just trying to make Carina stop pacing.

Lisa pressed the test into Carina's hands, and she disappeared into the bathroom. 'Keep talking to me while I do this, otherwise I'll freak out,' she insisted, from the other side of the door that had been left open, so they could hear her but not see her.

'Okay. I don't get it though – you never have sex without a condom.'

Silence.

'Carina?'

A small voice that oozed regret answered. 'But I did. Just once. The ball at the naval base. The guy I was seeing. Rod. We got carried away and I swear to God if you make another joke about his gangplank, I'll never forgive you.'

'Not saying a word.' The joke about the gangplank stayed inside with the fireworks from earlier, locked in by the crushing anxiety and fear she was now feeling for her friend. This could change everything for Carina. Ruin her plans. Devastate her. And her stroppy, snobby cow of a mother would have a fit. She'd already cut her off financially to try to make her go home. Who knew what she'd do if she found out about this.

'How are you doing in there?' Lisa asked, looking fearful.

Moira slipped her hand into her friend's and squeezed it.

Carina came out at that moment, clutching the stick, holding it out in front of her so that they could both see it. 'If a blue line appears in that box in the next sixty seconds, I'm screwed.'

For a full minute, all three of them stood, silent, still, and stared at a white stick.

14

THURSDAY, 3 JULY, 2025 – HONG KONG

Moira

It was only the third day since she'd left home – one day travelling and two nights sleeping in this big comfy slab of a swanky super king bed – and already Moira felt like she'd been gone for a week.

She had her phone propped up on a pillow so that she could see and talk to her pal, Jacinta, back in Glasgow, while putting on her make-up. 'Honestly, Jacinta, I'm heartbroken for the lass – Stevie. And devastated about Lisa. I still can't believe it. We were so close to being together again and…' A sob caught in the back of her throat and she raised her eyes to the sky, trying to halt the tears. This was the third time she'd tried to put her mascara on while telling Jacinta about the last couple of days, and she still hadn't managed it. Not that superficial stuff like her make-up mattered in the least right now.

'Change the subject until I get my act together here, love. Tell me what's happening with you.'

'Not much since my best pal deserted me.' Jacinta said, and

Moira knew she was just trying to do exactly as she'd asked, and raise her spirits. 'I'm about to go to sleep since the same chum rudely wakened me at 1 a.m....'

Moira pulled the mascara away from her lashes. 'I've already said sorry about that. Miscalculated the time difference.'

Jacinta's smile told her she was forgiven. 'But other than that, I've just been spending my days floating around here being windswept and interesting. The crowds outside have subsided since your son left for LA...' Ollie's fans had some kind of communication going on with social media, which alerted them to where Ollie was most of the time. Since he'd announced his involvement with the theatre academy in Glasgow, there was always a crowd outside, ready with their iPhones to film him or take selfies. Moira didn't know how he dealt with the relentless public scrutiny, but he somehow managed not to let it get to him most of the time. 'But the documentary crew are still here so I've had my lipstick on, my hair done, and I've been wearing two pairs of Spanx. I refuse to let them get me at a bad angle.'

Moira had finally got one eye done, so she moved on to the other one. 'I admire that dedication to your craft, my love.'

'Always the professional,' Jacinta assured her, tongue firmly in cheek. 'If this doesn't get me an offer to do *Strictly* I'll be outraged.' Moira smiled, mostly because they both knew there was a bit of truth in there. Jacinta had been a jobbing actress for decades, bagged a couple of short-term soap parts and been killed once on *Taggart* and once on *Shetland,* but the roles had dried up now that she was circling her sixties. The offer to be an acting coach at Ollie's academy couldn't have come at a better time for her too and Moira knew she was grateful for it, but there was still a tiny bit of ambition in Jacinta that had her convinced that global stardom could be just around the corner. Moira, on the other hand, had a whole different set of priorities.

Yes, she wanted to keep her feet on dry land and to be back in Scotland, putting her talents to good use, but now all her ambitions were for her work-life balance. She'd grafted for decades – time to focus on what made her happy outside work, if she could just figure out what that was.

'Anyway, love, I'd better go. I'm meeting Carina and Stevie downstairs in ten minutes. We're going to do a bit of a step back in time and show her our old haunts.'

Jacinta blew her a kiss. 'Have a lovely day, darling. You know, the fact that Lisa was coming all that way to see you after all these years, says something about how much she loved you and Carina. I hope you see that.'

'Aw, bugger, there's the mascara away again,' Moira said, swallowing back another sob. 'Thanks, lovely. You're not so bad really,' she added, trying to keep herself together. 'I'm away before I crumble again. I'll buzz you later.' With the blow of a kiss, she disconnected.

Keep busy. Keep going. That's what she was going to do, starting right now. She went on the hunt for a pair of flat shoes that would go with the yellow, floaty linen trousers and T-shirt she'd picked for the day. Cool cotton covered everything up so she was less likely to die of sun stroke. She'd learned thirty-odd years ago that her Scottish DNA couldn't cope with these kinds of temperatures. She grabbed her bag, slipped it over her head so that it sat across her body, pulled on a hat and sunspecs and was downstairs in time to meet Carina and Stevie, both already at the door and good to go.

She kissed them both. 'How are we today, ma darlins?'

'Tired, sad, stressed, but happy to be here and doing this,' Carina summed it up perfectly.

'What she said,' Stevie added, and Moira thought again how hard this must be for her. They had to change that. Maybe give her something to smile about. Something good had to come out of this week for them all.

'Right, well, let's shake off the cobwebs and go hustle up some memories. But only the good ones.' They'd already agreed last night that the first stop would be Kowloon and the guest house they'd once called home. Although Moira was fairly convinced it would have been condemned as an environmental hazard, torn down and turned into a car park by now.

'I like the sound of that,' Stevie agreed, with Lisa's smile. Moira felt another tug on the heartstrings. Dear God, she was going to have to work hard to stay chipper today. 'I can do it, Lisa,' she sent the silent promise skywards.

Outside the hotel, they went down the steps to the MTR, Hong Kong's underground system and Moira noticed the first change since they'd been here last. The station had been completely renovated and was now slick and spotless, with cookie shops and juice bars on the way to the platform. Carina had already advised them all to load a prepaid Octopus card onto their phones, so they breezed straight through, a quick scan replacing the need to buy tickets. When they got on to the train, Moira spotted another difference. Thirty-five years ago, the platforms were usually packed and there would be crowds of passengers pushing onto the trains, but now it was all far less busy and frantic. They even managed to slip into three seats when a group of teenagers left at the first stop. Moira watched Stevie looking around her, taking it all in, thinking this must be such a shock to the system. Only a few days ago she was at her mum's funeral and now she was here.

'The plan was to change at Admiralty, that's a couple of stations along, to the line that takes us under the harbour over to Kowloon, but I'm thinking now that instead of doing that, we should just head to the Star Ferry and go across that way,' Carina was saying to Stevie now. 'It's breathtaking and your mum insisted we took the Ferry every day coming the other way, from our hotel to work. She always said it was her favourite part of the day.'

Lisa also used to say that it blew out her hangover from the night before, but Moira chose not to share that. Stevie's revelations about Lisa's life had shocked them. It was clear that the mum who raised her was a completely different person to the one Moira and Carina had known. But then, Moira knew she was a different person now too. Age did that. Life did that. Having a family did that. Wasn't that why she'd come here? To find her old self?

'Yes, let's do that. Right, this is us, then,' Carina announced, standing up, and Moira felt another twinge of nostalgia that made her heart swell. Carina had always been the organiser, the planner, the one that got them where they were meant to be, when they were meant to be there. She'd slipped right back into that role and Moira was more than happy to go with it. It made a nice change from having to be totally self-sufficient and responsible for planning every detail of her day.

They got off the MTR, took the escalators back above ground, and then it was a ten-minute walk to the ferry, thankfully cutting through an air-conditioned shopping mall to get there. At the ferry, they scanned their Octopus cards again, and then got a shift on to catch the iconic green and white boat that was already filling up. 'Top deck or bottom?' Carina asked, speedwalking to the gangway.

'Top!' Moira shouted, focusing on keeping up. She should definitely have had a go at losing ten pounds before she got here.

They made it just in time, sliding into a row of wooden seats on the top deck just as the ferry began to move. 'You sit nearest the window, because that's where...' Carina stopped, and Moira knew why. The words had been snatched by the bittersweet pain of the memory.

Stevie sensed it too. 'That's where my mum always sat?'

Moira nodded. 'Yep, she'd climb over us to get there. Then she'd face out to the water and close her eyes the whole way.'

'I think I'll keep mine open,' Stevie said, with a smile. 'The view is way too stunning to miss.'

Moira didn't disagree. The journey took about ten minutes, cost less than a British pound, yet it was one of the most iconic sailings on the planet. Moira jumped into the empty seat at the end of the row behind, so that she had the full view too, then watched as the ripples in the water took them from HK island to Kowloon, incredible skylines on both sides. How many times had they done this back in the day? Her, Carina and Lisa, in full face make-up and sometimes in their stage costumes too, hair lacquered to the size of a small bush, sipping from hip flasks of vodka and orange that were stashed in their handbags.

She felt her cheeks begin to ache and realised she was smiling. This was what she'd come for. The memories. The connection to a time when they thought they were going to have the most incredible lives and that anything was possible.

By the time they docked at Kowloon side, she felt ten years lighter and her shoulders, weighed down by stress and age, had risen an inch.

'Let's walk along the harbour. I'm not ready to let this view go yet,' Moira suggested as they disembarked. They turned right out of the terminal and then made their way to the promenade that stretched right along the Tsim Sha Tsui waterfront. As they walked, Moira decided she didn't recognise some of what she saw. There were a couple of new buildings on this side of the road. New railings too. And glancing back over to Hong Kong island from here, she could see that the skyline had changed, with new structures added in front of the ones that had been there for decades. She'd read in the in-flight magazine on the way over that there had been a large swathe of land reclaimed from the harbour on both sides, and looking over from this side of the water, she could see it clearly now. So much change.

Across the road though, looking inland, there were still many familiar sights. Star House. Then the gorgeous old building that used to house the Marine Police HQ was still there, although ground level was now lined with luxury stores. Further along, she smiled when they reached the stunning façade of the Peninsula Hotel. 'How many times did you walk past that and say you were going to be able to afford to stay there one day?' Carina asked, reading her mind.

'Weekly,' Moira answered, touched that Carina remembered. 'Big dreams back then. Thing is, I really believed it would happen. Still, it's nothing a lottery win wouldn't solve. Or, you know, a bit of breaking and entering.'

They were still laughing as they crossed over Salisbury Road at the lights, then turned the corner of the busy street onto Nathan Road. Another crossing, then they turned left and kept going up Nathan Road, past the Sheraton Hotel until they got to Middle Road. Moira felt her heart begin to race, and not just because it was 90-odd degrees and she had no business walking around in this heat. She pushed her sunglasses up on to her head to get a better look as they went down the street.

She squinted against the sun to see ahead of her, realising with depressing inevitability, that their former home wasn't there.

It wasn't there.

It wasn't there.

'There it is.' Carina said, almost in a whisper, as she stopped dead on the pavement.

Moira almost crashed into the back of her. She turned her head, trying to see something she recognised. It took her a moment but... yes. The doorway. The same doorway. Same frame. Although, it no longer had five coats of chipped paint and a battered old door hanging off it. Or a tatty sign above it saying:

Kowloon Star Guest House

Now, the door was glass with long brass handles, there were topiary balls in big steel planters on either side, and a large gold sign on the wall said:

The Bendon

in vintage letters, with:

Boutique Hotel

underneath.

'Are we going in?' Carina asked, clearly not fussed either way. Moira could understand why – other than the location, this modern, flash hotel clearly had no connection to the hovel they'd lived in.

Moira was too busy recreating a memory from her first day here. Carina answering the door. Walking up the rickety stairs. And there, at the reception, Nate.

Her Nate.

Moira managed to force out the words. 'Yes, I think we are.'

15

CARINA

'God, if these walls could talk...' Carina said, her hands automatically going to the shiny granite tiles that now lined the walls that ran up each side of the staircase.

'Is it crazy that I feel really excited to be here, yet I don't know why?' Stevie asked, keeping in step next to her, with Moira bringing up the rear. Carina had noticed the new steel lift to the left of the door downstairs, but ignored it, because it was only one flight of stairs. She hadn't made it to the gym yet again this morning, and she usually never went more than two days without playing tennis or going to her thrice weekly yoga class, so she was glad of the exercise.

Moira, however, didn't seem to feel the same. 'You know, there's a reason that lifts were invented, Carina,' she was muttering behind her. 'It's to stop fit specimens like you feeling smug.'

Carina ignored her, but couldn't stop the corners of her mouth twitching in amusement. It was bizarre how natural and normal this felt. They'd just slipped right back into their old routine of love, affection, support and sarcasm. If she wasn't going through an existential crisis, facing the potential end of her marriage, and feeling nauseated at the very thought of that, and if poor Lisa had made it here as she'd planned, then Carina had no doubt that they'd be having the time of their lives.

In a twisted way, Lisa's passing had almost reinforced her need and desire to be here because it felt like they were paying tribute to her and doing the only thing they could do right now to honour her memory – they were taking care of Stevie. And the fact that it was keeping her mind off her own worries was a 'head in the sand', classic avoidance tactic, sanity-saving bonus. Of course, there was part of her that wanted to know how Spencer was reacting. Was he frantically trying to find her because he'd realised he'd made a mistake and he was desperate to fix it? Or was this a pattern and he'd cheated on her before? Had he made a choice between the two women and she wasn't it? Was he already moving Arabella in and ordering his lawyers to start divorce proceedings? She might find out the answer to those questions if she checked her voicemail and texts, but that would give him the power to encroach on her day and right now she wasn't prepared to give him another second of her life, especially because she was toying with the crunch question – *did she care?* She knew she absolutely should, yet the whole thing still made her feel numb. There was nothing. No pain. No panic. No devastation. Just numbness. And as long as it stayed that way, she was going to get up in the morning and spend the day with her friends – yes, Stevie already counted as a friend – find glimpses of joy in the moment, enjoy the memories of their past lives and ignore the rest.

That's why, when they got to the top of the stairs, Carina glanced around hoping for something, anything, that looked familiar. There was nothing. Where there used to be threadbare, sticky carpet, there was now marble floor. Where there used to be tacky mirrors on the walls, there were now cool wood accents on what looked like Venetian plaster. The old tatty spotlight tracks had been replaced by gorgeous brass and crystal downlighters. And the sight of Nate, behind the reception desk, had been replaced by a water feature, because the desk was now double the size and on the opposite wall, right where, if Carina wasn't mistaken, Moira's room used to be.

'Your room is now a coffee area,' Moira whispered. 'And look, this whole floor has been extended back there now.'

Carina could see she was right. A long thin corridor that used to have bedrooms on both sides, had now been opened up and become an open plan bar and lobby area, with signs directing guests to rooms, gym, spa, and roof terrace. Whoever owned this place now must have bought one of the adjacent buildings and knocked them both together. Quite an upgrade since 1990, yet Carina felt a pang of regret. She'd love to have seen the old place one more time.

'Shall we have a drink at the bar?' she suggested, suddenly thirsty. She'd forgotten how much the humidity parched the throat.

'Good idea,' Moira agreed. 'But just let me have a wee word with one of the receptionists.'

Carina and Stevie followed her as she made a beeline for one of the staff members standing behind the long black onyx desk.

'Excuse me, this might be the craziest question you'll get today...'

'I like a challenge,' said the smart, smiling man in accented English. If Carina had to guess, she'd say he was in his early thirties, and the dual-language badge on his jacket informed them that he was the duty manager.

'Excellent. I just wondered if there is anyone still employed here who might have been working here thirty years ago? You see, my friend and I...' she pointed to Carina. 'While we don't look a day over forty, actually lived here back in 1990, when we were in our twenties.'

Carina struggled to keep a straight face. This was what Moira did – charmed anyone she set her mind to. Warmth oozed out of her, and she viewed every interaction as an opportunity to make someone smile, laugh or chat. Why was she only realising now how much she'd missed that?

The gent behind the desk was shaking his head. 'I'm afraid not. We only opened in this location in 2005.'

'And what about the company that owned the building before that?' Moira pressed on.

'I really have no idea. As far as I know, it changed hands a couple of times in the years before that. It was fairly run down when we took it over.'

Moira nodded. 'Yep, it was fairly run down when we lived here. We considered that part of its charm. Okay, well, thank you.'

'You're very welcome. Sorry I couldn't help.'

Moira tried and failed to hide her disappointment by becoming nonchalant and breezy. 'Oh well, I suppose any other outcome would have been too good to be true. There was really no chance that Nate would still be here after all these years. He's probably back on the Gold Coast, on his fifth wife, and working three jobs to pay alimony to the other four.'

A very undignified snort of laughter was out before Carina could stop it. 'Your mind really does work in strange ways, Moira Chiles. Come on, I think this calls for a beverage.'

They settled down in a cluster of four vintage leather tub chairs around a smoked glass table, and ordered three waters and three coffees from a very efficient waitress.

'It's so strange to think that my mum was here. I still can't get my head around it. She climbed those stairs. Walked on this floor...'

'Actually, where we're sitting is roughly where her room was,' Carina realised, as she calculated the floor plan.

'I'd love to have seen that. Was she meticulously tidy and a bit OCD back then too?'

As usual, Moira struggled to contain her reaction. 'Do you want the diplomatic answer or the truth?'

'Truth. I think.'

Moira nodded solemnly, fishing the lemon out of the glass of water the waitress had just put in front of her. 'Well, her room permanently looked like a tornado had blown through it, she had an ashtray the size of a small pyramid and her wardrobe looked like Top Shop had vomited the clothes into it. She was the untidiest woman I've ever met in my life.'

'Hers was the party room. If Jack Daniels ever ran out of bottles, they could have bought her stash of empties,' Carina added hesitantly, taking Stevie at her word that she wanted to hear the facts.

'I mean this with love because I'm so grateful to you both for letting me gatecrash your holiday,' Stevie began, 'but I'm beginning to think you're both pranking me. Or that maybe your Lisa and my Lisa were two different women.'

'It makes sense though,' Carina tried to soften the shock. 'Time passes. Moira and I are pretty different from the two youngsters that lived here too.'

They were interrupted by the waitress, who'd come back with their coffees, and then they steered on to more neutral territory as they shared a few less controversial tales about living here.

After yet another story that involved Nate, Stevie's curiosity was piqued.

'So this Nate guy,' Stevie asked, 'did my mum ever date him?'

Carina shook her head. 'No, he was actually Moira's boyfriend.'

'A serious boyfriend?' Stevie asked.

Moira shrugged. 'First love of my life. Actually, there haven't been too many since then. If you rule out Robbie Williams and Gerard Butler, I'm still down in single digits.'

'Oh hon,' Carina sighed. If Moira was using humour to brush over something sad, it meant that she'd taken a dagger to the heart. 'Is being here bringing up feelings?'

Delaying her reply, Moira gestured to the waitress for the bill, then pulled out the 'kitty purse' to pay it. They'd all chipped in HK$1,000 each this morning, about £100, deciding that it would be easier to use that for food and drinks throughout the day, than all messing around with splitting bills and credit cards.

'Och, maybe I just thought that it would have been good to see him again. I've always wondered what happened to him. How his life turned out. Anyway, there's no point moping.' Shaking off her melancholy, Moira put some notes down on the leather bill holder the waitress had just delivered, and morphed back into her standard cheery self. 'Shall we make a move?'

They gathered up their bags, and headed back to the stairs, saying goodbye to a different chap who was behind the reception desk now. At the bottom of the stairs, Stevie opened the door and the three of them flinched as the heat outside slammed into them like a solid wall.

'This is why I've never liked a sauna,' Moira muttered, as Carina pulled on her sun hat and shades. They'd only taken a couple of steps outside when they heard a shout behind them.

'Excuse me! Hello?'

Carina turned around to see the duty manager they'd spoken

to on the way in. 'You asked about people that used to work here?'

Carina almost staggered to the side because Moira nudged her so hard in the ribs, as she exclaimed, 'Yes!'

'Well, I was on my break, and I had a quick look on google... There was a newspaper article... the corporation that owns this hotel now, bought it from a property company with an office over in Causeway Bay. I don't know if that helps or not, but I hope so. I wrote the address down here.'

Carina wasn't sure it helped either, but she appreciated the gesture and took the Post-it, then automatically slipped a note from the pile of hundred HK dollar bills she kept in her pocket for tips and handed one over.

'No, no,' the gent put his hands up. 'No need. I'm just happy to help. I hope you find the person you're looking for.'

'Thank you,' Carina said, as he retreated back inside.

'What does it say?' Moira asked. 'I mean, I know it'll be pointless, because Nate will be long gone and even if we contact them, they won't have a clue who he is. He was only working here to get enough money to travel on to somewhere else. I'm sure he would have left not long after me.'

Stepping back under the canopy of the door to get shelter from the sun, the three of them huddled together, all looking at the company address on the note. 'Means nothing to me,' Carina said.

'Nor me,' Moira agreed. 'Oh well, let's go back on the ferry and get the wind in our hair and maybe stop for a cocktail somewhere to get us out of the heat again. It's only our first day of sightseeing. We need to pace ourselves.'

Beside Carina, Stevie had other plans. 'Hang on a second,' she said, and they watched as she typed something into her phone. 'Okay, it's a company called Crocodile Realty that's at that address.' She clicked away a few more times. 'Managing director...'

Moira was now holding Carina's hand and squeezing it a bit too tightly.

'Nate Wilde.'

Silence. And a long pause. Until Stevie, misreading the shock for disappointment said, 'Wrong Nate? Is that not him?'

'That. Is. Him,' Moira said, her words dripping with incredulity. 'Oh, holy crap, it's him.' She was fanning her face again. 'It's Nate. And how on earth did he go from working on reception to being the managing director of the company that used to own the building?'

Carina had no answers, but despite being wildly disappointed in love, romance and the male species this week, she felt her heart soar with joy for her friend. Moira deserved something to be happy about, especially since the trip she'd been so excited about had been shrouded in sadness from the start.

'Only one way to find out,' Carina suggested, feeling beads of sweat pop out under her linen shirt. They really needed to get moving or to go back inside or they'd melt. 'Shall we go to their office now? It's in Causeway Bay, so we could detour on the way back.'

Moira was already shaking her head as she fished in her bag, then pulled out her phone.

'No, there's a number there. I'm going to call first. Who knows if he's even still there? I'm not getting my hopes up,' she added, sounding very much like someone who was definitely getting her hopes up. She pulled on her specs, then read the number on the piece of paper aloud, while punching it into her phone with trembling thumbs.

Someone at the other end must have answered, because the next words out of her mouth were, 'Hello? Yes, can I speak to Nate Wilde please?'

16

STEVIE

Stevie pushed her hands into the pockets of her black capri trousers, so that Moira wouldn't see that she had her fingers crossed. She figured they needed all the help they could get, and she so wanted some kind of win for at least one of them. After dinner last night, Carina had filled her in on what had happened on the night of her anniversary, and wow, her husband sounded like a prize dick. And not in a good way.

It was hard to imagine that anyone would cheat on this woman. Sure, it was impossible to know what went on behind closed doors, but she was gorgeous, smart, and by all accounts she'd dedicated her life to supporting him and bringing up their family. And then the utter scumball turns around and does this? A similar thing happened to her pal, Keli – equally as gorgeous and smart – a few years ago, when it turned out her actor boyfriend already had a live-in partner and was out scouting for other hook ups too. It was enough to make you lose faith in relationships. Or maybe that was just Stevie's way of justifying her decision to stay single all these years. There had been a couple of long-term relationships. She'd been with her ex, Dan, for over six years after meeting him at a pub quiz. Thanks to him, she now knew the answer to, 'Is it possible for a man to love football and motorbikes more than he loves his girlfriend?' And, 'Is it a red flag when your boyfriend thinks "commitment" is a swear word?'

After that, there had been Anthony, a nurse on the psychiatric ward, who'd analysed everything she did. And Dexter, a cop she'd met when he brought in a cumulative total of two broken jaws, a skull fracture and seven cracked ribs after a bar fight in Glasgow city centre. Maybe she should stop dating guys that she met at her place of work, but when you slogged twelve-hour shifts, often six days a week to cover sick leave and holidays, it was hard to meet guys anywhere else. The last thing she felt like doing on a weekend night was getting all dolled up and going out on the hunt for a bloke. So no. If she was going to meet anyone, it would have to be a burglar who broke into her house on a Saturday night and gatecrashed her 'Pizza and Movie' night with Caleb.

Sometimes she'd wondered if her mum felt the same, and that's why she'd never met anyone after her dad left. As far as Stevie knew, there hadn't been a single date in all those years. And if there had been, it didn't seem to have turned into any kind of permanent relationship – unless of course, her mother had been keeping that a secret too. Nothing would surprise her now. Or make her sadder than she already felt. She kept coming back to the same thought – who was the real Lisa? Was it the wild one that Moira and Carina described as their friend here? Or was it the quiet, reserved, cautious woman who had brought her up? Either way, it seemed that her mum had acted completely out of character for a large chunk of her life, and that chipped a piece off Stevie's heart.

Maybe that's why she was listening to Moira's call now and

praying for a positive outcome. If there was any karmic justice in the world, Nate Whateverhisname would remember Moira immediately, he'd declare that he'd been pining for her all these years, and they'd fall madly in love again and live happily ever after.

'It's Moira Chiles. Yes, I'll hold,' Moira was saying now. Stevie caught Carina's eager expression and was touched again by how much they had supported each other, and her, since she'd met them.

The other person had obviously come back on the line, because Moira was re-engaging. 'Yes, hello again. Oh.'

Oh, what? Stevie couldn't read her tone. Although that might be because she was getting heatstroke standing in this doorway.

'Right then. Yes, if I could leave a message that would be great. Please tell him that Moira Chiles called and ask him to call me back at the Harbour Lights Hotel in Wanchai. I'll be there for a few more days. Thank you.'

She put the phone back in her bag. 'He's travelling on business, and she doesn't know when he'll be back, but she'll pass on my message.' There was no escaping how crestfallen she looked for just a few moments, but then she pulled her shoulders back and shook it off. 'Right, I'm not getting my size sixteen M&S knickers in a twist over a bloke when I have you two ladies and the prospect of Peking duck pancakes tonight to keep me going. Shall we get moving then?'

'Gladly,' Carina answered. 'MTR or ferry over to the other side?'

Stevie answered first. 'Can we take the ferry again? I just want to see it going the other way too.'

'Done,' Moira proclaimed. They retraced their steps down Nathan Road, turned right on to Salisbury Road, then walked back along the harbour front to the ferry terminal, Stevie feeling more exhausted with every step. The ferry ride back over was as stunning as the first one, and this time, as she watched the buildings on Hong Kong Island come closer, she pictured her mum sitting in exactly the same spot, taking this in.

'No matter how many times I cross this harbour, it never gets old,' Carina said, and Stevie knew she'd feel that way too. This was so far removed from her life back in Scotland, and she wasn't ready to go back to the daily drive, usually in the rain, to Glasgow Central Hospital for her shift.

They'd fallen back into an easy silence, when Carina pointed to a tall glass building almost directly ahead of them. 'That hotel there is the Grand Hyatt. There used to be a nightclub in there that had a soul band, and sometimes, on our night off, we'd go there and as soon as your mum walked in, they'd invite her up on the stage to sing with them.'

The shocks just kept on coming. 'How did they even know her?'

'Everyone knew Lisa because she was an incredibly talented singer who put on a great show, and like we said earlier, she was always the centre of every party.'

'I can't imagine that,' Stevie said, honestly. 'I know I keep saying it, but I honestly have no idea who you're describing. And I can't tell you how much I wish I knew her then. How much I wish she'd told me about her life here.'

'Maybe it was just a moment in time,' Carina offered. 'It's hard to describe what life was like here back then. Millions of people, yet our world was small because all the entertainers and nightclub managers and DJs and door stewards... well, we all knew each other.'

'And we mean, *really* knew each other,' Moira interjected. 'Not like all those Facebook friends and Internet pals you have nowadays.' She laughed as she nudged Carina. 'Could you imagine if we'd had all that social media stuff back then? We'd have been cancelled. Struck off. Those were different times. No Internet. No mobile phones. Too expensive to call landlines. And those photos I showed you yesterday... the only reason I had those was because my mother bought me a cheap camera before I came here because she'd never been further than Blackpool and she wanted to see the sights. I had to run around on my last day taking pictures of landmarks because all I had up until then were photos of us lot partying and she'd have been furious. It cost me a fortune to get them all developed when I got home. Anyway, the thing about having none of that Internet stuff was that we were free. We made loads of mistakes. Oh God, so many. But the difference is that there was no one there to capture it for posterity, so we didn't have to spend a whole lifetime looking back with regret or living in shame. We forgave ourselves and each other, because we could. And no one ever had to know.'

Stevie registered that that was the second time Moira had mentioned that they'd made mistakes back in the day, but she didn't feel she had the right to pry so she let it go. For now. 'So what made you leave, then?' Stevie asked, genuinely curious. 'It sounds like you were all living your best lives.'

Carina shook her head. 'In some ways, maybe. But we were also just figuring ourselves out. Strange really... We all left for different reasons, and not to be all deep and meaningful, but sometimes I wonder if I knew then what I know now, would I still make the same decision?'

Before she could answer her own question, the ferry bumped into dock, and they followed the crowd off the boat and through the terminal to the street. Moira suggested that they get a taxi back to the hotel, but Stevie wasn't ready. 'If it's okay with you, I'm going to walk. I need some fresh air.' It was cooler now that the afternoon sun had begun to go down, and she knew if she went straight back to the hotel, the jet lag and tiredness would kick in and she'd end up sleeping for the rest of the day. She wasn't ready for that yet. Not when there were still streets to explore and thinking to be done. 'You're very welcome to join me, though,' she added, suddenly worried that they'd be offended. She should have known better.

'Stevie, I've had a lovely day with you today,' Moira replied, 'but I'd rather stick forks in my eyes than walk in this heat. I'd have heatstroke and hair the size of a motorcycle helmet by the time I got there.'

'But thank God you wouldn't be dramatic about it,' Carina deadpanned, sticking her hand out to flag down a passing taxi, then turning back to Stevie and giving her a hug when the cab stopped. 'Call us when you get back to the hotel if you'd like to have dinner. No pressure though. We'll totally understand if you'd like a night off from our scintillating company.'

'Never,' Stevie said, laughing. 'But thank you. For that and for today.'

Carina slipped into the car, while Moira gave her a hug too. 'See you soon, pet. And you know we're here if you want to talk, day or night.'

'Thanks, Moira.'

She waved them off, then pulled out her phone, put the hotel address into her maps, and then started walking. A twenty-two-minute walk, her app informed her. Plenty of time to clear her head. But first, she wanted to share everything that had happened with the one person she knew would be up at... she checked her watch and did a quick calculation... just after 6 a.m. in Scotland.

He answered on the first ring, and she could hear him panting. 'Wild sex or jogging?' she teased.

'Jogging, sadly,' Caleb replied. 'I wouldn't have answered if it was wild sex. Even for you.'

Passers-by probably wondered why she was wandering along the street laughing to herself. 'Good to know your love is conditional. Anyway, I'm phoning to give you the latest on the never-ending revelations of the secret life of Lisa Dixon.'

'That sounds like a book I would read,' he said, and she could hear the amusement in his voice. 'Okay, shoot.'

'Well, apparently she was a well-known singer and a bit of a star...' She began, then recounted everything else the ladies had said today.

'That's incredible. Sounds like she was a badass.'

Stevie was nodding now. 'I think she definitely was. And her friends are beyond kind, and cool. Hilarious too.'

'But?' he said. 'I can hear the "but" coming.'

He was as perceptive as ever.

'But...' she repeated. 'I still think there's something about my mother that they're not telling me. And I think I need to stay here until I find out what that is.'

17

NOVEMBER 1990 – HONG KONG

Carina

Carina barged into Moira's room, and then immediately wished she'd knocked, waited two minutes, then walked in wearing an eye mask. There were things in life she didn't need to see and one of them was Moira and Nate, all wrapped around each other in bed.

'Urgh, you two are seriously sickening, do you know that?'

'We do,' Moira nodded, grinning. 'In fact, we try really hard to be as nauseating as possible. It's our mission in life.'

Carina threw open the curtains, blinding the lovebirds with the daylight. 'Well, mission accomplished. Come on – it's time to go to work.'

The only thing that was worse than knowing she sounded like a prize bitch, was that the two of them were so happy in their little blissed-out bubble that they weren't even rising to the bait. They'd been like this for the last month since they'd got together – completely inseparable and disgustingly happy. As delighted as she was for them, the truth was that she missed single-fun-partner-in-crime-Moira. The last few weeks had been so different to their usual routine. Normally, they'd finish their set every night around midnight or 1 a.m. if the place was packed, then they'd head to an after-party or a club at least four or five nights of the week. They'd party until dawn, then come home, crash, get up early afternoon and do it all again. Now Moira was straight home to see Nate, and Carina had to come drag them out of bed every afternoon.

'I love it when you boss me around,' Moira teased, throwing off the sheet and stretching as she sat up, her oversize 'Frankie Says Feck Off' T-shirt falling off one shoulder. It had been procured a few weeks ago when they'd all had one drink too many with a crowd of girls from Dublin, and Moira had swapped it for the conical bra she wore every night when she sang 'Vogue.' There had been a complete panic the next day when she realised what she'd done, but luckily the Dublin girls had returned the bra the following night. They let Moira keep the T-shirt though, because they said it was the best night they'd had on their holiday.

Talking of Irish girls...

'Have either of you spoken to Lisa today? She's not answering her door.'

Nate was up now too, on his way into the bathroom. 'No. Didn't see her come in last night either. Wasn't she with you?'

'No. I came back early – wasn't feeling it...' They'd all – except Moira, of course – ended up at a club in Lan Kwai Fong, the area that was the epicentre of the night scene on the island. The real Michael Hutchence and Kylie Minogue had been spotted there last year when they were still dating, and they all lived in hope of bumping into him again there now that he was single. 'She was with our usual crowd from the bar and didn't want to leave. Last I saw she was sitting on Josh's knee and knocking back flaming sambucas.'

'Maybe she's at his place.' Moira went to the same conclusion that Carina had come to after banging on Lisa's door for five minutes. 'She stayed there a couple of nights last week. I asked her about it, and she pointed out that I'm not her mother.'

Carina headed for the door. 'Nope, apparently that would be me. Honestly, it's like trying to round up toddlers with you two. I'll go try her again.'

She'd just opened the door when she saw the missing person coming past reception, still in last night's clothes. 'Lisa! For God's sake, we need to leave in half an hour.'

'Sorry. Got sick last night. Stayed at Ben's place.' Carina was surprised. Ben was one of the regulars at the bar, and someone who often hung out with them, but not one of Lisa's usual guys.

'Give me half an hour. Don't stress, I'll be ready,' Lisa assured her, with her usual chilled out shrug as she carried on along the corridor to her room. That was her go-to mantra. 'Don't stress, it's cool'. Or 'Don't stress, I'm fine'.

Carina turned back to Moira, and she didn't need to say what she was thinking, because Moira said it first. 'Is it just me, or is she getting worse? I'm getting worried about her. That's the second or third time she's got sick.'

Lisa had always been the wild card, the party animal, the reckless one, but in the last couple of weeks she'd taken it to a whole new level. The drinking. The guys. Carina had caught her doing coke in the bathroom of a nightclub last week, and Lisa had just waved her off like it was no big deal.

'Don't stress, I'm fine,' had, of course, been Lisa's response to the situation. Carina had taken some loo roll, wiped the coke off the top of the cistern and flushed it. 'You're not fine.'

There had been a totally uncharacteristic blaze in Lisa's eyes, when she'd shot back, 'Yeah, well at least I wasn't the one worrying that I was knocked up.'

Carina had reared back like she'd been slapped. The pregnancy scare had been terrifying and even weeks after the blue line had failed to materialise in the little white box, she was still waking up in a sweat worrying about it. What would she have done? Her family were still not speaking to her, so there would be no support there. The guy she'd slept with was long gone, deployed to somewhere in the Middle East. Her friends would be there for her, but the reality was, what could they do? None of them had money, or a home, or a normal job – this wasn't a life to raise a child in. And if she made a different choice... she didn't even want to think about the trauma that ending the pregnancy would cause her. It was the most petrifying thing that had ever happened to her, and the negative result had left her relieved, but... different. There was a knot in her stomach that she couldn't seem to shift, and this didn't all seem like such a big, fun game any more.

And now, it didn't help that she spent way too much time trying to stop Lisa from royally screwing up her life too.

'I know, but what do we do?' Carina shrugged helplessly, in answer to Moira's worries. 'She won't listen to anyone.'

Moira got up from the bed and started pulling her clothes for tonight out of her wardrobe. 'It's like she's got some kind of self-destruct button. I'll speak to her again. Or maybe Nate can talk to her.'

At that moment, Nate came out of the bathroom, fully dressed now. 'Did I just hear my name? What are you two getting me into now?' he asked, laughing as he ran his fingers through his long dark hair. Carina loved him, but he'd never been her type. She didn't go for that whole 'shaggy haired, surf dude' vibe.

'We need you to talk to Lisa. You two have been friends the longest and she listens to you.' He'd carried her upstairs after finding her passed out at the door on more than a couple of occasions lately, so he knew what they were worried about. 'Sure, but, you know... it's Lisa.'

He didn't have to explain what he meant. Yet again, they didn't have to be psychic to know that her response would be a variation of, 'Don't stress, it's all cool'.

But she didn't have time to worry about that right now, because if they didn't get to the bar soon, she'd be adding, 'unemployed' to her list of problems.

It took another half hour to get out the door, and they were running late so they had to take the MTR instead of the ferry, to give them enough time to stop at a little noodle joint in Wanchai for a quick dinner before they got to work. Carina had chicken with beansprouts in an oyster sauce, Moira had steamed pork buns and Lisa had three Marlboro Reds and two beers, but she still went on to the stage that night and lit it up. Hungover, strung out Lisa was gone and in her place was Stevie Nicks, with a voice every bit as good as the original.

But only for a while.

As Carina and Moira came off stage after the second set, Carina spotted Lisa across at the bar, throwing back a shot. Carina recognised one of the guys she was talking to, but the other one had his back to her, facing the other way.

'I'm going to head home to Nate,' Moira announced, predictably.

Carina wasn't thrilled by this news, but it was hard to object when Moira was so visibly, crazily happy. 'You know, your vagina might actually fall off. I've heard that happens. It's a medical fact.'

'I'll brace myself to catch it,' Moira said, giggling as she squeezed her in a hug and then kissed her cheek. For the first time, Carina realised she was over this place tonight.

'Sod it, hang on, I'll come with you. Let me see if we can talk Lisa into an early night.'

'There's more chance of my vagina falling off, but okay.'

They fought their way to the bar, and Carina saw now that there was no chance Lisa was leaving, because there were two drinks in front of her and she'd never let them go to waste. Still, she had to try.

'Hey, Ben,' Carina greeted the bar regular, kissing him on each cheek. He was one of the nicest guys in the group, but Carina had never put him and Lisa together, even though she occasionally stayed over at his place. He was too normal, too safe. He had a real job, something to do with imports so they mostly saw him at weekends because he wasn't one of the 'out all night every night' group of bar staff, entertainers and bouncers that they hung out with.

'Lisa, Moira and I are going to head off. Do you want to come with us?'

'That's a shame.'

It took Carina a second to identify where the voice came from. When she did, she had to raise her head to meet his gaze and wow. Just wow.

Ben immediately took charge of the introductions. 'Carina, this is my brother, Spencer. Feel free to ignore him, because he's far too cocky to be encouraged. Spencer, this is Carina. And that's Moira.'

Moira gave him a wave, but Carina played it far cooler, especially when he said, 'I watched the show tonight. You were all amazing. Why have I never been here before?'

On anyone else, it could have come across as smarmy, but not this guy. In one sweeping glance, Carina took in the expensive suit and the Prada shoes. The Rolex watch on his wrist. The swept back hair and the chiselled jaw, both of which barely registered because they were only a momentary distraction from the glint in his gorgeous blue eyes. Her first thought was that this was a guy who belonged in her old world, the one that she'd grown up in. English. Money. A cut-glass accent. The effortless confidence that came with success. He wasn't much older than her, but it was obvious from his easy charm that he knew exactly who he was. Her second thought was that her family would love him. This was the type of man she'd been brought up to be with. Unlike her, he wasn't living in a slum hotel and gigging for a mediocre wage, pulling his friend out of toilets, and constantly teetering on the edge of messing up his life. A couple of months ago, she would have said she loved her life here, adored the freedom, the rebellion, and didn't want to change it any time soon. But lately it had felt as if something was shifting, like the good times were slipping away.

Now, looking into his eyes, she had the sudden thought that maybe it was time for her rebellious phase to end.

'Moira, you go on without me. I think I'm going to stick around here for a while.'

18

FRIDAY, 4 JULY, 2025 – HONG KONG

Moira

Moira called down to reception for the third time today. And yes, she was mortified at how pathetic that made her seem, but she couldn't help herself.

'Hello, this is Miss Chiles in the penthouse.' It made her even more mortified just saying 'penthouse'. In her opinion, there were many traits that could embarrass a working-class Scottish woman, but the most toe-curling thing was being perceived to be acting boastful or smug. 'Moira Chiles, you just take yourself down a peg or two,' her mother would tell her when she was a kid, if she ever showed the slightest sign of getting too big for her boots.

She tried to calm her red face of shame, and ploughed on. 'I just wondered if there have been any calls for me?'

At which point, just like the two previous times, the receptionist asked her to hold, then she heard the click of the buttons on a keyboard, before she came back on the line with a variation of, 'No, you daft old deluded bag, a bloke you hooked up with over thirty years ago hasn't been jamming up our phone lines looking for you.'

Okay, so what she actually said was, 'No, Ms Chiles, we have no messages for you. Would you like us to put any callers straight through to your suite?'

The red face now came from a place of disappointment. 'Yes, that would be lovely, thank you.'

It had been a day and a half since she'd called and left the message at Nate's office, and he still hadn't returned her call.

What did she expect? It was ridiculous to think Nate would have any reason to get back in touch with her, especially after how they'd ended, but she'd hoped that if nothing else, curiosity would have got the better of him. Apparently not.

However, now wasn't the time to sit and mope about it, because Carina and Stevie would be knocking on that door any minute to go for dinner. Moira pushed her feet into her hotel slippers and padded over to the dressing table. She'd already applied her make-up, so she just had her hair to fix now. Checking it out in the mirror, she decided there was no hope for it, so she shoved the whole lot up in a deliberately messy high ponytail, leaving a couple of tendrils on either side at the front, which she curled with tongs into loose waves, then dabbed some extra concealer onto the latest bout of puffiness under her eyes.

Tonight, she decided, there would be no more tears, because they'd had enough to last a lifetime last night and no amount of lymphatic drainage was going to shift this if it got any worse. The previous evening they'd gone to Madame Fù for dinner, a gorgeous restaurant that sat on the top floor of a beautiful old 1880s colonial building that was the police headquarters, barracks and training ground back when the British were still governing.

They'd started out fine, chatting about life, and even for a while, about Ollie. After the second bottle of wine had been popped, Stevie had said, 'I need to tell you – your son, Ollie. I've seen him in that *Clansman* series. I had no idea that we had any kind of connection to him or to you, but when I went home to visit my mum, she used to watch it religiously and now I guess I know why.'

Something about that touched Moira's heart and another lump of regret and sadness had begun to form in her throat. She had retired from working on cruise liners and returned to Glasgow five months ago. Why hadn't she just jumped on a plane or a ferry and taken herself over to see Lisa? Maybe even taken Ollie with her. It seemed so tragic now that two of her oldest friends had never met her son, and before now, she hadn't met any of their children either. Why had it come to this to make them realise how much they'd missed?

Moira had told them all about him, but of course, most of that was already public knowledge. The fact that his famous Hollywood wife, Sienna Montgomery had been filmed cheating on him with her co-star. And that he'd then had a lovely romance with a Scottish soap actress called Casey Lowden, that had regrettably ended because Casey's movie career had gone stratospheric in the last few months and, with their crazy shooting schedules, it had become impossible for them ever to be in the same place at the same time.

Stevie and Carina had been genuinely interested, and it had been a lovely diversion from all the heartache, one that continued when Moira asked Carina to tell them about her girls. One in Shanghai, one in Dubai, and they sounded like they were a credit to her. 'I'd love to meet them one day,' Stevie had said, then immediately followed that up with, 'I mean, that is, if you'd like to keep in touch after this.'

'Of course we would,' Moira had jumped in truthfully. 'Stevie, you only live half an hour away from me in Glasgow. I'll expect you for dinner every Sunday,' she said, only half joking.

'And I'm currently homeless, so I'll probably be in her spare room,' Carina had added, and the fact that she could find a way to joke about the hellish time she was having was a tonic to them all.

'Have you switched your phone back on yet?' Moira had asked. 'I keep waiting for Spencer to barrel through that door clutching a dozen roses and a ludicrously expensive apology gift.'

Carina was still in the defiance stage of post-adultery. 'Only to check that the girls aren't trying to get in touch – I don't want them worrying. But I switch it straight off again and ignore everything else. I just don't want to engage. For years I've been at everyone's beck and call and sod it. I'm over it. Spencer can wait. In fact, the whole of the outside world can wait until I'm ready. I've told Ben if there's an emergency to call me at the hotel, but other than that I'm still playing it ostrich-fashion, head in the sand. There's something quite liberating about it.'

Moira guessed exactly how that must feel. 'Like taking your bra off after a long hard day?'

'Exactly like that,' Carina had agreed, laughing.

The light-heartedness had been a blessed relief, but it hadn't lasted because just when their after-dinner coffees were being served, Stevie had switched to more difficult territory. 'Sorry – I know I've been relentless with the questions, but can I ask you both something else?'

Moira had a moment of fear. They'd told the lass so much about her mum, but there was even more that they'd left unsaid, because they didn't want to reveal anything that would tarnish

Lisa's memory. There were some things, so many things, that should stay in the past.

'Of course,' Carina had answered her.

Stevie had taken a sip of her coffee. 'I just wondered... what did my mum tell you about me? Did she talk about me? It's just that... I always felt like I disappointed her. Or maybe just didn't bring her much happiness. And I've got no one to ask whether that's true.'

Moira's heart had almost shattered into a million pieces. 'What makes you think that, love?'

Stevie had shrugged. 'She was always worried. Always sad. Always a bit... broken. There was no joy in her and I just never understood it, I suppose. And eventually it became too claustrophobic for me and that's why I went to university in Glasgow. So I just wondered... did she ever say that? That I'd disappointed her?'

Moira had met Carina's gaze and instinctively known that whatever she said, her friend would back her up.

'You have to understand that we only ever communicated by letters popped into birthday and Christmas cards, until the last few years when we did a couple of those Zoom calls. And I know that must seem strange to your generation, because you're much hotter on the communication stuff, but that was just the way it was with us.'

Moira tried to keep her expression neutral, tried to summon every ounce of strength and resolve, because she was about to lie to this poor woman's face. 'But honestly, pet, she only ever said how wonderful you were.'

'She was so proud of you,' Carina added, sealing her conspiracy after the fact.

The brutal, unfathomable truth was that Lisa Dixon had told them that she'd got married, that she'd had a daughter, but in the years that followed, she'd only ever mentioned Stevie in general terms. 'We are all doing fine'. 'All is well this end'. Always just brief, non-committal comments, and because the notes were just brief catch-ups in cards, that hadn't seemed too strange. At the tail end of the nineties, she'd mentioned that she was no longer with her husband, but that it was for the best, and that her and Stevie were perfectly happy without him. That was it. Nothing more in depth or personal than that. She'd certainly never shared her pride over the lovely woman who was sitting across that table from them. Never told them that Stevie had moved to Glasgow. Never said what she did for a living or that she looked exactly like a young Lisa. Moira didn't understand and she didn't condone it. In hindsight, they should have asked more questions, made more of an effort to learn about each other's worlds, but they were all just getting on with their lives and it hadn't seemed odd at the time. All she and Carina could do was support Stevie. She didn't know if they'd done the right thing embellishing Lisa's pride or not, until a single tear had dropped from Stevie's face onto her saucer.

'That's amazing to hear. I've never had anyone to ask how she felt. She was such a closed book, I guess. I suppose it's one of those things that always get talked about at funerals. You know, how much the person loved their husband, or wife, or kids... But we didn't get that chance.'

For a moment Moira had wondered if she'd missed something, but if she had, she could see by Carina's expression that she was just as confused. 'Why? Did none of her friends want to speak at the service?'

At that, it was Stevie's brow that had furrowed in confusion. 'No, sorry. I thought I'd told you about that. My mum left a letter of wishes, and one of them was a direct cremation. There was no official funeral service. No memorial. I guess she wanted to keep things private. The same way she lived her life.'

Now, sitting at her dressing table, Moira realised she was fighting a losing battle against the puffy eyes because the tears were back again, just as they'd fallen in every solitary moment today when she thought about Lisa, alone, no one there to commemorate her, to say goodbye, to tell her she was loved.

The doorbell through in the other room saved her, and she jumped up, desperate for any distraction from her thoughts. Halfway there, it struck her that it might be... just might be...

She threw open the door. 'You were thinking there that I might be Nate,' Carina declared with spooky accuracy.

Moira went right on to the back foot.

'I never thought any such thing,' she said haughtily, fully aware that they both knew the truth. Posh Pal's ability to read her mind had always been uncanny.

'Come on in. I just need to put my shoes on and then I'm good.'

Carina closed the door behind her. 'Moira, you know we need to talk about last night... about what we told Stevie...'

Moira nodded. 'I know, but not now. She'll be here any minute. Are you sure you're still okay with our plans for tonight?'

The game plan for tonight had been formulated earlier in the day, after they'd taken the iconic funicular Peak Tram up to the highest point on the island. They'd had lunch at the restaurant there, the views stunning, the food good, the service from their lovely Filipino waitress friendly and chipper. They all seemed to be on the same unwritten page, because they stuck to neutral, general topics of conversation like Stevie's job, Carina's travels, Moira's most outlandish stories from her cruises.

They were on their third glass of wine, when Moira broached the all-important subject.

'So what are we doing tonight, ladies? As always, you're both welcome to bail out and have a quiet night and we could regroup tomorrow.'

Stevie had come in first with her answer. 'If it's okay with you both, I'd like to meet up for dinner. I'll have plenty of opportunities for quiet nights in when I get home.'

Carina had held her hands up. 'I feel the same. And if I sit in my room, it'll just give me too much time to think. I'm enjoying living in this bubble of denial.'

Moira had nodded triumphantly. 'Excellent, because I've got an idea. My feet are killing me so I'm not up for traipsing far, so how about we just go downstairs to the bar in the hotel and check out where we used to work. To be honest, I've been dreading it, because I didn't think I could bear the memories, but I found out today that it's been turned into a karaoke bar, so I feel a bit better now because it'll be completely different from the place that we knew. And if it's not up to much, I can always get up and do a mean rendition of the "Shoop Shoop Song". It's my karaoke classic.'

Stevie had agreed immediately and with surprisingly little resistance, Carina got on board too.

Now, though, she seemed to be having a change of heart.

'I just keep thinking that my whole life changed down there. If I hadn't met Spencer that night...'

Her words drifted off. Moira, shoes now on her feet, threaded her hand through her friend's arm.

'Honey, it's going to be fine. We're going to go down there, have a nice dinner, a couple of drinks, a laugh at the folk on the karaoke and then we'll be in bed for 10 p.m. What could go wrong?'

'Your ex-boyfriend could show up and open a whole other big fat can of worms.'

'Don't be daft. There's no way he'd know we were there. And even if he did – I'm 100 per cent sure he wouldn't arrive uninvited.'

Her head was absolutely certain that was the case.

But there was a tiny bit of her heart that hoped she was wrong.

19

CARINA

Many times over the years, Carina had wondered how it would feel to come back here again. She'd spent many years living in Hong Kong at the start of their marriage, and she'd travelled back here on holiday countless times too, but somehow, until now, she'd never had the inclination to revisit old haunts. Perhaps there was a part of her that believed they belonged in another time, to another person. Not Carina Lloyd, wife of wealthy businessman, Spencer Lloyd, mother of two beautiful daughters, exquisite hostess, chairwoman of the school board, and benefactor of multiple worthy charities. No. That Carina bore no resemblance to the posh rebel who once lived in a slum hotel in Kowloon, and spent her nights rocking out in a riotous bar and partying until dawn.

Now, Carina wasn't sure which of those women she was prouder of. At least young Carina had been true to herself, and done exactly as she damn well pleased. She'd taken risks and chances and pushed herself right out of the rarefied bubble she'd been brought up in. Until she'd panicked and toed the line, she'd had a bloody good time. And it was telling that now, in probably the darkest time of her life, who was she with? Not the wives and friends she'd met over the last three decades. No. Her first reaction had been to come to Moira and Lisa. She wasn't entirely sure what that said about her choices over the last thirty-four years.

Those were the thoughts that were still running through her mind, when Moira, ahead of her, pushed open the door to the bar, then held it for her and Stevie to pass. Almost immediately Carina spotted the differences in the entrance way. Their bar had wood panelled walls, with glass and brass globe lights hanging from the ceiling in the hallway that led to the main room. Now it was decorated in a retro, old Hollywood, speakeasy vibe, the white walls lined with black and white photos of loads of celebrities who'd visited over the years. They all slowed down as they studied the images they were passing. Brad and Angelina sitting at the bar. Pacino eating with DeNiro in one of the booths. Sports teams from the Rugby Sevens, huddled in the centre of the frame, downing beers while holding trophies aloft. The Spice Girls. A couple of Korean boy bands on the stage singing karaoke. Take That. Debbie Harry from Blondie posing on top of the bar. It was like a *Who's Who* of pop culture that spanned years of recent history.

And then there was... Carina gasped. 'And then there was us,' she whispered, transfixed by a print in a black frame, about a foot square, that was right at her eyeline.

She glanced back at the other two, who were bending down, checking out an image of Kevin Costner, walking down this very same corridor, deep in conversation with another guy in a suit.

'Oh my word, I bloody loved that *Yellowstone*,' Moira was saying.

'Girls, look at this,' Carina beckoned them.

Moira's heels clicked as she walked towards her. 'Is it John Travolta? I heard he came in here once on my night off.'

'No, it's—'

She didn't have to finish the sentence, because Moira and Stevie gasped at the same time. 'It's us,' Moira blurted. 'Oh my word, would you look at us.'

'I know exactly what night that was. Christmas Eve, 1990. Look at the decorations hanging from the bar, and it was one of the few times we were all on stage together. We did an encore to count down to midnight, but we kept it going and ended up doing an hour together.' She turned to Stevie, not sure if she'd already explained the format of their acts. There had been so many conversations in the last few days it was impossible to be sure. 'I might already have told you this, but your mum and I did one set as Fleetwood Mac, and then Moira did her set, which was hits from musicals and general rock, pop and soul hits from female vocalists. I played piano on her set too. Never did work out why I didn't get paid double.'

'You did it for the love of it,' Moira quipped, still staring at the image.

Carina noticed that Stevie still hadn't spoken. 'Stevie? Is it too distressing?' Maybe this was a mistake after all. They'd just managed to get through the day with some degree of emotional equilibrium and now this.

'No,' Stevie said quietly, still staring. 'It's fecking glorious. Just look at my mum.'

All eyes went as directed to the blonde in centre stage, who was punching the air, her eyes closed, her mouth open in a roar, but her perfect face still exquisite.

'I remember that night. She had food poisoning and wasn't feeling great...' Carina didn't want to go for the truth, that Lisa probably had her usual post-party hangover, and yet she still went on that stage and set the place on fire.

'Look at this one too,' Moira gasped again, pointing to a frame Carina hadn't noticed. It was a newspaper review with the headline, THE STARS SHINE HERE! Underneath were photos of Moira in her Cher costume and Carina and Lisa doing Fleetwood Mac, and then a glorious account of their performances. They were sensational, it said. Yes, they were, Carina agreed, followed right up by another thought – when was the last time she'd felt sensational? When was the last time she'd felt true joy, or fulfilled, or inspired, or that she was making the most of her life? When was the last time she'd had unabashed fun? She honestly couldn't remember.

They all snapped pictures of the frames on their phones, then carried on into the bar. Carina's heart began to race. Moira had said the place would be different, and the décor definitely was, but Carina hadn't factored in that the layout would still be the same.

There in the corner, at the back of the bar, was the spot where she'd spoken to Spencer for the first time. It would be easy to say that she'd fallen in love with him at first sight, but now she suspected it was more complicated than that. Her family had cut her off. She'd lost Moira to Nate and Lisa to alcohol and partying. What had seemed like a wild adventure had turned sour. And of course, he was so handsome and charismatic that he'd swept her off her feet.

A barman approached them as soon as they pulled out their stools from the stunning walnut bar. 'Good evening, ladies, what can I get for you?' he asked, with the kind of wide smile and easy charm that suggested he probably made a fortune in tips.

'Gin and tonic please,' Carina said, returning the smile.

'I'll have the same,' Stevie echoed.

Moira was on a different track. 'Porn star martini, please,' she said sweetly, before turning to them, 'And I don't want to hear a word of judgement from you pair.'

The barman got in on the joke. 'I'll evict them immediately if they do. And can I get you menus?'

'Most definitely, thank you,' Moira replied, while Carina took her attention to the rest of the room. The stage was still in the same place, although the lighting rig above it was a testimony to modern technology. The back wall used to be where the drum kit sat, but now it was just a huge screen that she presumed would spring to life when the karaoke started. There were four microphones on stands in a line at the front of the stage, one acoustic guitar sat off to the left-hand side, next to a keyboard and a rack of tambourines, and in front of the whole lot was what looked like a glass teleprompter, which Carina assumed the singers used to read the lyrics.

The barman put the menus and two gin and tonics down, then got to work making Moira's martini. 'What time does the karaoke start?' Carina asked him, curious as to why the place was already pretty busy, yet there was no entertainment.

'Around nine,' he said, 'but people like to get here early to study the song books and pick their tunes.'

He took their food order – a sharing combination of flatbreads, mozzarella sticks, salad and chicken tenders, then keyed it all into a machine by the till.

'The televisions are still there,' Carina said, 'but they've changed more than a little.'

Back in the day there had been big, chunky TVs suspended from the ceiling. Most of them showed MTV music videos, but the one in the centre above the bar, ran a promotion video of their night time performances on a repetitive loop, as a way to encourage the daytime diners to come back in the evening.

The barman was back, and gently placing Moira's porn star martini in front of her. Carina took a sip of her gin, decided it was one of the best she'd ever tasted, then put it back down on the bar. A thought occurred to her, and she decided there was no harm in asking.

'Can I ask something else, please?'

'Of course,' he replied, and she mentally notched his tip up a bit more.

'If, say, thirty years ago there used to be a video of the act that played here every night, and they used to show it on a big, eighties television that dangled right above your head there, is there any long shot of a possibility that there would still be a copy of it anywhere? Would the hotel hang on to something like that?'

As expected, he appeared stumped – not a question he'd ever been asked before.

'I'm not sure but I can ask my manager. They have a huge store in the basement where they keep props, and memorabilia, and posters, and anything else that is relevant to the hotel. I can ask him to check there.'

'Wonderful. I'm in room 204. If he could just leave a message there, or with my porn star martini friend in the penthouse, we would very much appreciate it.'

'No worries at all. Do you have the name of the act?'

Carina pulled out her phone and showed him one of the pictures she'd taken of the prints in the entry way. 'This is actually us. We were the act. That's the porn star...' she pointed on the photo to Moira in her Cher fishnets and leather jacket, and couldn't resist, 'She hasn't changed much. Still wears that on a Saturday.' She pointed at the others in the photo. 'That's my friend here's mum. And that's me. It was a long time and a lot of wrinkles ago.'

'That's pretty cool. Do you still perform?'

Carina said, 'No', at the same time as Moira said, 'Yes.'

The barman slid a couple of song books over to them. 'Here you go. Just in case you fancy giving us a song here tonight.'

It was impossible to miss the way that Moira's face lit up as she took the book from him.

'What do you think, ladies? Fancy joining me? Carina, there's a keyboard up there.'

She cast her mind back to the last time she'd played. Her anniversary night. And the whole time, Spencer had been up in the bathroom, screwing Arabella.

'No, it's fine. I'll pass.'

Once upon a time, music had been her greatest joy, but she'd given it up for a man.

Now, it would always be a reminder that he'd given her up for someone else.

And she had no idea whether a ballad about forgiveness or a break up song was going to be next on the soundtrack of her life.

20

STEVIE

Was it wrong that she was enjoying herself? After the stresses of the last few days, tonight had been the first time that Stevie had felt anything even close to relaxation. The gin and tonics helped. So did the fact that the music was loud, so it made intimate conversation difficult. It felt like the best of both worlds – they were together, but they got to be happy, not sad.

There had been three or four singers up already and they were all surprisingly good. Over the noise of the music, Carina had filled her in about how popular karaoke was here in this region – almost a national sport. It was one Stevie could get on board with. When she was a student, she'd been a regular in Glasgow's karaoke bars and it was still her first choice of destination on her birthday. Her duet with Caleb to 'Endless Love' had wrapped up too many nights to count.

A short, suited gent who looked like an accountant brought his enthusiastic version of Meatloaf's 'Bat Out Of Hell' in to land, holding on to the last note like his life depended on it. Applause over, he took several bows, before the karaoke host jumped back up on the stage again to announce the next song.

'Ladies and gentlemen, please welcome the next singer... Moira Chiles!'

The crowd clapped politely as Moira slipped off her bar stool with a bashful shrug. 'Sorry, I couldn't resist.'

The lights went down, the opening bars of the unmistakable sound of Aretha Franklin's 'Respect' rang out, Moira opened her mouth and... Oh good grief, every single person in the bar snapped around to pay attention because the voice that came out of her was just incredible. For the first verse, the crowd listened in awe, by the middle of the song, they were singing along and by the time she got to the last chorus she had the whole room on its feet – Carina and Stevie included.

Stevie glanced at Carina and saw that despite her wide grin, tears were streaming down her face. Stevie instinctively understood. This wasn't just a performance that she was watching. They'd already said this was the same location, same stage, same songs – so what Carina must be witnessing was a re-run of her and Moira's past.

As soon as the song finished, the karaoke host returned, making a bowing motion to Moira, hailing her brilliance. It was difficult to be sure, under the lights, but Stevie thought she might be blushing.

'Thank you very much,' she said into the mic, acknowledging her audience. 'Thirty-five years ago, I sang on this stage every night, so I can't tell you how good it felt to do that.'

More thunderous appreciation, and a crowd of Americans at the table behind them began calling for an encore.

Stevie saw Moira's eyes go to the host, who made a shrugging/bowing motion inviting her to carry on.

Moira spoke back into the microphone. 'When I worked here, I actually sang with my two best friends and one of them is here tonight, so maybe she could come and join me?'

That set the crowd off again, all of them loving this idea... except the woman standing to Stevie's right, whose emotion appeared to have turned to a distinct reluctance to take centre stage. 'No,' she mouthed to Moira, shaking her head.

The Americans clicked that it was Carina that Moira was inviting to join her, and began cheering her on, until she must have realised that there was no point in resisting.

Carina picked up her drink, knocked it back and then leaned into Stevie's ear and said, 'Remind me later that I plan on killing her, please.'

'Will do,' Stevie agreed, chuckling. The cheer that went round the room carried Carina all the way to the stage. When she got there, Stevie could see her speaking to the host, who nodded, before stepping to the side and pressing a couple of buttons on the keyboard.

The whole time, Moira was grinning, which turned to laughter when Carina whispered what Stevie assumed was a death threat in her ear. She adored the dynamic between these two women. And she was grateful that her mum had been a part of it all those years ago.

That thought sparked a strange feeling, something that sat between regret and sadness. How different would her childhood, her teenage years, her twenties, her thirties have been if she'd known the other Lisa, the talented, badass one that she knew now had stood on that stage and entertained her audience?

Carina played a few test notes on the keyboard, twiddled a few knobs, and then began thumping out a beat that Stevie recognised immediately as the intro to a classic tune that had been written before she was born, but that everyone immediately reacted to. And as the sound of Cher's 'Turn Back Time' filled the bar, everyone was on their feet again. Moira raised the mic, belted out the first line, this time with Carina's harmony in perfect sync. Stevie knew they hadn't performed this for decades, yet they were flawless and fricking magnificent.

Again, halfway through the song, the rest of the audience joined in and there was a moment that she was sure they'd all talk about the next day, when they told friends, families, co-workers about the absolutely brilliant night they'd had tonight.

When the song ended, they hugged, hanging onto each other for a few moments, their emotion palpable, before they broke off and took a bow. By the time they were cheered the whole way back to their seats, the barman was already sliding fresh drinks towards them. 'On the house,' he said, laughing as he gave them a bow of appreciation.

'Aye, well that gave my lungs a workout,' Moira declared, before putting her hand up to stop any negative reaction from Carina. 'And don't you say a word, Carina Lloyd, because you know you enjoyed that every bit as much as I did.'

Carina was already taking a considerable gulp of her drink. 'Maybe. Okay, yes, so it felt good. Argh, I really, really hate it when you're right.'

Moira was beaming. 'Sorry, what was that? I was right? It was worth waiting thirty-five years to hear you say that.'

'Yes, well it probably won't happen again for another thirty-five, so enjoy it. Now come on – let's finish these drinks and get out of here while we're riding a wave of glory.'

They were entertained by a passionate performance of Christina Aguilera's 'Fighter' from an Italian chap in a Versace shirt, then an elderly lady belting out 'Like A Virgin', and finally the group from the next table took to the spotlights to give them 'American Pie'.

Moira signed the cheque, charging their food and drinks to her room, then slipped off her chair. 'Shall we go then, ladies?' With a parting wave to the barman, they headed off, and as they walked down the corridor, Moira said, 'You know, it never changes. That buzz when you come off a stage. We could never just go home and sleep after work. We weren't exactly filling arenas, but I understand why rock stars lose the plot, I really do.'

In the lobby, a pianist in the corner was serenading late night guests. 'Shall we sit here and have a night cap?' Moira went on, proving her point.

'I could do that,' Carina agreed. 'Stevie?'

Stevie hadn't sung a word tonight, hadn't felt the appreciation of the crowd, or the adrenalin of delivering a performance that rocked a whole bar, but she wasn't ready to sleep yet either.

A waiter took their order – three porn star martinis this time – and then left them to the sound of Andrea Bocelli's beautiful 'Con Te Partirò' being played on the piano. They sat in silence, appreciating the moment, but Stevie's mind refused to wind down and relax. It was as if everything they did, every place they went, every interaction they had, sparked another question about the woman she realised now that she'd never known.

'Stevie, you look like you're miles away there,' Moira said gently, perhaps wondering if the emotion of the song was making her sad.

'I was just thinking about all the things I've learned since I got here. I still can't quite take it all in or get my head round everything.'

'It must be a lot to digest,' Carina empathised.

Stevie could have left it there. Let it go. Enjoyed the music while they sipped their nightcaps. But her conversation with Caleb from the previous afternoon had raised a question that hadn't yet been answered. She was still sure that she didn't know the full story. Something was off. There were gaps in the narrative that hadn't yet been filled.

The song changed from 'Con Te Partirò' to 'My Heart Will Go On', and Stevie took that as a sign.

'Is it okay if we talk a little more about my mum?' she asked, her voice low, so that she didn't disturb the enjoyment of the people at nearby tables.

Carina was the first to respond. 'Of course.'

'It's just that something you said yesterday has been playing on my mind. You were talking about how you all made mistakes back in the day, but that you were lucky because there was no social media, or Internet or phones with cameras to record those mistakes.'

'That's true,' Moira agreed. 'And we were so much better for it.'

Stevie didn't disagree. 'What I keep thinking though, is that for the last few days you've been filling in blanks for me about my mum. And don't get me wrong, I really appreciate how lovely you've both been to me. But the thing I keep coming back to is that almost everything you've told me about my mum was positive, yet I know she could be complicated, and difficult and secretive. I get that she was your friend, and you're probably trying to protect her, but I want to know *all* of it, even the things I might not like. So I'd really appreciate if you would be honest with me and tell me – what were my mum's mistakes?'

21

DECEMBER 1990 – HONG KONG

Lisa

Lisa opened one eye, when she heard the footsteps coming out of the bathroom, then waited until her stomach settled before opening the other one.

'Good morning, gorgeous,' Ben said, sitting down on the edge of the bed beside her. 'Happy Christmas Eve.'

'Morning,' she groaned, in a voice that came directly from a packet of Marlboro Reds.

'I stuck around last night to make sure you were okay. You were pretty wasted.'

'Yeah... I'm, erm... sorry about that.'

'No worries,' he shrugged it off. 'But I need to get going. My flight is in a couple of hours and it's the last one that'll get me home by tonight. Should land in London about six this evening.' He'd told her a while ago that he was going back to England for Christmas. Said something about combining it with a work trip.

He leaned down and kissed the top of her head. 'I'm sorry I won't be here for tomorrow.'

Lisa pushed herself up so that she was sitting against her pillow. 'Don't worry about it. I'm working anyway and the show is sold out. You'll miss a good time.'

'I don't doubt it. Look, when I get back...' he began, and Lisa felt the familiar need to reject affection begin to creep under her skin. She knew what he was going to say because he'd hinted at it before. And she knew how she was going to reply. The same way that she always did.

This guy was way, *way*, too nice for her. She'd stayed over at his flat a few nights and he'd brought her home many times over the last couple of months, and he hadn't asked her for money, offered her money, plied her with booze, taken her for granted, or tried to have sex with her when she was wasted then escaped first thing in the morning, saying he'd call and then not bothered – all things that were far easier to deal with than someone who was just a genuinely nice guy and a friend. Last night pretty much summed him up. Like other occasions, he'd come home with her in a taxi to make sure she got back safely. But last night... the memories were hazy, but she tried to piece it together. Last night, she'd been blackout drunk, probably worse than he'd ever seen her before. He'd had to help her up the stairs because there was no way she was making it on her own. She remembered crashing out on the bed and when she'd woken up during the night to pee, she'd had a row of pillows along her back, that he must have put there to keep her on her side, just in case she threw up. On the other side of the pillows, he'd been lying sleeping, still fully clothed too.

All of it was evidence for the prosecution. Way too nice – guilty as charged.

'Don't be doing all that soppy stuff,' she warned him. 'What did I tell you about that?'

Laughing, he put his hands up. 'Okay, fine. But, how about we just try a proper date? You know, dinner. Drinks. Just us.'

She stopped him there. 'That sounds like more of that soppy stuff,' she warned him, but it did make her smile. 'Maybe. Just maybe. I told you...'

He put his hands up, conceding defeat, but still in the game. 'I know – you don't do relationships. I got the message. But I don't do random hook ups. So maybe we could just start out slow. Look, no pressure. Let's just wait and see how it goes. Maybe you'll miss me so much, you'll be driven crazy by lust and longing for me.'

'I highly doubt that, but sure, you can't knock an optimist.'

That made him laugh again, as he went over to the chair by the window and picked up his jacket.

'How long will you be away for?' she asked.

'See, you're missing me already. A couple of months. I should be back end of February or early March.'

'Okay. Well, look me up. You know where to find me.' It wasn't exactly a commitment, but it was a start. Maybe by that time she'd have her shit figured out and be ready to try to act like a normal human being. And if she was, then maybe this would be a pretty good guy to have proper relationship with.

As soon as he was gone, she ran through the rest of her morning routine. Cigarette. Paracetamol. This morning it was washed down with a bottle of water that he must have left by her bed. She stretched over, pressed 'play' on the tape recorder. Listened to the same message she'd heard every morning for the last five years.

'This is Netta Dixon. Don't leave a message because I don't know what to be doing with this damn contraption anyways. There. Are ya happy now, Lisa?'

Lisa closed her eyes and let the feelings of grief and loneliness consume her. She had no idea why she did this every morning, but she just knew she couldn't stop. It was her oxygen and also the thing that suffocated her. She felt the familiar urge to reach for the liquid that numbed it all, when her door opened and Carina and Moira came in carrying...

'Morning! We brought you a Christmas tree. Actually, we stole it from downstairs, but they'll never prove it was us. Nate agreed to turn his back when we went past reception with it so there are no witnesses. Anyway, since we're all too skint to buy each other presents, you need to get up, because we're going out.'

'Where to?'

'We're going for Christmas Eve lunch.'

'Does that mean getting cheap food from somewhere and going back and forward on the Star Ferry all afternoon?' Lisa asked. It was their standard celebration treat. Before Moira and Carina had got loved up, they'd spent many days off that way. They'd done the same thing whenever any local newspapers or radio hosts did a brilliant review of their show. And then again for Moira's birthday last month.

'It sure does.' Moira confirmed.

'Then I'm in,' Lisa agreed, gingerly pushing herself out of the bed. 'Let me get a shower and I'll catch up.'

In the end, it was past twelve by the time they were on the top deck of the ferry, boxes of chicken and rice on their laps. The weather was cooler at this time of year, so for once, they weren't melting in the heat.

'Guess what arrived for me this morning,' Carina teased, before using her chopsticks to pop a chunk of chicken into her mouth.

'Patrick Swayze's boxer shorts,' Moira guessed, before raising her gaze from her lunch. 'Wait, did I say that out loud?'

Carina wasn't amused. 'Your mind is a swamp of a place. Anyway, no, and I'm not letting you spoil my good mood by mocking me. It was a Christmas card from my parents.'

'No way,' Lisa said, as she pushed her food away. The ferry must be rockier than usual today because her stomach was churning.

'Yes. I think the photo I sent them of me and Spencer did the trick. Apparently, my father knows of Spencer's family, so they think I'm on the road to redemption after all.'

'And what did your mum say in the card?' Moira asked.

'That she hopes my new relationship means I've come to my senses and will be coming home soon.'

A cog turned even tighter in Lisa's stomach. Moira and Carina were the only people she had. Nate too. They were her family. She couldn't bear the thought that that could change. 'And will you? Go home?'

'I don't know. Maybe. At least, for a visit. Spencer is saying that he's planning to base himself in Hong Kong in the foreseeable future, so maybe I'll stay here. Depends how it works out. Either way, though, I'm thinking that there's going to come a time that I'll leave the agency. It's been great while it lasted, but we hate that I'm working six nights a week. Doesn't leave any time for us.'

Lisa felt like she'd been slapped and Carina must have registered her expression because she nudged her. 'Not yet though. Don't worry, I'll give you plenty of notice so you can throw me a party.'

There was a couple of minutes silence while they absorbed that, until Moira shook them out of it. 'Right, let's change the subject, because it's Christmas Eve and I refuse to be sad...'

So they weren't. They kept up the holiday spirit for the rest of the afternoon, and then all the way to the show, and right through two incredible sets that had the packed crowd on their feet and dancing well after they'd counted down the clock to Christmas Day. Lisa even went back on stage and the three of them did an impromptu hour together, nothing rehearsed, nothing planned, just a crazy hour of three chicks rocking that the crowd adored. They kicked off with one of their favourite songs, 'It's A Man's World', then ran through a few other hits that they'd sung together at parties for months, just for fun. It blocked out every negative thought and feeling, leaving only pure joy. It had always been the way that no matter how she felt, no matter what was on her mind, the second she was on the stage it was all forgotten until she sang the last note.

Tonight, that had never been more true.

At the end of the show, Spencer whisked Carina off to some flash hotel somewhere, and Moira and Nate were going to Lan Kwai Fong to carry on the party.

'You're coming, right?' Moira asked, probably expecting her to say yes, given that she never missed an excuse to drink and be merry. However, for once, she didn't want to join the revelry, because as soon as she'd got off stage, the nausea she'd felt earlier in the day had kicked back in.

'I'll catch up with you there,' Lisa lied to them. 'I'm not feeling great, so I just want to stop off and pick up something to settle my stomach.'

'I'll come with you,' Moira offered but Lisa had no intention of spoiling anyone else's night, so she fobbed her off with another lie. 'No, no – Zak and Joe are going to come with me.' The barmen didn't need to know that she was involving them in her lie.

Outside the Harbour Lights Hotel, she jumped in a taxi, then put the window down, breathing in through her nose and out through her mouth to try to fight down the nausea. There was a tiny bit of panic in there too. Had she damaged something by going too hard on the booze? Her gran used to warn her about this, about how easy it was to wreck your body, even when you were young.

In through the nose. Out through the mouth.

There was a dodgy moment when they were going through the tunnel that took them under the harbour to Kowloon, but she managed to keep it together right up until the taxi turned into her street.

'Stop here, please. Anywhere.' She threw some money into the front, then lurched open the door and threw up into the gutter.

Bed. She just needed to get to bed.

She practically crawled up the stairs to reception, where Wai, the night manager, nodded to her from behind the desk.

Almost there. Almost there. She made it down the corridor, into her room, then staggered into the bathroom where she threw up until there was nothing left in her gut.

Unable to stand, she pulled the basket that sat under her sink towards her, looking for any kind of anti-sickness pill or even just some water to make her feel better.

That's when she saw two things. First of all, a box of tampons. Unopened. Her mind tried to calculate when she'd bought them, but she couldn't remember. Felt like longer than a month ago, though.

The second thing she saw was the pregnancy test that had been left over from the box of two Carina had bought. 'You take it,' Carina had said, when her test had been negative. 'I won't need it, because after this, I'm never having sex again.'

Lisa had thought it was funny at the time. She'd just tossed it into this basket and forgotten about it. Now it didn't seem like so much of a joke.

She couldn't be pregnant. She was on the pill. And she used condoms most of the time too... At least, when she was sober enough to remember.

In some kind of slow, dread-filled trance, she opened the test and followed the instructions, then, back on the floor, held the stick in shaking hands while she waited for the results.

All day, surrounded by normal people, with normal lives and families and loved ones, she'd managed to block out that dark, creeping thought, that reminder that there were no Christmas cards with her name on them, no presents from any family, no calls from people across the seas that missed her. Nothing. Other than her skint friends here, she was completely alone in this world so no gifts would be coming her way.

But now, as she stared at her destiny in her hand, she saw that for Christmas, she'd just been given a faint blue line in the window of a white stick.

22

SATURDAY, 5 JULY, 2025 – HONG KONG

Moira

'Moira, you know you'll enjoy this so much more if you open your eyes,' Carina suggested.

Moira wasn't having it. 'I think a one-night stand once said that to me back in the eighties. I didn't believe him then and I don't believe you now.'

Why? Why had she let them persuade her to do this? Thanks to Carina bossing them out of the hotel and on to the MTR – she was definitely power crazy when she was in charge, Moira decided – they'd travelled across the territory, alighting at Tung Chung, and been first in the queue for the Ngong Ping cable car on Lantau Island. They were now soaring high in the fricking sky, which was particularly bloody terrifying given that Moira vehemently disliked being in any situation from which she could plummet to her death. Even the penthouse at the hotel made her queasy if she looked down over the balcony.

'You know, back when we were here last time we had to get a

boat to Lantau island. We used to come here sometimes on our day off and hang with all the hippies that stayed here. Now this feels more like a hostage situation.'

Stevie was on Carina's side. 'Honestly, Moira, it really is spectacular. You should definitely open your eyes.'

Heart racing, she decided to pull on her big woman pants and do it. She was already traumatised, so how much worse could it get?

The answer came the second she squinted open one peeper, looked down and then yelped, because she hadn't realised the gondola had a glass floor. Again, why?

'What kind of twisted soul would come up with something like that?' she gasped, pointing downwards, where the treetops and slopes of the terrain below them were clear as day between her Skechers. 'Like it isn't terrifying enough?'

Yep, they'd definitely got her at a weak moment when she'd agreed to this. It had been last night in the piano bar, long after the music had stopped and the rest of the guests had gone to bed. The three of them had still been sitting there, exhausted after a two-hour conversation that had run the emotional spectrum from tears, to sadness, to honesty and even, a couple of times, to laughter too. When Stevie had asked to know her mother's mistakes, they'd been as honest as possible with her. She deserved to know. All this week they'd been protecting Lisa, but now, they knew it was time to protect Stevie too, and that started with answering as many of the questions that were troubling her as they could.

And that's what they'd done. They'd shared the stories about her drinking, about her melancholy, about the darkness that sometimes consumed her. They'd said that she made questionable choices with men, and that she had no interest in being in a relationship, that she never let anyone get too close.

'We were her best friends, yet she shut us out too. She talked more to Nate...' Moira remembered, 'Because the two of them had been there the longest. I used to think he was like a brother figure to her. He looked out for her.'

Stevie took a second to get her head around that one. 'Nate, the guy you called? The one you dated?'

'Yes, but they were just friends – it wasn't a sharing situation,' Moira quickly clarified. 'We were wild, but not *that* wild.'

They'd talked a while longer, answering every question Stevie threw at them.

Stevie had taken it all in. 'I think that what I don't understand is why. Why was she so broken?'

Moira truly wished she had the answers to that. 'We don't know. It was just as if she had a self-destruct button, and she couldn't help pressing it. I suppose nowadays we're more aware of trauma and mental health issues, even things like PTSD, but back then, we were just young, with no experience or knowledge of anything like that. We just accepted her for who she was. She never talked much about her family, and she shut us down when we asked. All we knew was that her mum had passed away and her gran raised her, then died a few years before she came to Hong Kong.'

'By the time I came along, there was no one left,' Stevie said. 'Mum would just say her family was all in heaven. As a child, you just accept that and let it go. I'm so sorry now that I didn't ask her more, but like with you, she never wanted to share her feelings.'

'Maybe that was just who she was, and we need to respect that?' Carina had suggested.

That was the point when they'd decided to call it a night. 'Any thoughts about what to do tomorrow?' Carina had asked in the lift.

Stevie had a suggestion. 'Actually, I did read about one thing that sounded really cool. The Big Buddha on—'

'Lantau Island,' Carina had finished for her. 'That sounds like a great idea. It hadn't been built when we lived here, so no sad memories.'

Tired, aching, desperate to make Stevie smile, Moira had agreed without researching it. That's why she hadn't known that this morning she'd be dangling in a tiny box in mid-air, with the ground terrifyingly far below her.

'Look, there it is!' Stevie exclaimed, and Moira turned her head so quickly that she almost heaved. But actually, it was worth it. It even took her mind off her terror for a few seconds. There, rising from the trees at the top of a hill in the distance, was a gigantic, breathtaking Bhudda.

'I looked it up – it's thirty-four metres tall and it's made of bronze and steel,' Tour Guide Carina informed them.

It was enough of a distraction to get Moira through the rest of the journey without more fear-induced sweating, just in time for the doors to open, the heat to hit them and the sweating to start all over again. She was definitely beginning to wonder if she was cut out for this tourist stuff. When she'd planned the trip, she'd envisaged a bit of nostalgia, a lot of relaxing, a fair amount of singing, long chatty lunches and even longer chatty dinners with loads of great food and wine. This most certainly wasn't any of those things.

'Right, I think it's this way.' Tour Guide Carina was back, and Moira and Stevie were happy to follow her along a wide walkway, with shops on either side selling touristy things, jewellery, snacks and drinks. There was even a Starbucks, which they detoured into for water, before carrying on, most of the rest of the tourists around them going in the same direction, towards the huge statue that sat on a hill and towered over them. When they got to the bottom, Moira stared upwards, puffed out her cheeks. 'You have got to be kidding me.'

There, stretching up in front of them, was the tallest, most intimidating staircase she'd ever seen in her life.

'I wouldn't want to have to sweep that,' Moira mumbled, mostly to herself.

'Two hundred and sixty-eight steps to reach the Buddha,' Carina informed them, reading the information on a pamphlet she'd picked up from the cable car station.

Stevie was already eyeing her expectantly. 'Shall we?'

Moira was still looking skyward. 'I hate to be Captain Obvious, but I've got that bloke's figure,' she said, nodding to the bronze chap at the top. 'If I climb up there, there'd better be water, a defibrillator and a surgeon to replace my knees.'

'And yet again, I'm so glad you're not dramatic,' Carina piped up, taking the sting out of her mocking with an affectionate nudge on the shoulder.

'I feel I need to point out that I'm a trained medical professional who could intervene in the case of an emergency,' Stevie added, laughing.

'And I'm a trained professional singer, but I'm not standing in for Celine Dion,' Moira jested back, enjoying the banter, despite the prospect ahead of her. At that point, an elderly lady, maybe in her eighties, marched past her and began taking the stairs at rapid speed. Moira took it as a sign that the Buddha was laughing at her too.

'I suppose we can't come all this way and not do this...'

Carina took a sip from her water bottle. 'Correct.'

'Okay, let's do it. And if I die, make sure they put up a plaque here.'

With the renewed determination of someone who doesn't like to fail, a steely stare, and a prayer of hope, she set off first, with Carina at her side and Stevie one step behind them.

They were a third of the way up, when the phone in her pocket began to ring. 'That's God telling me he didn't build me for stairs,' she said, managing to keep walking and check the screen at the same time. A Facetime call. There was only one person in the world that she would answer to at this moment, and his photograph was on the screen. She pressed the green button.

'Ollie,' she panted, 'I just want it known that these women are trying to kill me. If anything happens to me, Carina will return my personal effects.'

Still climbing, still panting.

That TV star grin of his made her heart melt as he said, 'Good to know, Ma. Where are you?'

'Climbing the stairs to the Big Buddha. Look it up and you'll understand. Where are you, son?' she asked, squinting at the screen while still climbing, still panting.

'LAX. Just about to get on my flight back to the UK. In sixteen hours, I'll be back in Glasgow.' He looked like he was happy about that, and Moira didn't blame him. Last year, with all the travelling he'd done, he'd worked out that he'd spent twelve nights in his Glasgow home in five months. Now that he'd founded the drama and music school, he was aiming for a better balance.

'Okay, well, I'd love to chat, son, but my cardiovascular system is shutting down and every breath could be my last. Have a safe flight, ma darlin'. I love you and I'll see you when—' She paused, a wave of light-headedness taking her words for a second. Then another. Then... She reached out to try to put her hand on the stone banister, but it was too far away and... now she couldn't catch her breath. Couldn't feel where her feet were. Couldn't make herself go forwards, or backwards, until... It all went black.

And the last thing Moira heard as she began to fall, was her son shouting 'Mum?'

23

CARINA

The temperature in the hospital corridor was cool, but Carina felt like she was melting from the inside out, her panic stoking a fire underneath her skin, her mind ruminating, repeating the same words over and over. Please be okay. Please be okay.

Sitting beside her, Stevie was leaning forward, elbows on knees, hands clutched together, head bowed as if in prayer as she said, 'I just keep thinking that we somehow brought this on. The way we were joking about the climb causing a medical emergency... maybe we put it out there into the universe. You know, all that manifestation stuff.'

Carina pulled at the neck of her T-shirt to get some air. 'Do you believe in that?'

Stevie shrugged, a sad smile on her face. 'No. But I just feel so guilty about suggesting coming here this morning. If I hadn't done that...'

Carina reached over and took one of her hands. 'If you hadn't done that then maybe this would have happened somewhere else. Look, we just need to keep telling ourselves that she's going to be fine. She is.'

Stevie looked up at her with Lisa's eyes. 'Based on?' It was exactly the kind of cynical response that Lisa would have had too.

'Blind faith and optimism. Moira used that to get through every tough thing in her life, and I'm sticking with it now.'

'I still feel responsible.'

Carina went straight in to refute that. 'Stevie, you're not responsible. If you hadn't been a couple of steps behind her and caught her so quickly, she would have rolled down who knows how many more stairs and banged her head on each one. You didn't harm her, you saved her. We were so lucky that you were there.'

'I just couldn't bear it if—' Stevie began, and Carina forgot her own worries for a second, desperate to comfort this young woman who'd been through so much in the last month. 'Don't say it, Stevie. Blind faith and optimism. Stick with that,' she said softly.

'Okay, but I'm going to go try to find a doctor and get an update. I want to know if she's fully regained consciousness yet, and if they've found out what caused her to fall. They'll already have run the preliminary tests so if it was a heart attack they should have some indication by now.'

'All right, but I'll wait here in case anyone comes looking for us.'

She watched as Stevie went down the corridor, then through the double doors at the end, in the same direction they'd taken Moira earlier.

When Carina could no longer see her, she leant her head back against the wall. As soon as she closed her eyes, her mind began replaying the moment that everything had changed. One second, Moira had been on a Facetime call to Ollie, laughing and talking about how she'd see him again soon. Then, in what seemed like a heartbeat, she'd collapsed, fallen to the side, her phone smashing as she crumpled to the ground, banged her head on the stone balustrade and then began to slide downwards, rolling down a couple of steps, before Stevie had thrown herself behind her to break her fall.

What happened next was a blur. Moira, on the ground, unconscious. Stevie down there too, checking her vital signs, her pulse, her breathing, trying to bring her round. Tourists had swarmed around them, many of them trying to help. One gave them water, another put an umbrella above them to give shade. Someone else ran back down the stairs to the ticket office at the bottom, to ask them to call an ambulance. Carina had no idea how long it was until they'd arrived – probably only fifteen minutes or so, but it felt like hours. They'd stretchered Moira back down to the car park, loaded her into an ambulance, allowed Carina and Stevie to ride with them as they'd driven, blue lights flashing and siren wailing, to the hospital on Lantau. Moira had been flitting in and out of consciousness on the journey, and as soon as they'd arrived, she had been whisked away, and they'd been asked to wait. That's why she was now sitting in a hospital corridor, waiting to find out if she was about to lose another friend.

Despite reassuring Stevie that they were going with blind faith and optimism, Carina felt panicked to her core.

She couldn't lose Moira. She just couldn't.

They'd only just reconnected after all these years, and now... no, she couldn't lose her. She damn well refused.

'Cary?' She recognised the man's voice and his nickname for her before she even opened her eyes.

'Ben! You got my message. Thank you so much for coming.' She stood up and let him wrap his arms around her. Her brother-in-law had been one of her favourite people for all of her adult life and she'd texted him as soon as they'd arrived at the hospital. He'd lived in Hong Kong for over thirty years now, so he'd been her first thought for advice, and for just being here and helping her to navigate getting Moira the best care.

'Of course. How is she? Have you heard anything?' he asked, releasing her and then taking the seat that Stevie had just left.

'I don't know. All I do know is that they're running tests on her now to try to find out what caused it. Stevie mentioned that a heart attack is the obvious possibility, but I guess it could be anything. And she banged her head when she fell, so they're probably testing for a head injury too. She started to come round in the ambulance, but she wasn't making much sense and the blood pressure monitor kept going off so... Actually, I don't know what that would mean. It's all a bit of a blur.'

He took in everything she was saying. 'That's understandable. Everything I say right now is going to sound like a cliché, but let's just keep the faith until we know more.'

Carina nodded. 'I just gave that same speech to Stevie. Blind faith and optimism would get us through this, I said. But I don't think I believed it either. All I can think about was that we were too late to find Lisa again. Surely, I won't lose Moira too?'

'You won't lose her. Let's stick with that optimism stuff. I still can't believe Lisa is gone.'

When she'd called him a couple of days ago to tell him what had happened to Lisa, he'd listened to the whole story as she'd poured it out, stunned. 'Christ, Cary, I'm so sorry to hear that. Poor Lisa. That's tragic. And her daughter... she came to Hong Kong to tell you that she'd passed away?'

'Yes. I couldn't talk to you about it when you called earlier because Stevie was with us,' Carina had said.

'Stevie?'

'Yes. Would you believe Lisa named her after Stevie Nicks?'

His voice had oozed sadness. 'Yes. I think that's probably the most "Lisa" thing she ever did.'

When she'd hung up, Carina had told herself that was the last of the sadness for this week. She could never have guessed that now, just a few days later, she'd be here.

They sat in silence for the next few minutes, until Carina's gaze fell on a clock on the opposite wall, just a couple of metres away. Every tick seemed to last forever.

'You know, the strange thing is, I didn't feel this way when I left Dubai. When I left Spencer...' She paused, tying to formulate her thoughts. 'I thought I'd be grief stricken. Panicked. Devastated. But this... this is so much worse. I think maybe that tells me something.'

He sat with that for a few seconds before he replied. 'He knows for sure that you're here. I'm just warning you. You used your credit card somewhere and he saw it on your bank transactions.'

She had a sinking moment of realisation. 'Shit, I bought the tickets for the cable car online. I must have used those card details. Damn it. I'm sorry if that puts you in a difficult position. I don't want you to get stuck in the middle of me and your brother. That's not fair.'

'Don't apologise. Pissing off my brother is one of my favourite sports. He already had a hunch that you'd come here, but that confirmed it. He called me, raging that I'd lied to him.'

Carina could picture that scene perfectly, hear every word that would have come out of Spencer's mouth. He wasn't a man who took kindly to not getting what he wanted. That was one of the things she used to love about him.

'What did you tell him?'

'I told him not to come here, to give you space to figure this out and decide what you want to do.'

'Did he listen?' Carina already knew the probable answer to that.

Ben gave a gentle shrug. 'Who knows. If he did it would be a first. But I told him he could risk everything if he tried to pressure you, so maybe that got through.'

Carina sighed. 'It's what, five days now? I'm surprised I got that long before he found me. Where is he now?'

'He was in London when he called. I think he'd gone there to see if you were staying at your family's house.' Her dad was in his nineties, living in a wonderful care facility, in the grip of Alzheimer's for over a decade now. She now co-owned her family estate with her brothers and often stayed there when she was visiting her dad – she got on well enough with them but they weren't the people she'd turn to in a crisis.

'I'd like to have seen him explain that one away if my mother was still alive. Although, given how much she adored him, she'd probably have taken his side.' Her mother had passed away four years ago, and right up until her last breath she was still talking about how wonderful her son-in-law was, and how he'd saved Carina from a life unbecoming of her status. So yes, she had no doubt her mother would blame his affair on her. All those years ago, she'd thought that marrying Spencer would earn her family's respect, but no. As far as they were concerned, she was lucky he'd chosen her. It had taken her a long time to have the experience and emotional maturity to realise that her mother was just one of those females who vehemently disliked other women. She was a bully who cared so much more about appearances than happiness. And where had that got her? She'd died a bitter old lady, still complaining and gossiping. If that was what living the 'correct' life got you, Carina wanted no part of it. Maybe it was time to let everyone else's opinions go and do what she damn well pleased. It was telling that this week, she hadn't missed a single thing about her life with Spencer, other than her daughters. Maybe it was time to live an 'incorrect' life on her own terms – one where she chose her own way and didn't put up with people who hurt her.

Carina stared at the clock again. *Tick. Tock. Tick. Tock.* So slowly. At least talking stopped time from standing still.

'Did he say where things stood with him and that woman?' She couldn't stomach saying Arabella's name out loud. Not here. Not now. She didn't matter. She was inconsequential in Carina's life, especially when there were far more important people to care about right now.

'No. But I do know that Imogen kicked her out of the house when she found out what had happened. Apparently Spencer finally confessed all to her yesterday and Imogen was furious with him. She hadn't even realised that you'd left before the end of the party because Spencer had spun her some bullshit story about sending you on some surprise spa trip for your anniversary. Imogen hit the roof, ordered Arabella to leave and told him he was a disgrace and that he needed to sort himself out – said she'd quit if he didn't make this right.'

It surprised her that Imogen had stood up to Spencer so forcefully. Just like with Ben, Carina hadn't wanted to involve her daughters, to force them to take sides. She usually called Erin once a week, and she'd spoken to her on the night of the party, so her younger daughter would be blissfully unaware of the drama. As for Imogen, it was even more personal because Arabella was her friend. The fact that Imogen had sided with

Carina... if she were anywhere else than right here, right now, that might even have given her a little surge of pleasure.

'Did Imogen tell you that?'

'Yes, she called too,' Ben went on, 'And I hope you don't mind, but I told her you were here and safe, and with Moira and Stevie.'

'That's fine. I'll call her later and I'll—' Before she could finish the sentence, three uniformed staff flew round the corner pushing a crash cart, all of them running towards the doors Stevie had gone through. Carina's hand jumped to her mouth.

A few moments later, an ashen faced Stevie came back through the same doors. Carina felt all the air being slammed out of her chest.

Her words came out in a strangled burst. 'Tell me she's okay—'

Stevie shook her head. 'They wouldn't let me see her. All they would tell me was that the doctor would be out to speak to us soon.'

'Okay. Okay. So it's not bad news. We're staying positive.' She wasn't sure who she was trying to convince. With a jolt, she realised she hadn't introduced Stevie to the man beside her.

'Sorry! Stevie, this is my brother-in-law, Ben. Ben, this is Lisa's daughter – Stevie.'

Ben reached out and shook her hand, and Carina could see his shock at just how much Stevie resembled Lisa. 'I wish we weren't meeting under these circumstances. I'm so sorry about your mum. She was a special lady.'

'You were friends?' Stevie asked.

'We were.'

Carina zoned out of their conversation as the sound of the clock on the opposite wall once again became the soundtrack to this moment. *Tick. Tock. Tick. Tock.*

With every tick came a realisation. She didn't care that her marriage had fallen apart. Didn't care that she'd left her home. Didn't care that she had no idea what she was going to do next. All she cared about was watching that door at the end of the corridor, waiting for a doctor to come through it and tell them the fate of the only person who mattered right now.

24

STEVIE

Stevie was beginning to lose hope. They'd been there for hours now, and no one had come to see them. What did that mean? If this was back home, and they were at her place of work, Glasgow Central Hospital, she'd have known exactly who to speak to, she'd have known where to go, she'd have had a rough idea how long each step in the process would take. But here, she was just a tourist, waiting for information about someone they cared about, and scared to death what the news would be.

Carina's brother-in-law, Ben, had gone to see if he could track down some coffees, so once again, it was just her and Carina, sitting with their heads against the wall, listening to that bloody clock tick.

And then bang...

Stevie and Carina both gasped and shot upright, as the door at the end of the corridor opened and a woman in a white coat came towards them. Stevie tried to read her face, but couldn't. Neutral. Could go either way.

Stevie reached for Carina's hand, and squeezed it, while both of them kept their eyes fixed firmly on the doctor.

'Good afternoon,' the doctor said in perfect English. 'I believe you're with Miss Chiles? Brought in today from Ngong Ping?' she said, giving the location of the Buddha its proper name.

'Yes,' Stevie replied, noticing that Carina's mouth wasn't moving.

'I'm Doctor Lin, and Miss Chiles has been under my care. We've run many tests to establish the cause of Miss Chiles' accident. We were concerned that there could have been a cardiac incident, but we were also concerned about the possibility of deep vein thrombosis, given that she had a long flight earlier in the week. Of course, no tests are absolute, but we're confident that we've ruled out both of those possibilities.'

Stevie felt like someone was lifting a giant weight off her chest, as her lungs kicked back into action. 'Sometimes,' the doctor went on, 'The simplest answer is the correct one. We think she was acutely dehydrated and suffering from the effects of the heat and humidity. She's managed to tell us that she hasn't been sleeping this week, and she's had a considerable amount of stress. Our conclusion is that those factors, combined with a lack of fluids, caused her to faint, in the first instance.'

More relief. Dehydration. Exhaustion. Heat. That made total sense.

'However, Miss Chiles did take a considerable knock to her head, causing her to lose consciousness. We've scanned her head and there's no obvious injury, but we'd like to keep her in overnight for observation as a concussion is a potential issue and one that we need to monitor.'

Beside her, Carina's whole posture changed, as her shoulders lifted, her chin raised and she found her voice again. 'I can't tell you how grateful we are, doctor. Thank you for everything you've done. Can we see her?'

'She is very sleepy at the moment, so perhaps only for a few minutes? After that, please let us take care of her and come back in the morning. We should have a full picture of the situation by then. If you'd like to follow me, I'll take you through now.'

Just at that moment, Ben came down the corridor, carrying three coffees. 'Ben, she's okay. We're just going to nip in and see her for ten minutes.'

Stevie noticed that he had a kind smile. 'That's great news. I'll wait right here. No rush. Take your time. And tell her I said hi.'

They followed the doctor down a maze of pristine corridors, until she stopped to open the door of a small room and there, propped up in bed, was the smiling face of Moira Chiles. But only for a second, before she winced. 'Ouch, it hurts when I smile.' Stevie thought she looked tired. Maybe still a little groggy. But oh, it felt great to see her.

Carina, so incredibly worried outside, now reverted right back to their usual mode of communication. Tender jibes and sarcasm. 'The things you'll do to get attention, Moira Chiles.'

In the bed, Moira gave a hopeful smile. 'Did it work? Are they putting up a plaque that says, "Moira Chiles fell here"?'

Carina nodded. 'They are. And they're giving you free tickets for the cable car for the rest of your life.'

Stevie stepped forward, unable to stop smiling. 'You gave us a fright. I'm so glad you're okay. They've said they just want to keep you in overnight for observation.'

There was no mistaking the glisten in Moira's eyes as she nodded. 'I gave myself a bit of a fright too. What happened? I remember starting to climb the steps, then I remember waking up here. Nothing in between.'

Carina brushed her off. 'Don't worry about that now. The

important thing is that you need to rest. Sleep. We'll be back in the morning to collect you. If you need anything at all, just call.'

'I will,' Moira agreed. 'Although, I don't have my phone.' She scanned the room. 'Any idea where it is?'

Stevie pulled it out of her bag, and placed it on the nearby counter, where Moira's clothes sat in a neat pile. 'I lifted it, but it was smashed up when it bounced down the steps, I'm afraid. But don't worry. I'm sure they'll let you use the landline here and we can get a new phone for you tomorrow.'

Moira seemed happy with that solution, and her eyes were already getting heavy, so with a kiss on the cheek from each of them, they said their goodbyes. 'Oh, and Ben is here,' Carina told her. 'He said hello. He'll pop over and see you tomorrow, if you're up to it.'

Moira's eyes were closing now. 'Tell the handsome big devil I said hello back and I always thought he was much sexier than Spencer. Sorry, Carina. That might be the concussion talking.'

Moira's breathing changed as sleep claimed her, and Stevie felt nothing but relief. She was okay. She would be fine. The x-rays and all the tests were clear, so worst case scenario this was a concussion – best case scenario, Moira walked out of here tomorrow with nothing but a bit of bruising.

They left her to sleep and they were halfway back to the hotel in Ben's car, exhausted, depleted, but still bathed in relief, when a thought occurred to Stevie.

'Carina, was Moira still on the phone to her son when she fell? He might be worried.'

'I'm not sure. Damn. I don't have a number for him – it would have been in Moira's phone.'

Stevie felt a pang of guilt that she was ramping up Carina's stress levels again.

'I'll send him a direct message on social media and I'll see if I can track down a contact number for him.'

It took the rest of the journey home for her to type out a private message to Ollie Chiles on Instagram, and then she googled the name of his agent and manager, and called their offices too. At both offices, she got the security staff, because it was the middle of the night in LA, so she left her number there with a message saying she was calling about his mother, stressing that it was urgent, and asking them to call him straight away, despite the late hour. She came off the phone hopeful that they'd pass it on.

Back at the hotel, Ben came into the lobby with them, and suggested a drink in the lounge.

'I've never needed one more,' Stevie replied, meaning it. How could it be 7 p.m. already? The time had gone so slowly today, yet now it felt like it had flown by. Carina, however, looked dead on her feet.

'Darling, thank you,' she said to Ben, 'But if you both don't mind, I'm going to go upstairs and take a bath. It's been quite a day. Quite a week.'

'Yes, it has,' Stevie said, feeling for her. 'I'll call you in the morning and we can arrange to go back for Moira when they give us the okay.'

'Excellent. And both of you, thank you. I'm very grateful you were with me today.'

With a squeeze of Stevie's hand, she left them to it. Although, suddenly Stevie felt hugely awkward. This poor guy had invited his sister-in-law for a drink, and instead he'd been landed with her and he was probably now desperately thinking of a way to escape.

She tried to give him a light-hearted off-ramp. 'Erm, if you'd rather give a drink a miss now that Carina is gone, I'm very happy to raincheck.'

'Not at all. You grab that seat and I'll order. What would you like?'

'White wine? Any kind.' At home she barely drank alcohol, maybe a couple of glasses of wine a week at most, but the last few days definitely came under exceptional circumstances.

He came back with two glasses, and they made polite small talk until the wine began to kick in and relax them, and he brought up the subject of her mum again.

'I know I said earlier, but I really was sorry to hear that you'd lost her. She was a pretty special person.'

How many times had she heard that this week? Who was this woman that they all had such fond memories of, despite all her flaws and complexities? It still boggled her mind.

'It's been quite a revelation, being here. I don't know if Carina explained, but there's a whole chunk of my mum's history that I never knew existed. I didn't know she lived here. Or that she was a singer. And I've discovered she had some pretty wild ways.'

'She did,' Ben said, nodding fondly. Stevie decided she liked this man. He had a kind vibe, a decent manner about him. 'But she also had a good heart.'

'Did you date?' Stevie realised what she'd said, and immediately backtracked. 'I'm sorry, that was intrusive! Please don't answer that if you don't want to.'

He had an easy laugh too. 'No, no, it's fine. But no, we didn't date, as such. We spent a lot of time together and I liked her very much, but mostly we were just good friends.'

Mostly, he'd said. Stevie wondered if that meant there was more to their relationship, but she'd already invaded his privacy enough, so she let it go.

'Actually, though, the last time I saw her was on Christmas Eve that year. I was leaving to catch a flight back to England for a couple of months, and by the time I returned she was gone. I always wondered... well, what would have happened if she'd still been here.'

'I guess we'll never know,' Stevie said, sad for all the possibilities, the potential, all the chances her mum might have missed to have a better life than the one she'd had – just the two of them, in a tiny house, in a very ordinary little village. This was a different world.

Stevie drained the last of her wine. 'Thank you so much for the drink and it was lovely to speak to you, but I think I'm going to follow Carina and head up for an early night.'

So much to think about. Her mind just needed to decompress, to take it all in and process the craziest week.

They said their goodbyes, and Stevie went to her room, and lay down on the bed, just for a few moments. She closed her eyes. Definitely just for a few moments.

At 5 a.m. she opened them again, and saw that she'd lost the whole night.

Her body didn't know if it was tired or awake, jet lagged or full of nervous energy. Looking out of the window, she saw the dark skies were streaked with the orange beginnings of the sunrise, so she decided to go for a run.

Outside the streets were quieter than she'd seen them, and it gave her space to run, to breathe, to feel the pain and pleasure of her feet hitting the pavements. She cut down onto the harbour front and ran along the promenade, looking out over the water towards Kowloon. On the other side of the harbour, she could make out the Sheraton Hotel. She remembered it was at the bottom of Nathan Road, right round the corner from where her mum lived, and she thought again how she had walked in her footsteps all week.

Her chest tightened and she stopped, put her hands on the railing, stared up at the beautiful sunrise coming up over the harbour now, casting sheaths of light down on to the water.

Without thinking, she threw her head back, her gaze heavenwards. 'Can you see me, Mum? I'm right here. Back in your world. And do you know what, Mum? I wish you were with me.'

For the first time since she'd got the call to say that her mum was gone, she buckled over and she sobbed until there were no tears left, releasing all the resentment, knocking down the walls that had always been between her and her mum. Only when she'd surrendered it all, let all the pain go, did she steady herself, take a deep breath, and began to run again, her world suddenly feeling so much lighter than before.

When she got back to the hotel, for once, the lobby was almost deserted, with only a few people milling around. Cleaners buffing floors. Watering plants. Just a couple of guests checking out at reception, leaving several members of the reception staff free. She thought back to her last conversation with Moira, when she'd told her to call from the hospital if she needed anything, and decided she'd better check for messages.

'Excuse me,' she disturbed the very smart young lady at the first desk. 'I wonder if you could check if there are any messages for me? Stevie Dixon. Room 610.'

'One moment, madam.' She began tapping on her screen, leaving Stevie to glance around at... at...

There was a new arrival, a guy practically storming across the lobby, looking frantic, harassed, and oh so familiar. He made a beeline for the free agent at the next desk.

'Excuse me, can you please call up to my mother's room. Moira Chiles. She's in the penthouse. It's really urgent.'

Stevie turned, so that she was staring straight at a face that she'd only ever seen on TV.

'Ollie? Your mum is fine, but I'm afraid she isn't here at the moment.' She stepped toward him. 'I'm Stevie. Her friend Lisa's daughter. Shall we go have a seat and I can explain?'

25

JANUARY 1991 – HONG KONG

Moira

Moira rolled onto her side, and stared at the envelope on her bedside table.

She'd known it was coming, but somehow, seeing it there made it so much more real. The contract with the Night Stars Talent agency had only been for six months, and she was already a couple of weeks past that. So now they'd made it official. Her time here would end in two weeks, unless she committed to another contract, this time for a year.

A year. And she only had another forty-eight hours to confirm, or they would terminate, effective immediately.

Forty-eight hours to decide between this life or the one she'd left behind in Scotland.

Forty-eight hours to decide between a future here or the dreams she'd left at home.

She had always intended this to be a six-month adventure on the road to a career in theatre, not a goodbye to everything she knew. Her theatre ambitions were what she'd trained for, worked for, given up her childhood and teenage years to study. It was why her parents had sunk every extra penny they had into supporting her with dance classes, acting coaching, singing lessons. It was the only life she'd ever envisaged for herself... until now. Now she had Nate and these incredible friends. But would this life here ever be enough? And could she even contemplate a future so far from her family? It would break her mum's heart. And hers. But so would leaving Nate.

As if he heard her thoughts, Nate nuzzled into the back of her neck, murmured a half-awake, 'Morning, babe,' before going right back to sleep again.

She had forty-eight hours to decide between 'with' Nate or 'without' Nate.

'Morning, my love,' she replied, quietly, so that she wouldn't wake him properly, because when he was asleep, she didn't have to look at his gorgeous face and think about saying goodbye. Or think about staying here with him and living a different life to the one she'd always thought she'd have.

'You could come back to Scotland with me,' she'd said last night, when they'd been discussing it, as they'd done every night for the last month.

He hadn't even pretended to consider it. 'Come on, Moira, we both know that's not an option. I was only staying here until I had enough money to move on. I've just about got enough to take a year off. Thailand. Singapore. Bali. I want to travel. Want to see the world. Want to surf at sunset on the beach in every country in Asia.'

'Scotland has surfing...' she'd tried to argue, not mentioning that for most of the year it was a dice with death from hypothermia. He didn't take the bait.

'Come with me,' he'd said. 'We've got something special here, babe, you know that. Let's travel. You can pick up jobs wherever we land, and I'll do the same. Let's just see where it all takes us.'

Moira immediately heard her mother's voice in her head. 'See where it all takes you? That lad's not got a sensible bone in his body. A proper job, that's what he needs. With a union. And a pension.' Her mother had always supported her career dreams because she believed in her. Saw how hard she'd worked to take every step forward. That's the world she came from. Grafters. 'Let's just see where it takes us' would have her mother going for a lie down in a dark room. And before she met Nate, Moira would have felt that way too. But now?

There was a quiet knock on the door, then it opened, and Carina poked her head in. 'Are you awake?' she whispered.

'Would it matter?' Moira asked, knowing the answer, but finding Carina's charade of consideration amusing anyway.

'No,' Carina conceded. 'Lisa's room, two minutes.' It was clearly a command, and Moira knew there was no point resisting. When Posh Pal was on a roll, the only thing to do was to give in willingly. Besides, it usually resulted in a good time, a good bit of gossip, or a good moan, and Moira would be happy for any of those things to take her mind off her own woes right now.

Using the kind of contortion that belonged in a circus, she managed to slip out from between Nate's arms without waking him again. Forty-eight hours to decide if she was going to leave them forever. Or at least, for a while.

Wearing just the vest top and shorts that she'd slept in, and slipping her feet into a pair of flip flops, she padded out into the hallway, and then along the six feet to Lisa's room.

Forty-eight hours to decide whether she could bear to leave her friends.

As soon as she walked in, she scoped out the room and still couldn't believe the transformation. No ashtray. No dirty clothes on the floor. No fast-food containers. No used condom wrappers on the bedside table. No bottle of Jack Daniels next to them. And no random guy under the covers. The transformation had begun around Christmas, and they still had no suitable explanation.

'When are you going to admit that you were beamed up by aliens and they've tampered with your brain?' she asked her lovely Irish pal, who now looked more like Stevie Nicks than ever, because her shaggy blonde locks were washed and flowing down her back, and she had a bit of colour in her cheeks and a tiny bit of weight on her face, since she was no longer subsisting on a diet of nothing much more than Marlboro Reds and alcohol.

'I told you, it's my New Year resolution. New healthy me,' Lisa insisted, for the hundredth time this month. 'Fed up with the hangovers and feeling shit.'

Moira wanted to believe that there was nothing else behind it, but Carina had a theory. 'I think she's met someone that she's madly in love with so she's sorting herself out. It must be someone who's squeaky clean. Maybe a vicar. Or Jason Donovan.'

Moira stuck to her guns. 'I think the aliens are more likely than Jason Donovan.'

Looking at Lisa now though, whatever had transformed her beyond recognition could only be a good thing.

'Okay, why did you get me out of bed at this un-godly hour?' Moira asked, sitting down on the bed and for once, no longer having to worry that Lisa's sheets were harbouring something contagious.

'It's nearly 2 p.m.,' Carina shot back.

'Exactly.'

Since Carina had met Spencer, she'd started living more of a normal existence. No more partying after work – just straight home or over to his place, and then up at the same time as normal people in the mornings. Moira missed their old nocturnal activities, but Carina was unapologetic and too loved up to care.

'Okay, so before we get to the really crucial stuff, have you decided whether to go home or stay here and then go travelling with Nate?'

Moira sighed. 'I don't think I can leave him. I really don't. But... Argh, I don't know. I'm not equipped to make life changing decisions. Either way, I'm going to hurt someone. If I stay, my family will be devastated. If I go, I'll break his heart.'

'And what about you?' Lisa asked. 'What will make you happy?'

Moira couldn't answer. 'Right now, the only thing making me happy is sitting here in my pants with my pals. I can't bear the thought of leaving you two either, but I know the agency will move you both at some point too and we won't be able to do anything about it.' Carina and Lisa factored into her dilemma too. Carina had been candid about the fact she was considering giving this all up now that she'd found romantic bliss with Spencer, but Moira couldn't stand the thought of leaving Lisa here alone – not even in her new, clean, non-wasted, celibate state. The creeping feeling of anxiety that had been making her stomach go like a tumble dryer for the last fortnight kicked up again and she knew she had to get off this track and stop thinking about it all. At least for now. 'Okay, distract me. Tell me what is so crucial that you got me out of bed.'

Carina reached for two black dresses that were hanging on the front of Lisa's wardrobe, and, with a theatrical flourish, held them up in front of her. 'I need help to decide which one to wear tonight.'

'That's what you needed me for? To pick a dress?'

'No, to pick the outfit I'll be wearing when my mother finally comes to see the show. And you two have to be nice to her.'

'Carina, the last time your mother met me, she cut you off and didn't speak to you for months.' Moira pointed out.

'That wasn't because of you. That was because... well, okay, you might have been a tiny part of it. And Lisa. And the bar. And the job. And because she's a snobby cow, who didn't even watch our performance last time she came to the bar because she felt it was beneath her. But I need my allowance back because I hate being skint. And Spencer is winning her over, so I just need to sway her on my job here and I'll be back in the fold.'

'I don't know if I want to shoot myself or you,' Moira sighed, flopping back on the bed. 'Lisa, talk some sense into her. Tell her she doesn't need the damn money.'

Lisa took a sip of her tea. Tea. With no Jack Daniels in it. 'She kinda does. She's terrible at being poor.'

'See!' Carina said, vindicated. 'I'm going with this one,' Carina said, holding up the dress in her left hand, making her mind up with zero input.

'I'm disowning her,' Moira groaned, rolling her head into Lisa's lap. 'Let's bomb her out and we can just be the cool kids without her.'

Lisa didn't reply. No smart-ass comment. No agreement. Nothing.

Moira squinted open one eye and saw a red rash creeping up Lisa's neck.

She pushed herself upright. 'What's going on? Red rash on your neck. That only happens when you're stressing.'

Lisa didn't say anything for a few moments then she cracked.

'I was going to wait and tell you later, but you know my contract with the agency is up in March...'

Oh no. Oh no. Moira knew exactly what was coming.

'Well, I've told them I don't want to renew. I'm going to go home to Ireland. To where I grew up. I've still got my gran's house there – it's been rented out since she passed away, so I'm going to make it mine.'

Carina's chin dropped. 'But you said you'd never go back.'

'I guess I changed my mind. I'm over this. Like I said earlier, new me.'

They spent the rest of the day trying to persuade her to change her mind, but Lisa would just shrug and say it was done. 'I love you guys, but I'm over this life. I want a bit of normality.'

'Okay, well that's settled then. Moira, you can't leave,' Carina demanded. 'I can't lose two best friends at the same time. Because, you know, it's all about me.'

As usual, that made Moira laugh. 'You've got Spencer. You don't need friends any more.'

'That's not true!' Carina argued staunchly, before letting out a chuckle and reverting to her usual brand of caustic humour. 'I need to keep you around as a fall-back plan in case he ditches me.'

Moira was laughing on the outside, but on the inside, one more reason to stay had just dropped off the consideration list. Lisa was leaving, so Moira wouldn't be abandoning her.

Hours later, as she got ready to leave for the show, that thought and a million other ones were still going round in Moira's mind. She was as torn and confused as she'd been all week when Nate, on duty out at reception, shouted to her. She opened her door to see him dealing with a guest who was either checking in or checking out. Even now, when she watched him chat to people, that gorgeous smile and easy charm, she would get a thrill that he was hers. She loved him. That was all there was to this. She. Loved. Him.

Something in her heart took charge and after wrestling over the issue for weeks, she had a blinding moment of clarity. Nate was the first man she'd ever fallen in love with and she could quite honestly say she wouldn't mind if he was the last, if this was the one for life. When was she going to find this kind of love again? Why would she ever want to say goodbye? Carina was right. She had to stay. Had to give it a try. If it didn't work out, then she could go home in a month, or six, or a year, or whenever her mother persuaded Interpol to come drag her back. She was so relieved, so happy that she'd finally made a decision, that she almost missed that he was now holding out the cordless handset to her. 'Phone for you, babe.'

Puzzled, heart thumping, she took it back into her room. The only person who'd ever called her here was her mum, and that was on her birthday, and she'd only stayed on for thirty seconds because international calls were way too expensive.

'Hello?'

'Hello, darling, it's your favourite agent. You know, the one you abandoned to go off travelling the world.'

'Calvin! Och, I miss you.'

Calvin had been her agent back in Glasgow. He was only a couple of years older than her, but he already had big plans. He swore he'd own his own company one day, but Moira wasn't convinced. He seemed way too nice to be a ruthless businessman.

'I miss you too, my sweet. I call with news, and I'll get straight to the point because if I don't, they'll dock the cost of this call out of my wages. *The Rocky Horror Show.* The touring production. Remember you auditioned for them last year?'

Oh yes. She remembered every shimmy and song from that

day. She thought she'd killed it, done enough to win the role of Magenta, but they'd passed and she'd been devastated.

'They just offered you another callback. The actress who got it left and they need cover quickly. It's your dream role, babe. The one you always wanted. First reaction?'

His words delivered a resounding reminder that since she was a kid, belting out songs from old Judy Garland movies, practising high kicks from *Chicago*, mimicking Liza Minelli in *Cabaret,* all she'd truly ever wanted to do was be on the stage. Everything else was just filling in until she got there.

'When do they want to see me?' she asked, biting her bottom lip.

'I know it's tight, but next Monday.'

Four days from now.

'Can I get back to you tomorrow, Calvin?'

She heard the surprise in his voice, but he didn't pressure her. Probably because the call was costing a fortune. 'Of course, my love. But Moira... things like this don't come around very often. This is what you've been waiting for.'

'I know,' she said softly. 'And thank you. You're amazing.'

'Telling me things I already know, my darling.' And with that there was a very final click.

Moira was frozen to the spot, an explosion taking place in her head. She'd just decided to stay, but... This call could change everything. A show. A touring production. A dream role. One that she'd have given anything to join six months ago. And sure, she might go back, audition again and still not get the part, but could she really take that chance? She was right back at square one on the quandary scale – take a chance on her dreams or take a chance on Nate?

'Moira! Get a move on. Places to go, one snobby boot of a mother to see!'

That came from Carina, who was thudding her door once again. Moira grabbed her bag, put on her bright red lippy, and shot out of the door. At reception, she returned the phone to Nate and then gave him a kiss. 'Are you coming to the show later?' If he was free, he usually came to meet her, and they'd go down into Lan Kwai Fong for drinks and karaoke.

'Babe, I'd love to but I'm doing a double shift tomorrow. 6 a.m. start. Extra money and we need all we can get,' he said pointedly. Moira knew what he was saying. *We need it*. They were a team. And he wasn't even going to think about the possibility that she wouldn't be with him when he left to go travelling.

'Come on, love bird, let's go,' Carina bossed her, as she passed, Lisa right behind her.

Moira leaned over and kissed him again. 'I love you.'

That gorgeous grin reappeared. 'I love you too. Hurry up and come home.'

They took the usual route – stopping off at a street stall for chicken and rice, then on to the Star Ferry, Lisa sitting right at the edge of the seats so that she could feel the breeze on her face.

The bar was already packed out when they got there. Moira headed for her usual spot to watch Carina and Lisa play the first set, while Carina spotted her guests and went to greet them. Moira saw her beam when she kissed her mother on each cheek, then kissed Spencer too, before going up on stage with Lisa, and giving the best performance she'd ever turned in. They had the whole crowd in their pocket from the opening bar of 'Dreams', until Lisa whipped around in a frenzy as she belted out the last line of 'The Chain'.

When their set came to a close, Moira got ready to take over and keep the party going, but it turned out there was an unexpected half time act. She watched as Spencer Lloyd walked up onto the stage and, with the kind of confidence that came with money, status and a tad of overindulgence, he proposed to her best friend in front of a cheering crowd.

Carina let out a very un-Carina-like shriek as she accepted, sending the whole place into raptures yet again. Even her mother's face had cracked into a wide grin of approval. This was the future that Carina's mum had wanted for her and now she was going to get it – and look how happy it had made them all.

As Moira cheered, clapped and cried for her friend, the balance on the scales of her decision tipped in a different direction yet again. Lisa was leaving. Carina, the future Mrs Lloyd, definitely would now too. Nate wanted her to stay with him, but only on his terms. Meanwhile, her family wanted her home, and her dream job was in touching distance.

There was only one thing that made sense.

'Lisa, I think I need to go home,' she whispered to her friend, standing next to her. 'Will you cover my next two weeks for me? You know my sets off by heart.' The two weeks left on her contract would have to be completed.

'Aw feck, are you sure? And yes, you know I will. Jesus, are we really doing this? We're really all going?'

Moira wrapped her arms around Lisa's tiny shoulders. 'I think so. At least for a while. You know I love you, Lisa Dixon. This has been the best time ever.'

'Right back at you, doll,' Lisa murmured, with a loud sniff right in Moira's ear, before she let go, dried her eyes. 'But we need to stop all this emotional stuff or I'll be right back on the drink,' she said, forcing a smile. Moira knew she was joking. Something had happened in her friend that she couldn't quite put her finger on, but she seemed so much happier. Whatever it was, Moira could see it was a good thing.

'Eeeeekkkkkk,' the very unladylike shriek came from Carina,

who'd sneaked up beside them, and was now waving a left hand with a very large rock on it in front of them. 'Christ, you could play snooker with that thing,' Moira said, before the three of them went into a hug huddle. 'Congratulations, pal. We're so happy for you. He's a lucky guy to get you.'

'I can't believe it. My mother is over the fricking moon. This might be the best day of her life – her daughter is no longer the family fuck-up. I think she's about to start a conga round the bar.'

The three of them turned to see Carina's mum, who was positively beaming as she gave her new son-in-law-to-be a very restrained, elegant embrace. 'That's the closest she gets to excitement,' Carina chuckled. 'But, oh, look at my fiancé. I'm getting married!'

She shrieked again, before grabbing Moira's hand. 'Right, come on, let's go get this set done, so I can get out of here. I'm calling the agency first thing in the morning and telling them that regretfully I'll be leaving their crap-paying, hovel-living job of a lifetime with immediate effect. Spencer just told me he has booked us on a celebration trip to Singapore, leaving tomorrow. Please don't hate me for leaving you.'

Moira decided this wasn't the time to tell her she was going too, or that Carina had just made it easier for her to say goodbye. There was only one person now that Moira was letting down by going... She just needed to find the heart to say goodbye to him too.

Still holding hands, Carina and Moira went up onto the stage, and Moira went straight to the mic. 'Ladies and gentlemen, let's give it up one more time for our newly engaged fiancée, Carina!' The crowd, so many of them familiar faces that they'd got to know over the last six months, cheered, stamped their feet and did drum rolls on the tables.

'This is a very special night for all of us...' Moira felt the words catch in her throat, but her pause was filled by another enthusiastic cheer from the crowd. She could feel the tears running down her cheeks as she went on, 'So we thought that we'd do something really special. If you were here on Christmas Eve, you might have seen all three of us, Carina, Lisa and me, up here together. So tonight, we thought we'd do that one more time...'

She raised her eyebrows questioningly at Lisa, over at the bar, 'What do you say, Lisa? Fancy joining us up here for one more night?'

The crowd wasn't giving her the option to say no, as they cheered her all the way to the stage. Moira had a mic waiting for her, and Lisa went straight into an intro.

'You know, you see us up here every night and we love you all for being here. But what you don't see, is that away from this stage, these are the best friends I've ever had.'

Moira raised her mic. 'Until forever,' she agreed, giving in to some more very unprofessional tears.

Back to Lisa. 'So how about we start with this and see where we go...'

With pitch perfect clarity, she belted out, acapella, the first line of 'Ain't No Mountain High Enough', by Marvin Gaye and Tammi Terrell, a song that was in Moira's Motown playlist, so she knew exactly where to go with it. Moira joined in on the second half of the verse, Carina came in on keyboards, and everyone in the bar joined in the absolute celebration of love, of friendship and of always having someone to call on.

For the next two hours, long after they should have finished, they moved through all their favourites, taking requests from the audience, hyping up the party so that everyone in the bar – even Carina's mother – knew they were sharing something special.

It was almost 1 a.m. when Moira, high on the performance and glowing with the heat and electricity in the room, stepped forward to say goodnight. 'Thank you so much to you all. You've made this an incredible night for us. There's no one in the world that I'd rather sing with than these two ladies here...' Carina and Lisa both took a bow to more applause. 'And I love them both beyond words. But all incredible things have to move on sometimes and no matter how much you love someone or something, you have to let it go so that they can fly on to better things...'

The crowd obviously thought she was referring to Carina's engagement, so the cheer was rapturous, and Carina responded with an elaborate curtsy. They didn't realise it was about so much more. Lisa was going back to a very different life, but for whatever reason, it was her choice, and she'd never looked more at peace. Moira knew, deep in her soul, that the only choice she could make tonight, no matter how much it broke her heart, was to choose dreams over love, at least for now. 'So tonight, there's only one song, that feels right to leave you with...'

She didn't even have to tell the others. Carina instinctively knew, and began playing on the keyboard.

And as the introduction of 'Landslide' filled the room you could hear a pin drop, until three gorgeous voices, in perfect harmony, came in with the most incredible, heart-twisting tale of change, of saying goodbye to a piece of your heart, and rising above to a new place to find happiness.

As the crowd cheered the final note, and the three of them exchanged glances that said so much more than words, Moira knew there would never be a more perfect way to say goodbye.

Except...

'Come with me,' Carina said, when the lights came up and the bar began to empty. 'I've told Spencer and my mum to wait in the lobby bar, so I only have a minute.'

Moira and Lisa followed her up the back staircase, and out through the fire exit to the pool terrace, overlooking the harbour and bathed in moonlight.

'Will you still be here when I get back?' Carina asked them. Moira shook her head. 'I don't think so.'

'You're going?' There was no surprise in her voice.

'I need to.' Moira told her, feeling the truth of that.

Carina turned to the third friend in the trio. 'Lisa?'

Lisa shrugged, smiling. 'Can't play without Christine McVie so I guess it's time.'

'Promise me that we'll keep in touch. I mean, I'll be far too busy living a windswept and glamorous life, to hang out with you two...' Moira and Lisa both rolled their eyes at exactly the same time, and Carina grinned at their desired reaction. 'But promise we'll always know where we are. You know. Just in case...'

Moira nodded. 'Promise. Lisa?'

'Promise.'

'Okay, I need to go before Spencer spends more time with my mother and changes his mind about marrying me. Love you both.'

'Love you too,' Moira choked. 'Although, you're definitely way too posh for me.'

'And you're definitely way too fricking sensible now,' she added to Lisa. One more hug, and then Carina bolted off.

'You coming too?' Lisa asked. 'I'm going to go say goodbye to the guys at the bar.'

Moira shook her head. 'I'll catch up with you.'

She didn't. Instead, she sat there for another half hour, thinking everything through, watching the moon glisten on the harbour in front of her, then she went home and packed her bag. Nate was sound asleep in her bed, and she couldn't bear to wake him, couldn't bear to see his face when she broke his heart.

Instead, she wrote him a note.

Need to go home for audition. Will call you and be back soon.
Love you xx

She would go home, audition for the part, and if she didn't get it, she'd be back. And if she did get it, she'd let him know and she'd come back after the theatre run. Six months. Maybe a year. As long as they kept in touch, she'd know where to find him. If Nate loved her, he'd understand that. She thought about leaving her mum's address then changed her mind. If he came to find her, she didn't trust herself to refuse him. No. She knew where he was. She'd find him. She kissed her fingers, then laid them on his sleeping head, a silent goodbye to the first love of her life.

Grabbing her bag, she remembered to lift the open return flight ticket that the agency had given her when she came here. She'd get it validated at the airport.

Crossing the room without making a sound, she opened the door and spotted a piece of paper that had been pushed under it. Lisa's name. An address in Ireland. She'd know where to find her too. And Carina... well, she'd never be difficult to track down. Just to make sure, she borrowed a pen and two pieces of paper from Wai at reception, jotted her mum's address and a note on both, and pushed them under Carina and Lisa's doors.

There was one more moment downstairs, when she walked outside into the quiet dawn and her resolve crumbled. She could stop. Turn back. He would never need to know. That's when a taxi came around the corner and she jumped in before she could change her mind.

As the taxi drove off down Salisbury Road, she watched the

sun come up over the harbour, and in her mind, she said goodbye to the island she'd loved.

'I'll be back,' she promised silently. She wasn't done with Nate. She wasn't done with her friends. She wasn't done with Hong Kong.

One way or another, she'd get back to them all one day.

26

SUNDAY, 6 JULY, 2025 – HONG KONG

Moira

'Okay, watch the steps,' Carina said, as they got outside the hospital and into the blinding sunlight.

'Is that a joke?' Moira asked, one eyebrow raised, thinking it was a bit too soon to be mocking the afflicted. Carina took a second to get her point, then dissolved into a fit of giggles. 'No! Sorry – I genuinely mean it, look!'

Moira's gaze went a few metres ahead, to where her friend was pointing, and yes, there were indeed two steps down from the hospital entrance to the ground.

Carina's laughter suddenly became infectious, and Moira began laughing so hard she had to reach for the handrail beside her – a motion that was a day late and a mighty headache short, apparently.

'Oh God, that hurts. Don't make me laugh. Don't make me laugh.'

The descent into hysteria took hold, but somewhere along

the line between comedic relief and anxiety over what could have been, the laughter morphed into big fat droplets of tears.

And those hurt too.

Moira took a deep breath, then exhaled, then paused for a moment to gather herself and formulate a way to express what she was feeling. 'I was so scared, Carina,' she whispered when she finally found the words. 'I got such a fright when I woke up in there yesterday. And I'm so grateful to be in one piece, but now I'm going from happy to sad to relieved to scared to weepy all in the same five minutes. This is like the bloody menopause all over again.'

Moira was grateful when Carina hugged her gingerly, careful to avoid the bruises. 'I know, darling. You gave us a fright too. But the doctors have said you're fine, so let's just get back to the hotel, put our feet up and be glad it all turned out fine. And you might want to avoid stairs for a while – you clearly can't be trusted. Right, the car is just over there...'

Moira looked up to see several vehicles parked in a pick-up zone a few metres away, with one of the drivers coming towards them. Then she looked again. And again. 'Jesus, that bloke is the spitting image of my... my...'

Now her emotional pendulum had swung right round to joyful. 'Ollie!' she gasped, as her son reached her and hugged her gently.

'Oh my God, I can't believe it. You're a sight for sore eyes. And a sore head. What are you doing here?'

'Couldn't live without you, Ma. And the studio sent me to see if you'd be interested in a bit of stunt work.' Ollie had well and truly inherited her need to handle stress, anxiety and scary moments with humour.

'I'm too expensive for them,' she told him, her smile so wide it was making her cheeks hurt.

And his happiness, or maybe it was relief, was coming right back at her. 'Come on, Ma – let's get you into the car.'

Half an hour later, they were approaching the foyer of the hotel. He'd filled her in on the Facetime call they'd been having when she fell – she had no recollection of it at all – and then told her how he'd cancelled his flight to the UK and flown straight here instead, how Stevie had found him in the lobby, and how panicked he'd been until he'd found out she was going to be okay.

'Me too, son. Me too. But I'm fine now, and you're a busy man, so if you need to go…' She let that hang there. Much as it was wonderful to have him here, she'd never been a burden to her son, or asked him to take care of her, and she wasn't going to start now.

'Meh, it's no big deal. I thought I'd just wait and come back with you in a couple of days. Make sure you don't do any more stunt work.'

The thought of him staying warmed her soul. 'Does that mean you've upgraded me to all that business class nonsense on the flight home too? Because, you know, I don't approve. Although I do like the swanky cutlery.'

As they drew into the foyer, Moira spotted Stevie waiting there, waving to them. As soon as she got out of the car, the younger woman threw her arms around her. Moira still found it hard to believe that this time last week they didn't even know each other. Now she felt like family.

'I'm so glad you're okay!'

'Me too, love. And thank you. I hear you stopped me falling any further and then took care of me until the medics got there.'

'It was the least I could do after suggesting going there in the first place. I'm so sorry about that.'

In the car, Carina had told Moira that Stevie was racked with guilt, so she made sure to wave that comment away. 'Don't be daft. It was pretty spectacular right up until I decided on a bit of gymnastics. And besides, it made the cavalry come,' she said, gesturing to Ollie. 'So it was worth it.'

'Thanks, Moira. I'm guessing you're going to take it easy for the rest of the day? I was going to go to the gym, but I can leave it until later if you want to have lunch?'

'You go ahead, love. I'm looking forward to a bath and a nap this afternoon. Why don't we meet up later for dinner?'

Stevie kissed her on the cheek. 'Sounds like a good plan. Right, I'll head off...'

'Actually, if it's all right with you, I'll come join you?' Ollie suggested. Moira knew he had to work out daily to keep his body looking like a sixteenth century Scottish warrior in the show. 'The gym is next to the pool?'

Stevie nodded. 'It sure is. I'll see you there.'

She went off, leaving Carina and Ollie to walk across the busy lobby with Moira.

She'd gone a few steps when she had a thought. 'Hang on, I just need to check something at reception first.'

'Do you mind if I go on up to my room? I just need to nip to the loo, so I'll come knock on your door later,' Carina said, giving her another hug and then heading in the direction of the lifts.

Ollie was happy to wait with her for a couple of minutes until a receptionist was free.

'Can I help you, madam?'

'Yes, I'm in the penthouse, Room 810, and I just wondered if there have been any calls for me. My name is Moira Chiles.'

The gent checked something on his screen. 'No, madame...'

Her heart sank. Tracking Nate down had been too good to be true.

'But we did call your room earlier, because there's a gentleman over by the bar who asked us to let you know he was here.'

'A gentleman by the...' her words trailed off, as she turned around, and no, he wasn't at the bar. He was walking towards her. He was almost here. Yes, it was him.

'Hello, Moira.'

This time it wasn't the bang on the head that was making her dizzy.

'Nate.' She was smiling, staring, speechless. If this was a movie, there would be fireworks. Nate. Here. Now.

Time froze for seconds, until she managed to snap herself out of it. 'Oh, we're in the way.' She took a few steps to the side to free up the reception desk, Ollie and Nate doing the same. Then she stared at him again.

'Sorry! My manners. Ollie, this is an old friend, Nate Wilde.' Ollie was grinning as he watched her, and Moira knew that it was because he'd never seen her flustered or stuck for words.

'And Nate, this is my son, Ollie—'

'Chiles,' Nate finished the sentence. 'I watch you on *Clansman*. It's a great show. I never made the connection with the names. To be honest, even though you play a Scot in the show, I just assumed you were American and great at accents.'

Moira immediately thought how she used to love this about him. The easy way he chatted to anyone, whether it was a backpacker checking into the hotel or... well, or a famous TV star who just happened to be her son.

'Don't let my mum hear you say that,' Ollie laughed. 'She's a bit territorial.'

Moira jokingly pursed her lips, but she was glad of the chance the conversation was giving her to find a way to breathe again. And to take in every detail of the man she'd once loved.

The long hair was gone. Now it was short, but still there. Grey. He used to look like a surfer from the front of *Sports Illustrated*. Now he was more 'Ideas for Christmas Gifts for Dads' from the front of the *John Lewis* catalogue. But it suited him. Handsome and cool – that was his vibe, as Ollie would say. Absolutely fricking gorgeous, is what she would say. Every nerve under her skin was standing to attention, causing full body goosebumps while her stomach was doing somersaults. He was beautiful. Perfect. So strange and yet so familiar. And now his eyes were back on hers.

'Sorry it's taken me so long to contact you. I was in Singapore on business and only got your message when I landed this morning.'

'That's okay. I'm just glad you got it.'

'I thought maybe we could talk?' he suggested, and Moira saw Ollie's surprise ramp up another notch. This was excruciating enough, without worrying about her son's amused reactions.

'Ollie, weren't you going to the gym with Stevie?'

'I sure was.'

'Then why don't you go on. Nate, why don't we go up to my room?'

She realised that could be taken the wrong way and immediately blustered, 'It's a suite. With a couch and a terrace!' Ah, she was making a tit of herself, so she leaned into it with an exasperated, 'And a mini-bar that I'm feeling a dire need for right now.'

'I think that sounds pretty good.' Nate agreed, and she saw that easy smile again. More goosebumps. Lord, she was a wreck. She wanted to hug him. To hold him. To tell him it was incredible to see him again. But she had no idea how he was feeling, so – against every habit of a lifetime – she acted with polite restraint.

She led the way, with Ollie getting off at the floor below hers, saying goodbye to Nate and giving her a cheeky wave that made her summon her very best expression of disapproval. Her and Nate went the rest of the way in silence, nothing said until they were in the suite. 'Beer?' she asked him, heading for the minibar.

'Sounds good.'

She pulled out one for herself too. Medicinal purposes. When she gave it to him their hands touched, and she felt a jolt of something that she hadn't experienced in a long time. Longing. But still, the restraint was in charge of her actions.

There were a few moments of silence, staring at each other, until he spoke first.

'It's so good to see you.'

She motioned to him to join her on the sofa. 'It's good to see you too,' she said, as both of them sat on the couch, facing each other, half a sofa of of space between them.

Another pause.

'You know, I had loads of things rehearsed to say,' he admitted. 'Can't think of any of them now.'

'Shall I give you some hints? How about you hit me with "Where have you been for the last thirty-odd years?" Or, "You're a complete cow for running out on me that night."'

He grinned. 'Yeah, sure. I'll start with that.'

'Okay. Then I'll start with "I'm sorry".'

'I'll take it. Am I allowed to ask what happened?'

She went with the truth. 'I got offered an audition for my dream job. I knew I wouldn't be able to go if I had to tell you to your face, so I did the cowardly thing and bolted.'

'Did you get the part?'

'I did. A year, touring the UK with *The Rocky Horror Show*.'

She'd always wondered what this meeting would look like.

Would he be furious? Resentful? Bitter? But now, there was nothing but calm acceptance as he took that in.

'I always knew you'd make it.'

'I don't know that I made it, but it was maybe the best year of my career.'

'And you never thought about coming back when the year was done?' Ouch. Arrow to the heart.

'I did,' she answered honestly. 'About a month before it ended, I wrote to you at the hotel, but no reply.'

'I'd left by then.'

'I figured. I should have written long before then but I didn't trust myself. I was heartbroken to leave you, you have to know that. And it would have taken just one moment of thinking about you to make me come back. So I think that... ah, we were stupid when we were young, but resilient too. I think that's why I compartmentalised it all, focused on making the reason I left worthwhile. I just concentrated on work and told myself I'd get back to you one day.'

'But you didn't...'

'No. When you didn't reply, I told myself you'd moved on. You'd got over me and gone off to surf at sunrise somewhere exotic.' Would she have come back if he was still there? She didn't know. Maybe. But he hadn't, and then *The Rocky Horror Show* had led to other gigs, and then she'd just got busy, until...

She told him all about it. A couple of years of work until she'd gone on holiday to Tenerife, and had a brief holiday romance that had led to Ollie and a whole new life. She'd given up theatre, become a mum, supported them by singing in pubs and clubs, until Ollie went to college to study drama and she'd gone off to work on the cruise lines.

'You never married?' he asked. Second arrow to the heart.

'No. Working and bringing up Ollie took all my time.'

She realised she'd been doing most of the talking. Her mouth always went on to overdrive when she was nervous.

'Enough about me. Tell me about you. Married?'

'Divorced.'

A comment she'd made at the start of the week came back to her.

'How many times?'

'Once.'

'Ah, I had my money on four. Maybe five. Did you meet your wife when you were travelling? What countries did you go to?'

'Erm, I never actually left.' That stunned her, so she said nothing as he went on, clearly a bit uncomfortable. 'I waited a few months to see if you'd come back, and then... I met my ex-wife. Her father owned the building that our hotel was in. We dated for a while and then married a year later. By that time I was working for her father's real estate company and in the years before the territory was handed back over to China, a lot of property changed hands. Right place at the right time. Eventually I set up my own company, worked day and night for a lot of years to make it a success. Ended up buying the hotel building from him, and then I sold it to the company that has it now.'

'Wait, so the free-spirited surfer who wanted to watch the sunrise in Bali...'

'He sold out.' He admitted, almost apologetically.

Moira's mind was whirring. He hadn't left. His longing to travel had been the reason he wouldn't come back to Glasgow with her, and yet he'd given that dream up to settle down with someone else. A large chunk fell off the rock of guilt that had been on her shoulders for thirty-four years. And was she imagining it, or now that her nervousness had begun to settle, did this feel easy? Warm. Just like before... She was just thinking that when her body betrayed her with an irrepressible yawn.

'You're tired. I'll go...'

Shit! He clearly thought he was boring her.

'No, it's not that. It's just that I was in hospital last night. I fell... Hang on, let me go back to the start.'

She fired off a text to the others, saying she was going to skip dinner, and then she rewound to the beginning. Over the next couple of hours, they switched to tea and ordered food from room service as she told him about the fall at the steps, then they moved on to why she was here, the letter, about Carina, and then finally, she told him about Lisa.

'Oh no,' he groaned. She could see he was visibly upset, and she understood – Nate and Lisa had been such good friends. 'And that's how we met Stevie. Her daughter. She's here in the hotel with us. She found the letter and came here to tell us about her mum. It's the craziest thing. Lisa had never told her that she'd lived here, or that she was a singer, or about us. Nothing. And the Lisa that Stevie describes is so different to the one that we knew. It's been incredible getting to know Stevie but it's raised so many questions for the poor lass that we don't have answers to. We just can't fathom how Lisa could have lived two completely separate lives. And looking back to that last month here, in hindsight, we should have tried to figure out what was going on. She changed so much in that final few weeks. And then suddenly deciding to go back to Ireland? Why didn't we make her tell us why? She just blew off our questions and you know what she was like... she hated talking about personal stuff. My heart aches for Stevie because we have no answers for her and it's all just impossible to understand.'

He sat with that for a couple of moments before he spoke. 'I think I'd like to speak to Stevie. Do you think that would be okay?'

'I'm sure it would. She's in room 610, if you want to give her a call.' Moira checked her watch. 'Although, she's probably out for dinner right now. Maybe you could call her tomorrow.'

Before she could say anything else, another yawn crept up on her. Bloody hell, her body was letting her down. She didn't want this to end. This moment. Just him. Her.

'I'm going to go and let you sleep,' he said, and she wondered if she heard a tug of reluctance. No, she was imagining it. It was just an incredibly comfy couch. It had been so long since she'd felt attracted to a man, her hormones were playing tricks on her mind.

He got up, and she followed him to the door, heart thudding. Hormones again. She was going to have to go back on the HRT.

'It's been so good seeing you, Moira. I'm glad you came back. Even if it was three decades later.'

'Me too.'

He put his hand on the doorknob, then stopped, turned back to her.

'I know this is crazy, but do you think there's any world where you could stay longer, so we could maybe get to know each other again? Maybe a month or two?'

An involuntary groan gave the answer before she found the words. She wanted to. She truly did. Every swirling hormone in her body wanted to be here with him, to touch him, to talk to him all night long. But...

'I can't. The drama school I'm running now... It opens on the first of September. There's no way I can take any more time off, probably for the next year or so.'

He gave her a rueful smile. 'Bad timing again, I guess.'

'Bad timing,' she agreed, sadly. She thought he was going to leave it there, but no.

'Do you ever regret not coming back?' he asked.

Moira felt a lump begin to form in her throat as she nodded.

'Sometimes. But then I think maybe it just turned out how it was supposed to. I loved you so much, Nate, but I guess, at the end of the day, there was a little piece of me that wanted a man who would change his life for me. Who would give up his dreams for me. Not the other way around.' Even as she said that, she knew it was true. In the end, she'd surrendered her dreams to be a mum, because it was the right thing to do for her son. Because that's what you did for someone you truly adored. Maybe her and Nate just hadn't loved each other enough to do that. Or maybe they'd just been too young to make the right decision.

She could see that his sad smile came straight from his heart as he nodded. 'You deserved that, Moira. I wish I'd realised that at the time.'

'Me too.'

He reached over, kissed her softly, his thumb tracing her cheek the way it had once done every time their lips met. 'Goodbye, Moira. You take care.'

'You too, Nate.'

After he left, she put her forehead against the door, and stayed there until the tears stopped falling. Youth, her family and her dreams had been her excuses for walking away from him last time. Could she live with herself if she let him go again?

27

CARINA

Carina lay in bed, staring at the ceiling, listening to the honking horns and revving engines of the traffic outside. This was why Spencer would only stay in rooms on high floors and with verified triple glazing. It was just another of his standards that Carina accepted and accommodated.

Well, sod him, maybe she liked listening to the traffic. It was weirdly relaxing and comforting to know that there was a whole world out there that would keep turning no matter what she decided to do with her life after today.

Since she'd arrived in Hong Kong, she'd put her marriage issues in a box and ignored them, choosing to stay in a little bubble of bliss and denial. In a strange way it reminded her of the first time she'd come here. Back then, she'd ignored the reality that her family would be outraged that she'd left her piano teaching post to perform in a bar. She'd lived in denial that they'd ever find out. And she'd gone about her life doing exactly as she pleased.

These last few days had definitely reminded her of that time. She'd ignored the reality of her broken marriage, lived in denial that she'd have to face it and gone about her daily life with Moira and Stevie, blocking everything else out. Until this afternoon.

When she'd returned from the hospital, she'd come up to her room, planning to let Moira sleep and then meet up later. She'd just been in the process of taking her shoes off when there was a knock at the door.

Must be Stevie. Or maybe Moira was bored already and had come to find her. Her friend didn't have the longest attention span or the greatest capacity for being alone.

When she'd opened the door, she'd seen immediately that it was neither.

'Hello, Mum,' Imogen had said, as if she'd just returned from popping down to the shops for a loaf of bread or a pint of milk. Not that she ever had to do that. That was their housekeeper's job and Imogen and Erin had led privileged lives where all such things were taken care of.

'Hello, love.' She took in her daughter's calm, almost business-like demeanour and realised immediately that this wasn't a woman in the midst of a career crisis or reeling from the betrayal of a father she adored. Which meant one thing. Spencer had talked her round. Placated her. Given her a solution she could live with. And now, she was here, so that meant...

'So he sent you, then,' Carina said, with calm inevitability. It had occurred to her that this was like a scene from every *Godfather* movie, when the consigliere was sent in as an advance party to smooth the waters before the boss arrived.

Her daughter didn't even try to deny it. 'He did. Can we talk?'

'Of course, darling,' she said, pulling back the door to the smallest room in the hotel. She wasn't going to make this difficult for Imogen. She'd been a daddy's girl her whole life and she'd just lost a best friend. Beneath the calm exterior, she had no doubt that her daughter was hurt. 'I would suggest we go downstairs, because this room is more than a little bijou, but I'm guessing this is going to be the kind of conversation that we don't want other people to overhear.'

'Probably not,' Imogen agreed, before stopping to let Carina hug her as she passed her in the doorway, then carrying on into the room.

'Anyway, this is just fine, Mum. Cosy.' She hopped onto the bed and plumped up the pillows, while Carina took a seat in the cool, leather bucket chair by the window.

'How are you, sweetheart?' Carina asked. This couldn't have been a happy week for Imogen and Carina wasn't sure that she had someone to talk to about it. There had been no calls from Erin, so the news hadn't reached her other daughter in Shanghai. The sisters had a friendly relationship, but they'd always been much too different to be close. She definitely wouldn't have been Imogen's first call in times of crisis.

Imogen paused, and Carina watched her take a deep breath, then exhale a rapid burst of an apology. 'Mum, I need to say I'm sorry.'

'You have nothing to be sorry for, sweetheart,' Carina said, surprised.

Imogen flicked back her long, glossy mane of chestnut brown hair, and Carina thought again how lucky her daughter was: smart, beautiful, confident in her decisions, fully aware of what she wanted out of life. Carina was in touching distance of sixty, and she still didn't have that level of self-belief.

Imogen was still pressing her point. 'Mum, I have. I saw her flirting with him and I said nothing. I thought it was harmless. He's my father, he's almost double her age, and he's married – all factors I would have thought were blockers to a relationship.'

'A reasonable assumption,' Carina agreed. 'I've known

Arabella for a long time too – I'd never have thought she was capable of this either. I guess we were both wrong.'

'I threw her out of our house. Honestly, Mum, I never want to see her again. Traitorous bitch.'

Carina wasn't surprised by the reaction. It was perhaps inevitable that her daughter would direct the blame to her friend instead of the father she adored.

'I'm sorry, darling. That must have hurt. Losing friends is a heartbreak, no matter how it happens.' She hesitated, thinking through what she was going to say next. 'But the thing is, darling, Arabella owed us nothing – except, perhaps, a bit of decency – so none of my anger is aimed towards her. Your father is the one who broke a promise. He's the one who betrayed me. Betrayed us. He knew she was your friend, he knew she was almost thirty years younger than him, and unless he has amnesia, he knew he was married. So, all in all, he should have known fucking better.'

Imogen's eyes widened and Carina realised it was probably the first time she'd ever heard her mother swear. And maybe that was long fucking overdue. Over the last week, she'd had so much time to think, and she could see now that she'd created this perfect world for them all, and in doing so, she'd faded into the background, her role in the family somehow becoming the person who facilitated everyone else's happiness. It had taken all this for her to realise that. Maybe now it was time that everyone else started to see *her*, to consider *her*, to give a damn about *her* happiness. And if that called for a couple of bursts of profanity every now and then, she could live with that. Fuck, yes.

Imogen took a second to recover before agreeing. 'He should, you're right. And Mum, please don't think I'm taking his side on this...'

Carina kept her mouth zipped on that one.

'...but I just don't want anything to change. I want our family to stick together. I want you guys to work this out so that everything can go back to the way it was. So...'

When she paused, Carina had a sudden foretelling of what her daughter was about to say.

'He's here, isn't he?' It should have been so obvious. Imogen had paved the way, so now it was time for him to follow up and seal the deal.

'He is.'

'Where?'

'Downstairs. In the hotel bar. He says it's where you met. And where he proposed.'

Oh, he was good. Go for the nostalgia. The sentimentality. Rewind this whole shit show back to what she'd always considered to be two of the best moments of her life.

Was it working?

She could refuse to go. She could pass on a message that he should leave. But wasn't that just delaying the inevitable? They were going to have to speak at some point, so she could either avoid this or get it over with.

She got up from her chair and slipped her feet into the Ugg slippers she knew he hated. Then she went to the wardrobe and pulled on an old comfy sweatshirt that she knew he hated even more.

She was done dressing for this man, done with keeping up the image of perfection, done with giving a damn what he thought.

'I'll go speak to him.'

'Do you want me to come with you, Mum?'

Carina didn't have to consider the answer. 'No. I think this needs to be just between us.'

Carina was almost at the door when Imogen said, 'Okay,

well, I'll go back to my hotel and leave you to talk. I'm staying at the Grand Hyatt tonight and flying on to Tokyo for meetings tomorrow morning. Call me there later and let me know how it goes. I love you, Mum. And for what it's worth, I really am sorry. Maybe when you come home, we can talk more?'

It was a small step to being seen, but she'd take it. 'I'd like that, darling.'

On the way down in the lift, Carina knew she should be thinking strategy, preparing speeches, getting her points in order, but all she felt was a slow, insidious lava of anger ooze around her chest. He'd done this. He'd taken a wrecking ball to them all, to their whole family.

The lunchtime crowd in the bar had subsided, so now there were only a few people sprinkled around, most of them on laptops or nursing solo coffees.

Except for one. Spencer Lloyd was sitting at a table, facing the door, watching her as she approached.

When she pulled out the chair opposite him, he was first to speak.

'Thank you for coming.'

'I wasn't going to refuse my daughter's request,' she said calmly, thinking that infidelity didn't look too bad on him. He was more casual than usual, in an open-neck, short-sleeved shirt, but the Dubai tan, the outline of his shoulders, the lean abs, and the swept back hair made him look exactly what he was: a wealthy, successful businessman, who took care of himself.

As always, he went straight to his point.

'Carina, I'm so sorry. I screwed up.'

'You screwed a thirty-year-old in our bathroom at our thirty-fourth wedding anniversary party,' she bit back, but her words were quiet, calm, measured. She wasn't going to let him see the hurt. That was all hers.

'I did. And I'm sorry. I need you to know—'

'I don't need to know anything.' Still cool, still calm, and she could see him sliding onto the back foot. This wasn't a Carina that he recognised.

His hand moved to the side, and she saw it was reaching for a small red velvet box. Cartier.

She cut that off right there, with, 'Don't do it, Spencer. Don't insult me. I'm not some cheap tart you can buy off and I'm not going to be swayed by a piece of fucking jewellery.'

He gave a sigh of exasperation. 'What else can I do, Carina? I'm sorry. She was a mistake. I know that. And I'll apologise another hundred times but I can't take it back. All I can do is ask you to forgive me.'

'How many others have there been, Spencer?'

'None. It was one mistake, Carina, I swear.'

She'd bet that Cartier box that he was lying, but she said nothing. She wasn't going to challenge something she couldn't prove. Once was enough.

After a few moments, he was the one who filled the silence.

'Carina, forgive me. Please. Come home. We are almost sixty years old. We've spent more than half our lives together and for the most part it's been wonderful. We've set ourselves up for an incredible future together. Please don't let one mistake take that away.'

The case for the defence rested, and he sat back in his chair, waited. When she was ready to speak, she did.

'You know, Spencer, I'm not laying all the blame at your door. I played a part in what got us here. I lost myself. I think I became... uninteresting. And uninterested in life too. Disengaged. After the girls left home and I was no longer the person who steered the ship, I just settled for a quiet existence. Lost my spark, my purpose. I wasn't prepared for this stage in my life. Neither was our marriage. We've taken each other for granted, stayed in our own lanes for so long that we don't even know who each other is any more.'

'I know who you are,' he said. 'You're my wife. And I want you to come home. Please, Carina, come back. Let's fix this.'

She already knew the answer to that.

'I'm not ready. I'm going to stay here for a while longer.'

'Because Ben's here?' he asked, both the question and the edge in his voice shocking her.

'Ben? Why would he make me stay here?'

'Oh, come on, Carina, he's been in love with you for years.'

What the hell was this? 'Don't be ridiculous,' she scoffed.

'He has. He just didn't have the balls to do anything about it.'

'Or maybe he just had too much decency to even contemplate such a thing,' she snapped, tired of this. 'I'm not here because of Ben. I came to see Moira.'

It took him a second to catch on, and even then he was confused. 'Moira? Who used to sing here?'

'Yes. She's here for a few days on holiday and I wanted to see her. Lisa was supposed to be here too...' She went on to tell him a brief account of what had happened to Lisa, but he had only met her briefly, so while he expressed his sympathies, she could see it didn't carry the sadness that she'd felt.

'And how is Moira?' he asked, obviously keen to keep her engaged in amenable conversation.

'She's good. It's strange, but I feel like being back here, thinking about the past after all this time is giving both Moira and me a different perspective.'

'And what's that?'

'When I came here in my twenties, the only thing I loved was performing. Even though my family objected, I had this hope, deep down, that one day I'd make it in that world. Neither Moira's life nor mine has turned out how we thought. Moira gave up love for the dream. I gave up the dream for love. Neither of us got it right.'

'I still think you did,' he said. 'I just need you to come home and give me the opportunity to prove it to you.'

'Maybe...' she said sadly, softly. 'But not now. I need to decide what I want on my terms. To be sure I'm doing it for me. And I'm going to need more time. I'll let you know what I decide.'

'When?' he asked, his eyes wide with surprise as she stood up.

'When I'm ready.'

Those were her final words to him this afternoon.

Now, lying in her room, the whole world turning outside, she kept hearing his words. '*...give me the opportunity to prove it to you.*'

All she had to do was decide if she should give him that chance.

28

STEVIE

Stevie flipped open the jar of cashews from the mini-bar, and popped one in her mouth, deciding she deserved it after working out harder than she ever had before at the gym. And yes, the fact that she was training beside an incredibly fit Hollywood actor may have spurred her on to the point where her muscles were applying for transplant to a body that could hear them screaming that it was time to give up and go lie on a sun lounger.

They'd got there eventually. After the workout, Ollie had suggested a drink at the outdoor bar and pool terrace overlooking the spectacular view of the harbour. Like everywhere else she'd been this week, Stevie had wondered if her mum had ever been there, right in that spot. She hoped that answer was yes because it was breathtaking. She'd lain out there with Ollie for a couple of hours swapping life stories. In what had already been the most surreal week of her life, a roller coaster of twists, turns and shocks, having frozen margarita's with Ollie Chiles in the middle of the afternoon, had to be up there with one of the most crazy.

And yet, it had felt perfectly normal at the time. Not that she'd prejudged him – okay, maybe she had – but before she'd met him, she'd expected him to be, well, a bit of an arrogant arse. Weren't most famous celebrities? She'd treated a few in hospital over the years, and could honestly say that no matter how attractive they were, she hadn't found a single one of them to be endearing or charming. In fact, the previous Hogmanay, she'd x-rayed the broken foot of drop-dead gorgeous Corbin Jacobs, star of *The Clydeside* soap, and he'd been such an utterly obnoxious dick, she hadn't watched the show since.

In hindsight, though, when it came to Ollie, she should have factored in the fact that Moira was his mum, and realised that once you got past his job and the whole 'Top Ten Sexiest Hunks In Hollywood' thing, he'd be just a normal, down-to-earth, self-deprecating, nice guy.

Even more surprising, he was just as interested in talking about her life as she was in hearing whether he knew what moisturiser Margot Robbie used.

When they'd met at the crack of dawn this morning, after he'd stormed into the hotel looking for his mum, she'd given him a brief account of who she was and why she was there, but that had been inconsequential, given that what they both really cared about was poor Moira, lying in a hospital bed. However, now that his mum was back and relatively unscathed, they'd strayed on to loads of other subjects. She'd told him about moving to Glasgow to go to university when she was eighteen. About her job at the hospital. Her friends. The things she did for fun, when she could squeeze in a day off to do them.

They'd talked about their mothers, and his face had lit up when he'd described the theatre academy he'd founded and was about to open in Glasgow for kids from underprivileged areas. 'I'm calling it the Moira Chiles Academy of Drama and Song, as a tribute to how talented she is, and how hard she has grafted my whole life. But she doesn't tell anyone that because she says it's too boastful,' he'd said, laughing. 'I'm thinking about putting her face on the front of the building just to tip her over the edge.'

Stevie had felt a pang of something when he'd spoken about that. Envy, maybe? Ollie and Moira obviously adored each other and had such a close relationship. She wished that she'd had that with her mum, and it devastated her that she was too late to try. Too late to know the real Lisa. Too late to ask her so many questions. Why had she kept such a big part of herself secret? Why had she stopped singing? How had she gone from being a wild rock chick who travelled the world, to being an uptight, anxious, overprotective mother who could never let her guard down and just be happy?

It broke Stevie's heart that she would never have the chance to ask her and she'd been thinking about it ever since she and Ollie had left the pool area. Ollie said he had some calls to make, and she'd come back to her room for a lie down.

'See you at dinner?' had been his parting words. 'I'll come knock on your door.'

'Sure,' she'd agreed. This. Was. Surreal. So was the fact that she hoped her mum could see this. 'You know, Mum, just Ollie Chiles from the telly, casually stopping by for me on the way to dinner.'

What would her mum think of that? What would her mum say to all of this? Would she be happy? And again why, oh bloody why, had she never told Stevie that this world and these people had been part of her life?

An incoming text from Moira disturbed her thoughts and she tossed another cashew nut into her mouth while she read it. Moira was bailing on dinner tonight. Stevie felt a little surge of happiness for her. Go Moira. Ollie had told her that Nate had shown up at reception earlier, so Stevie hoped that skipping dinner with them was a sign that their reunion was going well. Although, there was also the possibility that it was going really badly, and Moira was having a lie down in a dark room to recover.

Stevie replied with a thumbs-up and a heart emoji, and then she must have dozed off for a while, because the next thing she knew was that her phone had sprung to life and was vibrating between her cheek and the pillow. She pulled it out and squinted through sleepy eyes. Facetime call. Caleb. She answered straight away, and the smiling faces of Caleb and Keli filled the screen. 'Hello, lovely!' that was from Keli. 'We're on our day off and just about to head out for brunch, so we just thought we'd check in. Caleb has been bringing me up to speed on everything, and holy shit, it sounds like you're having a crazy week.'

'Oh, it's definitely that. And it got even more crazy yesterday. Wait until I tell you about our trip to the Big Buddha...'

The two of them listened intently as she recounted the events of the day before.

'Oh. My. God. Is Moira okay now?'

'Yes, but the guy who was her boyfriend when she was here thirty-five years ago showed up at reception earlier, and she texted a little while ago to say she's going to skip dinner with us, so I'm hoping it's going well. Oh, hang on – there's someone at the door. Probably housekeeping.'

Still carrying the phone, she crossed the room, opened the door, and...

'Hey. Just checking in to see if you still want to have dinner now that we've been ditched by my mother? I did text...'

'Shit, sorry. I fell asleep, and then I went straight on to a call with—'

'Stevie Dixon, is that who I think it is? You raise that phone right now or you and I are finished. Done,' came a loud demand from the direction of the phone.

'...with my mates,' Stevie said, holding the phone against her chest now. 'That voice you just heard would be one of them. Caleb. He, erm, enjoys *The Clansman* very much so I think he might be having a moment.' What she really wanted to say was that Ollie was his celebrity crush, but she didn't want to breach a confidence or make this moment any more cringe-inducing than it already was. She'd deliberately avoided mentioning that Ollie was here because she knew they'd make it a big deal and, well, point proven.

'Stevie!' Keli's voice this time. 'I swear we'll disown you.' Stevie held the phone even closer to try to muffle the sound.

Now leaning casually against the doorframe, Ollie, however, seemed to be finding this whole thing highly amusing.

'Can I?' he asked, gesturing to the phone.

Stevie felt her toes curling. 'Are you sure? You don't have to.'

'It's cool,' he said, reaching out for the handset.

'Okay... but come in...' She handed the phone over and then stood back to let him pass.

The next thing Caleb and Keli saw was the grinning face of Ollie Chiles. In her bedroom. This. Was. A. Pure. Beamer.

'Hey, I'm Ollie.'

Not a sound. Not a single sound. For what felt like a week. Caleb recovered first.

'Sorry, just taking this moment in, since our good friend, Stevie, seems to have omitted to tell us that you were there.'

Ollie raised a questioning eyebrow in her direction, and she shrugged. 'Didn't want to name-drop.'

'Understandable,' he agreed, still smiling.

He turned his attention back to the screen. 'Well, it's good to meet you both on here. I've just come by to see if Stevie is going to let me take her for a romantic dinner... wine, music, moonlight... all that stuff. So is it okay with you if I hang up now and she'll call you back later?'

'Absolutely!' It was Keli this time. 'Good to meet you too, Ollie. And erm, Stevie, we'll be waiting for your call,' she said pointedly.

He hung up, laughing properly now and Stevie groaned as she slapped her hand to her forehead. 'Really? Wine and moonlight?'

'Did you like that bit? Just thought I'd give them something to talk about.'

'That's cruel. I swear they'll be in a state of flux right now. You're Caleb's celebrity crush, but I'll deny ever having told you that.'

'My ego needs all the crushes it can get,' Ollie joked. 'Anyway, dinner? No wine and moonlight, but I hear the bar downstairs does a mean Korean beef. I've texted Carina to see if she's still joining us, but no answer from her either. See what I mean about my knocked ego? My texts and dinner invitations are getting rejected all over the place today.'

Before she could answer, there was yet another knock at the door.

'That's probably Carina now,' Stevie said, before adding a cheeky wink. 'She clearly likes me more than you.'

She was still giggling when she opened the door and... not Carina. A guy. Vaguely familiar. She tried furiously to place him, but it wasn't coming to her.

'Hi, I'm sorry to bother you...'

'That's okay.' Was he the manager of the hotel? Definitely familiar.

'I'm Nate. I was a friend of Moira's back in the day...'

That was it. One of the photos Moira had shown her from the nineties had a younger version of this guy in it.

'...and a friend of your mum's too.'

'Yes! Pleased to meet you.' She stuck out her hand, but realised he was so fixated on her face that it took him a few seconds to respond.

'Sorry!' he said, catching up. 'You just look so like her. Took me by surprise there for a second.'

Stevie now took that as a compliment. 'I've heard that a few times this week.'

'I bet.' He shook it off, as if he'd decided to get to the reason he was here. 'Anyway, Moira was telling me about everything that happened to your mum and I'm so sorry for your loss.'

Ah, he was just here to pass on his sympathies. 'That's kind of you, thank you.'

'And she was also telling me that this week has thrown up a few questions and how sad she was that she couldn't explain everything. The thing is, your mum and I, well we used to talk. And Lisa told me some things about her life, and we shared some experiences that might help you understand what happened to her. If you'd like to hear them, that is.'

'Yes,' Stevie could barely breathe as she stood back to let him come in. 'I think I'd like that very much.'

29

FEBRUARY 1991 – HONG KONG

Lisa

'Any word from Moira yet?' Lisa asked, as she lay on her bed popping grapes in her mouth.

Lying across the end of her bed, Nate took a sip of his beer. 'Nope. And I'm trying not to open that wound, so let's just skip right past that and change the subject. Can we talk about how I've known you for a year and I've never seen you eat fruit?'

Lisa flicked a grape in his direction, and he caught it with one hand, then put it in his mouth, laughing.

It was good to see him smile, because he hadn't been doing much of that lately, not since Moira had done a runner. Lisa loved them both, so it was hard to take sides on this. All she knew was that it tore Moira up to leave Nate, because she loved him. She'd left Lisa a note with her home address, 'so that they'd never lose touch,' it said, but it also asked her not to share it with Nate until Moira knew whether she was coming back in a week, or a month, or a year. Lisa had already decided that she would drop her a card when she got home to tell her about the baby.

Carina was long gone too – moved out the morning after she got engaged and was now on holiday somewhere in Singapore being the glamorous rich chick she'd always been on the inside. Even now that they were both gone, Lisa still meant what she'd said a couple of weeks ago, on that last performance at the bar. Along with Nate, Moira and Carina were the best friends she'd ever known. At school, she'd been the kid whose mum had died of an overdose. Who didn't have a dad. Whose granny had to raise her. And a couple of those kids were fecking merciless. That's why she'd spent most of her teenage years in her room, with music that sang to her, took her mind off a world that – with the exception of her lovely gran – made her feel like crap. Nate, Moira and Carina hadn't treated her like that though. Someone once told her that the best thing about being an expat was that you could be anyone you wanted to be, and no one knew any different. Her friends hadn't judged her on her past, they'd just accepted her as she was and loved her anyway. They hadn't cared about her flaws, and they'd never pushed her to give more than she was able to. They'd supported her, even when she was a fecking mess, which, let's be honest, was often. They were her first true mates, and now that Moira was gone and Carina had quit the bar and moved into Spencer's swanky apartment, she'd miss having them in her life. And she'd miss the guy that was lying on the end of her bed popping another of her grapes in his mouth.

'I suppose you're still set on leaving me too?' Nate said.

Without thinking, Lisa put her hand on her stomach as she answered. There was no bump there yet. When she'd first realised she was pregnant, she'd tried to work out her dates and she reckoned she was about ten weeks gone now. Ten weeks. No time at all. And yet it already felt like forever.

'I'm sorry. I have to. For me and for the baby.' Her hand was still trailing back and forward across her non-existent bump.

She'd told Nate about the baby the night after Moira and Carina left, because she wanted him to understand why she wasn't drowning her sorrows in a vat of Jack Daniels. He hadn't judged. Hadn't criticised. 'The dad?' he'd asked but they'd both known the answer to that.

'Messed up as this sounds, I have no idea,' she'd admitted. There had been way too many men, way too many risks, way too many nights when she couldn't remember what happened. Way too many nights when she hadn't cared about her own safety or her own life, because what did it matter? She had no family to miss her when she was gone. Now, she wasn't proud of that, but it was too late to go back and change it. All she could do was make it different from here on.

That's why she was sitting here tonight with Nate, instead of out raising hell and life had never felt so right.

How could she put into words how happy she'd been for the last month? Since the day her gran died, she'd had no family, no-one to belong to, nothing, except a deep void of sadness in her soul, one that no amount of alcohol or men had filled. And God knows, she'd tried. Drinking had been the only way she'd been able to block out the loneliness of having no one on this earth who loved her, who really knew her, who needed her, who cared if she was alive or dead. And the men... the physical stuff was a distraction. Just for that moment, that hour, that night, she didn't feel alone, until she woke up in the morning and hated herself for settling for some bloke she didn't even know. And so she drank, to numb that disgust... and on and on that cycle had gone, until there had been a reason to break it.

Because now... there was a baby. And her baby needed its mother. Needed *her*. For the first time in a long time, she had something to look forward to. That's why she'd changed everything. No booze. No cigarettes. No drugs. No men. She'd cleaned up her room so that she was living in a healthy environment. The reason she'd known what changes to make was because she'd seen the other side of it. When she'd been a child her mum had been a mess, her life ruled by drugs and alcohol, both substances far more important to her than the daughter who loved her, the little girl who'd been devastated when the drugs killed her. She would never let her child experience that pain, the fear of waking up every morning, not knowing if her mother would be sober or wasted, calm or raging, loving or dismissive, alive or dead. She was going to create the kind of childhood the other kids at school had – one where they never had to worry because everything was always the same: their worlds were calm, organised, safe, secure, protected. That was the life she was going to give this child.

And perhaps Nate deserved an explanation about that.

'Did I ever tell you about my mother?' she said, surprising herself by talking about the one subject that she'd avoided her whole life.

'Only that she was dead,' he said, and she saw the genuine interest on his face. He'd asked her about her family before and she'd shut the subject down.

'She was an addict. Coke. Weed. Booze. Anything she could get her hands on. Died of a heroin overdose when I was eight and left me to be brought up by my gran.'

'The one who passed away a few years ago?'

She'd forgotten he knew that detail. He'd walked into her room one morning when she was listening to her gran's voice-mail recording, and she'd been caught off guard and explained what it was. He'd hugged her, but she'd shrugged it off. Sympathy was the worst. It was the thing that should make you feel so much better, yet it always made her heart ache just a little bit more.

'Yes, that was her. She was nothing like my mother though. My mum partied, got wasted, would bring home all sorts of guys to our house...' If he recognised a pattern, he was kind enough not to say it. 'It was a tiny village and that kind of thing didn't go on there – she was the only addict most of them knew and they were horrified by her. Thing was, so was I. If she showed up at school, it was to embarrass me, or scream at another parent, or to cry because another man had fucked her over. I was terrified every day of my life with her and when she died...'

She felt her voice begin to crack, and cleared her throat, refusing to shed another tear for the hell they'd gone through. She tried to start again. 'I've never said this aloud to anyone before, but when she died, all I could think about was that I wouldn't be scared any more. I was relieved that she was gone. And I know that makes me the worst person in the world, but it's true.'

'It doesn't,' he said, softly. 'All it makes you is a scared little girl who wanted the pain to stop.'

'Maybe.' She couldn't quite give herself that grace. All she could do was look forward. 'That's why I'm going to be different. I can't bring a baby into this life here – me out every night and clubbing until dawn. It deserves better. That's why I need to go back to Ireland. I've given the tenants in my gran's house notice, so that I can go home, get a normal job, be a normal mum, with a normal life, and I can break the cycle. Sure, there'll be the older ones in the village who'll judge me for being a single mother – they're the ones who'll be praying for my soul on a Sunday while turning their noses up at me in the street every other day – but I couldn't care less. All that matters is that I'm going to take care of this child so well and love it so much. I'll protect it from all the shit I've dealt with, and it'll never know that kind of pain. My kid will never see what I've seen, I promise you, and I'm going to make sure nothing bad every happens to it.'

'You won't miss singing? That's a pretty big love to give up.'

'I will. It's all I've ever wanted to do, but I'm going to have another kind of love to take its place.'

He pushed himself up on one elbow, so he was facing her. 'Lisa Dixon, in case I forget to tell you,' he began, and she could hear the emotion in his voice too, even when he added, 'Or, you know, you do a runner like my girlfriend...' That made her smile. 'You're a pretty fucking incredible human being.'

She shook her head. 'I'm not. But I'm going to try.'

There had been something freeing in sharing all this with him, but predictably, the self-consciousness, insecurities and habits of a lifetime were beginning to make her chest flutter, so she diverted the focus back on to him. One painfully brutal revelation was more than enough for one night. 'Anyway, that's my sad story over and now you know. So let's talk about your fuck-up of a life,' she teased him, switching the mood. 'What are you going to do next?'

Lisa wasn't sure how long after that she fell asleep. All she knew was that when she woke up, the bedside lamp was still on, Nate was sleeping soundly on the end of the bed... and an excruciating pain was stretching across her stomach, twisting it with such violent fury that she gasped and buckled over where she lay.

'Nate! Nate!' she sobbed, pain taking her breath away. 'Nate, please wake up. Help me. Help me! There's something wrong with the baby.'

30

MONDAY, 7 JULY, 2025 – HONG KONG

Moira

Moira had slept for eighteen hours straight, wiped out by the fall, the sleepless night in the hospital afterwards, the remnants of her jet lag, and the sheer emotional toll of seeing Nate again yesterday and reliving the end of the most bittersweet young love she'd ever known.

Now, showered and dressed, it was just after 6 p.m. on their last night in Hong Kong, and she was finally feeling fully recovered from her tumble. The pain she was now experiencing wasn't physical, it was her heart being ripped out as she sat in the lounge area of her suite with Stevie, Carina and Ollie, listening to Stevie share the information that Nate had told her the night before, a story about Lisa.

'Oh no. She lost the baby?' Moira wept, devastated for the pain that Lisa must have felt. So many things made sense now that they knew Lisa had been pregnant. The way she'd changed in their last month together. She'd been happy. Calm. She'd shunned all her vices and decided to go home, to give up her whole world for a child that would never be born.

'She did,' Stevie whispered, leaving them all silent, grief-stricken.

Eventually, Moira used her sleeve to dry her face. 'I just wish she'd told us she was pregnant in the first place. I would never have left her. Or I'd have taken her home with me. My mother would have welcomed her with open arms and we could have taken care of her when the worst happened.'

Carina was on the same tear-stained page of regret. 'And there was me, so giddy and excited about getting married, that I didn't even think to sit her down and delve into what was going on in her life.'

'Going by what Nate was saying last night, she was planning to write to you both and tell you she was pregnant after she got home to Ireland,' Stevie consoled them. 'He says he was the only person she ever told in Hong Kong and even then, he was shocked because it was so out of character for her to share something personal.'

Carina agreed with that. 'It was. She kept everything so close to her chest, never shared her feelings no matter how many times we offered to listen.'

'But then she lost the baby before she could tell you about it. Nate was with her when that happened. He said she was distraught, because she'd been so happy to be pregnant.'

Moira ached for the heartbreak Lisa had endured. And now Stevie, the poor lass, had more to share. 'What he told me made something else make sense too. When I was going through Mum's documents I found her marriage certificate. May 1991. My dad was a guy she'd known from school, and he'd lived next door to her when they were growing up. Now, knowing the timings of when she left here, she was only home for three months when she married him. I can imagine he was bowled over by her – this gorgeous creature, who'd come back after years away, must have seemed irresistible to him. I was born ten months later. All she ever told me was that they should never have got married because they didn't really know each other, but now I think it was deeper than that. I think that maybe she was so desperate to recreate that feeling of having someone to love, that she rushed into it all. She got married because she wanted a baby. Someone to belong to, no matter what. And as soon as she had that, I think I became an obsession that my dad couldn't match.'

Moira listened to every word she was saying, and knew Stevie was right, it all made so much sense. Lisa was a lost soul. Damaged. A bit broken. She didn't share her life or her thoughts, so it wasn't difficult to see how she'd made the choices that she had. In that first couple of years after she'd come home, Moira had sent a few cards to the address Lisa had given her but received nothing back. She'd been about to give up, when she'd received the Christmas card, saying she'd married and had a baby. After that, even when they'd exchanged cards at birthdays and Christmas, there had never been an offer to meet. In fact, on the couple of occasions Moira had suggested it, Lisa had always had a reason why she couldn't do it. Work. Lack of time off. A backache. A broken ankle. Moira had taken the hint and stopped asking until she'd given up cruising and returned to Glasgow earlier in the year. Thirty-four years of excuses and she'd just put it down to life getting in the way. Now she knew it was Lisa protecting her secrets. She'd told Stevie nothing of her past life, no mention of her singing career, or of the friends she'd made in Hong Kong, and she wanted to make sure that chapter of alcohol, partying and the pain of losing a child stayed in the past too.

'I'm so sorry, Stevie. This is all a heavy load for you to bear, pet.'

Stevie reached for the coffee pot in the centre of the table and topped up her mug. 'In some ways. But in other ways, there's something really comforting in knowing the full story. The fact that her mother overdosed, and that my mum had issues with alcohol... I get now why she was so over-protective, always so strict and suffocating. I think it just all came from a place of fear that I'd follow their paths. But she could never really break down the barriers of self-protection because of everything she'd been through, so that made her seem cold. All those years she was so scared of losing me that she inadvertently pushed me away. And yet, now I feel closer to her, and understand her more than I ever did.'

Moira dabbed her face with her sleeve again, wondering if there had been a single day this week that she hadn't lost her mascara by nightfall. 'I'm just grateful that you found the letter when you did. Painful as it is, I'm so glad you know her story now. And selfishly, I can't bear to think about never meeting you.'

'Me too. I know I sprung a whole lot of heartache on you, but I'll never be able to thank you enough for letting me stick around. Is it crazy that in a weird way, it feels like Mum engineered this because she knew I needed it? It's as if she couldn't share who she really was when she was alive, but she wanted me to know her after she was gone.'

Stevie's positive attitude broke the sadness and lifted the mood, and Moira saw that Carina was nodding at that suggestion. 'I'm going to believe that she engineered it because we all needed it,' her posh friend said. 'I don't know what I'd have done without you both this week. I can't even begin to explain how grateful I am. And to you too, Ollie. It's been an absolute joy to meet you. You're one of the gang now. God help you.'

If there was anything that warmed Moira's heart more than someone she loved saying how lovely her son was, she couldn't name it. Although, she didn't want him getting too big for his boots, so she gave him a nudge. 'Aye, he's not bad. A bit too flash for my liking sometimes though.'

'I'll work on that, Ma,' he assured her, feigning repentance.

'I hope so, son. Talking about flash, what time is Spencer coming, Carina?'

Moira had thought when Carina came in that she looked shattered. She'd told them about the conversation with Spencer and that she had to decide whether to go back to him or to leave him. Moira knew what her own choice would be, but she kept that to herself. This had to be Carina's decision, so she didn't want to say that she'd have had his clothes in bin bags in the garden within an hour of catching him up to no good.

Her question evoked a deep sigh from Carina. 'I told him I'd meet him downstairs in the lobby lounge at eight. There's more chance of us keeping it civilised if we're in public. I haven't got the energy for recriminations or going over what happened. I just want to go forward. Move on. Whatever that looks like.'

Stevie asked the question they were all thinking. 'Have you decided what you're going to say to him yet? Are you going to go back to him?'

'I really don't know. I know that sounds ridiculous, but my head and my heart and my loyalties and my vows... they're all saying different things. When I saw him yesterday, I was so angry, but I'm clearer now on what he wants. I'm just hoping that when I see him, I'll feel what's right for me too. I'm going to have to decide one way or another because I need to know where I'm going when I leave here tomorrow.'

'You know you can always come back to Glasgow with me?' Moira offered, thinking how wonderful that would be – but again, she didn't want to influence Carina's decision so she didn't labour the point, just smiled when Carina squeezed her hand and said, 'Thank you.'

Meanwhile, Ollie decided to get Moira back for the dig earlier by putting her on the spot.

'What about you, Ma? Were you swept off your slippers by your old flame yesterday?'

If they'd been alone, Moira would have brushed off the question, but she could see Stevie and Carina were waiting for her answer too. She didn't know where to start. Seeing Nate had brought up a million feelings that had been strangers to her for a long time: attraction, longing, emotional intimacy and a warm familiarity that was still undeniable, even after all these years. After he'd left, she'd wrestled with the question of changing her mind and staying in Hong Kong for a bit longer. But every time, her answer was the same. No. She'd just put down her roots again in Glasgow, with a new home and a job that she felt passionate about. She was back with her son and they were creating something that would make a real difference to the kids in those communities. She didn't want to give that up for anyone. Not even Nate. And not thirty-five years too late.

She filled them in on the gist of everything that was said, closing with, 'So it was wonderful to see him, but I know I did the right thing.'

'Are you sure, Ma? I'll understand if you want to take a break from the academy and stay here for a while.'

'Thank you, son, but I'm sure. I was on the cruises for sixteen years, and all I want to do now is stay in one place with the people I love. Besides, if I don't go home, Jacinta will be over here with a documentary team dragging me back.'

Before Ollie could agree, there was a ping on his phone. 'That's the bar downstairs reminding us we have a table booked at 7 p.m. Do we still want to go down?' He turned to Stevie. 'Would you rather give it a miss? You've had a pretty heavy day.'

Moira couldn't help but notice that they'd struck up quite a rapport. It was nice to see.

Stevie didn't even need time to think about his question, though. 'No, I think we need to celebrate our last night. This time tomorrow I'll be heading back to Galway to clear out my mum's house, and we'll all have gone our separate ways. So tonight, let's have drinks, have dinner, and make the most of it. Is that okay with you, Carina?'

'It certainly is. I could do with a gin and tonic before Spencer arrives. Moira?'

'Oh, I'm in. If I ever say no to a karaoke bar, you'll know I definitely do have concussion.'

They didn't waste any more time. Ten minutes later, they walked into the bar, past the photos of their younger selves on the wall, and they were greeted by the same barman they'd spoken to earlier in the week.

'Welcome! Your table is right there,' he said, pointing to the one directly behind them. 'And I'm so glad that you came back, because we found a surprise for you.'

'Oh really? What's that then?'

Ollie had pulled out her chair, and Moira was just taking her seat when the barman answered her question by picking up a remote control, and pressing a button that made the TV screen above him come to life.

It wasn't the promo video that they'd asked about a few nights before. It was even better than that. There, in glorious technicolour was a recording of their show on Christmas Eve, 1990.

There was Moira.
There was Carina.
There was Lisa.
And they were all having the time of their lives.

31

CARINA

Carina couldn't have looked away if her life depended on it. It was so long ago, yet she remembered every detail of that night. The three of them were on stage together and wow, they were magnificent.

They were singing 'It's A Man's World', all taking different parts, the way they'd done so many times at parties and gatherings and to keep them amused while going back and forwards on the ferry.

Moira's rasp was smoky and gravelly, a Christina Aguilera before the real one came along.

Carina was playing the tune on the piano like it was a bluesy concerto, her pitch perfect voice testimony to all those years of expensive singing and music coaches that her mother had once insisted that she'd wasted.

And Lisa. She was spectacular. In her leather trousers and white blouse, she worked that stage, every move transfixing her audience, every lyric delivered with intoxicating sass.

'She's breathtaking,' she heard Stevie murmur, awestruck. 'I've never seen this side of her, never seen her perform or sound that way or move like that.' Carina could see the glistening tears in Stevie's eyes, the stricken expression on her beautiful face. 'It kills me that she gave this up so that I'd have a quiet, secure, protected life, away from the craziness of this world. I wish she'd just followed her dreams, even after I came along. Maybe it would all have turned out so differently. She was a star.'

She was. They all were.

No one said a word. They barely breathed. The whole world disappeared, and they only remembered where they were when the song ended, and the scattering of guests at the other tables in the bar broke into spontaneous applause.

None of them had a single clue that two of those gorgeous, sexy, fierce young women on that video, were the middle-aged ladies sitting at this table, tears falling down their faces as they ached for the loss of their friend. And the loss of themselves.

Carina couldn't reconcile that joyous, vibrant woman with the one she was now. When had that happened? When had she become quiet? Let her world become small? Let all that potential go?

She'd had a good life. She'd travelled. She'd had children she adored. She'd led a life that many would consider glamorous and luxurious. She'd married a man that she'd been in love with for many years.

If she could go back, would she change it?

No. She wouldn't.

But now she could see that she'd lost a huge part of herself in the process.

Had it been worth it?

Before she could answer that question her phone buzzed. She'd switched it back on last night, now that Spencer knew where she was. Unable to sleep, she'd called Ben, Erin, and Imogen. She'd spent a lifetime pressing her feelings down, putting a smile on her face, smoothing over the cracks and being the elegant paragon of grace and calm.

Well, in the words of this week's version of herself – fuck that.

Being uncharacteristically vulnerable, open and frank, she'd given them all an update on the situation. And they'd all reacted in very different ways.

Ben had given her no opinion on what she should decide, just told her to do whatever made her happy. Carina had omitted to tell her brother-in-law about Spencer's ridiculous suspicions that Ben had feelings for her. Jealousy and fabrication were such unattractive qualities and she'd never seen Spencer displaying them before now. But then he'd never been caught with his pants down before now either. His allegations were pure projection, nothing more.

On the subject of her marriage, her daughters had been more direct.

Imogen had asked her again to take their father back.

Erin had said it was up to her – but that her dad was an asshole and Carina deserved a medal if she forgave him.

That had made her laugh and feel a glimmer of hope for a new kind of relationship with her daughters. A non-sanitised version. One that was based on truth and honesty and full disclosure about her life and her feelings.

The phone buzzed again, and this time, Carina read the text message.

> I'm in the lobby. Meet me there. Sx

'I'll be back,' she told the others, not entirely sure if that was true.

'Spencer's there?' Moira asked.

'Yes. He's waiting for me in the lobby.'

Moira squeezed her hand as she passed. 'Whatever you say will be the right thing, Carina. Just tell it from your heart. Bugger, all this emotion is making me talk in song lyrics.'

Thankful for the pep talk, Carina walked into the lobby with the kind of posture and poise that her mother had drilled into her from childhood. She saw him immediately, sitting over at a low table by the window, two large glasses of red wine on the table in front of him. He'd ordered for her, as always. When had she become so voiceless, that he'd just taken for granted that he knew what she wanted?

Chiding herself for being petty, she joined him, and he said the same thing he'd said to her on a thousand other nights.

'You look beautiful, darling.'

Tonight, though, it didn't land the same. There was no frisson of pleasure. No gratitude that he still paid her compliments. But she still had manners, so...

'Thank you,' she replied, then lost her words. Nothing else. The opposing arguments in her brain had collided and shut her down, so there was nothing but an awkward silence that he broke first.

'This is ridiculous, Carina. I feel like I'm waiting to hear my fate. And I hate that I have no control over it.'

'Welcome to my life,' she said, then immediately backtracked on the bitterness. 'But that's my fault. I was the one that gave up control. I allowed it. I've been doing so much thinking, and I can see that now.'

'Can you also see that I need you back? That the girls need you? That we need to be a family again?'

All about everyone else. Did he even consider what she needed?

She avoided the questions. 'I can see that I needed this time to breathe and to think about how we got here.'

That seemed to exasperate him and he lifted his wine, clearly in need of liquid fortification. 'I've already said I'm sorry so many times, Carina. If I could take back what I did I would.' There was an irritation in his tone that evoked the same emotion in her – did he think a simple 'sorry' would fix this?

'But you can't. It's done, and I feel like everything is different now. I'm different. And it's not just what you did that changed me. It's being here. With Moira. With Lisa's daughter, Stevie. With the ghosts of who we used to be.'

He leaned forward in his chair, the way she'd seen him do so many times when he was negotiating or sharing an idea with a business contact. 'But Carina, that can only be a good thing. Maybe that's what we needed. For you to find your old self again, the one I met here. Christ, we were madly in love. We couldn't get enough of each other, and there was so much excitement and joy and promise for the future. Maybe what happened will turn out to be the biggest blessing we could have had.'

Wow. He was honestly going down the line that inserting his dick into another woman was going to be the hallelujah-shot in the arm that their marriage needed.

Maybe the old Carina would have gone with that, but the new Carina, the one in her 'Eff That Era' had a very different point of view.

Fifteen minutes ago, she'd walked across the lobby unsure of what her answer would be.

Now she knew. She just had to explain it.

'You know, Spencer, after what happened to Lisa, there's a question that's been plaguing me this week. What would have happened if she'd known she was going to die that day? That month? That year? Would she have made changes to her life? Lived it a different way? Taken chances? I've no idea. But I do know that I get to choose now. You've had my life since I was twenty-three years old, and I'll never regret it. But you've had enough of it, Spencer. I've decided that the rest of my days are going to be for me.'

She stood up, gave him a smile that said goodbye. 'So I'm sorry, Spencer, but being your wife... well, that just doesn't work for me any more. From now on I want to make my own plans, my own decisions and order my own bloody drinks.'

Naturally, he wasn't giving in that easily. 'You're emotional. Still raw. And I don't blame you because I let you down. But I'm going to keep trying to get you back, Carina.'

'What you do is up to you, but it won't change anything. I want a different life, Spencer.'

'And what will that be, Carina? Where will you go?'

She smiled at the man she'd loved for a lifetime.

'Wherever I damn well please.'

With that, she turned around and walked out of the lobby and out of her marriage.

And she didn't even think about turning back.

32

STEVIE

Stevie was standing at the bar, lost in a world of her own when Ollie came over from their table. He had a baseball cap on his head, and fake glasses on his unshaven face, but his deliberate disguise hadn't fooled everyone. So far tonight he'd had at least six requests for selfies, four for old school autographs, and a marriage proposal.

Thankfully, the adoration of his fan club had died down in the last hour or so, because the bar had become so busy he was able to fade into the background.

The strange thing was, despite all the evidence to the contrary, the more time she spent with him, the more she forgot that he was famous. He made her laugh, and he had such a caring, easy way about him, such a genuine openness, that all the actor-y superficial stuff seemed irrelevant.

He stood next to her at the counter and nudged her shoulder. 'Everything okay or are you getting ready to flee the scene?'

'I'll warn you if I'm about to do a runner. Depends on the size of the bill. But yes, I'm fine, thanks. The waiters were busy, so I just decided to come for the drinks myself.'

He didn't seem to be buying that. 'That's all?'

She wasn't getting away with it. 'Well, maybe I wanted to clear my head a little. Every time I think we're on smooth emotional sailing, someone comes along and torpedoes the boat. Watching the video of my mum... I can't get that image of her out of my head. She was so different. They all were.' She shook off the melancholy. 'But I think your mum and Carina needed to see it too. Carina has been like a different person since she came back from meeting that husband of hers.' She glanced back over at Carina and Moira. 'How's your mum doing?'

Ollie followed her gaze. 'Okay, I think. But then, if she wasn't, we'd never know. Don't get me wrong, she's not afraid to vent her thoughts when she's pissed off about something, and she'll go to war with anyone who crosses her or hurts someone she loves, but when it comes to her own life...' He smiled back in Moira's direction, 'well, she's one of those people who does what she needs to do and just gets on with it.'

'I can see that in her. She's been right there for me and Carina this week.'

Back over at the table, the two women were deep in conversation now, heads together, and Stevie saw a lightness to Carina's face that she hadn't seen all week.

'I'm so glad that Carina didn't go back to her husband. Not that I'm judgemental, and this is based on never meeting him and only anecdotal evidence, but I can't stand him and she's way too good for him.'

That made Ollie chuckle. 'You're sounding like my mum. I've heard her offer to bury his body at least twice in the last couple of days.'

The barman was back, and he slid the first two drinks from her order across the bar top. Two margaritas for the ladies who'd been together now for a week, but still appeared to have engrossing stuff to talk about.

'It's hard to believe they haven't seen each other for over thirty years. I keep thinking that it's such wasted time. And for my mum too. Why didn't she make an effort to see them? Why couldn't they all be in each other's lives? They could have brought so much strength and joy to each other. I know that my mum could have done with friends like that.'

Obviously he didn't have the answers, but he threw it back to her.

'Why do you think she kept this life secret?'

'I think she was scared of opening the door to this world again. She wanted to keep everything controlled, just her and me, no one else in our lives, especially people who knew about her past. I think she was probably embarrassed. Scared of who she'd been. And if she pretended that it hadn't happened then it couldn't harm her or me.'

The thing about him being such a good listener was that it made her want to talk more. And it felt so good to just let it all out.

'I used to think she was just being a nag and stomping all the happiness out of my life. I'm no expert but I wonder now if a lot of her behaviour was a trauma response. So much loss. Her mum. Her gran. The baby. And no other love to get her through those things. That definitely changed her.'

'In what way?' he asked, encouraging her to go on.

'Look how different she was from the stories we've heard about her here. When I was growing up, she was nothing like that. She'd stopped drinking, stopped smoking, stopped going out, stopped being who she was. Watching that video earlier was one of the highlights of my life, but it makes me sad to see that she was so free and she had so much talent. Yet, to me, she spent her whole life terrified. She refused to give me any freedom or allow me to make mistakes. That girl who'd flown to Hong Kong on her own when she was barely out of her teens, became a woman who refused to take chances and she wouldn't let me take them either. That's how I ended up doing the job I'm doing now. It was a safe move. It's a great job, but I just don't know if I'd had free rein to pick that I'd have done the same thing.'

The barman slid their other two drinks over to them, but Stevie wasn't ready to go back to the table yet, too happy to be talking this through with him. At home, everything was discussed with Caleb and Keli and she got her maternal fix from Gilda, who cared for her in a way that made her feel that whatever choices she made, good or bad, she'd be supported. That was all she'd ever wanted from her mother. She understood now that Lisa was too scarred and too scared to let that happen.

'What else would you have done if you hadn't chosen your line of work?' Ollie asked.

She took a deep breath. This was it. Time to put it out there. Let it go.

'I think I terrified her when I was a little girl because I wanted to sing. I had no idea that she'd been a singer – I just loved it and wanted to perform. She shut that down so quickly. Wouldn't allow it, even when I begged. Again, I can see now that she was just petrified that history would repeat itself.'

'I'm sorry. It's hard for me to relate, because my mum pushed me to do whatever I wanted to do. But I'm so sorry that happened to you.'

'Thank you.'

Around her, she heard the track that three gents were murdering on the karaoke come to an end.

'The thing is,' she went on, 'I think I'm over not taking chances.'

The karaoke host took to the stage.

'Thank you, gents,' he crooned. 'Ladies and gentlemen, please give it up for our next singer... Miss Stevie Dixon.'

Ollie's eyes widened, but they didn't leave hers. 'Really?' he asked, grinning.

'Really,' she said. 'So I'm going to start taking them now,' she told him, unable to contain a high that didn't come from her drinks. She was about to step away, when she stopped, leant towards him, and kissed him on the lips until she could barely breathe. And she felt a jolt of happiness when she realised he was kissing her back.

'I won't be long,' she murmured. 'Then I'm going to do that again.'

She felt his eyes on her back as she walked to the stage, and she saw Moira and Carina jump to their feet as she passed them, now watching her, cheering her on.

When she took the mic she didn't even have to look at the words on the screen because she knew them off by heart.

And as the opening bars of 'Landslide', by Stevie Nicks, began, she closed her eyes. And she sang. She sang for herself. For the two women she'd met only a week ago. For the guy she'd just snogged at the bar. And she sang for her mum.

And when she let go of the last note, she opened her eyes and Moira and Carina were on their feet again... and so was every other person in the bar.

The noise brought her back to earth, broke the spell, and she blushed furiously as she walked back to her seat, into Moira's waiting arms.

'I wish my mum could have been here to see that tonight.'

Moira held her tight as she whispered in her ear.

'Stevie, I've never been more sure that your mum was right here the whole time.'

EPILOGUE
MONDAY, 1 SEPTEMBER, 2025 – GLASGOW

Moira

The flashes from the photographers' cameras were clicking like strobe lights, as Moira walked onto the red carpet at the opening ceremony for the Moira Chiles Academy of Music and Drama. No, she hadn't been able to persuade Ollie to change the name, and yes, it was mortifying to think that people might accuse her of getting too big for her... she glanced down at her feet... sparkly, red cowboy boots, but at least he hadn't carried out his threat to project her face onto the front of the building. She had, however, forgiven him because he'd gone with her suggestion to rename the music school in the building. The coaches in 'The Lisa Dixon Studio of Song' would nurture the kids of this area and help them become the stars they dreamt of being.

'I preferred it when I was the star around here,' said the gentleman next to her. Her son's cheek made her smile. In partnership with his friend and her former agent, Calvin Fraser, this was Ollie's project, his investment and his way of giving back to the working-class community that they came from. She could not have been prouder or loved him more. However, the smile for the cameras never left her face, as she responded to his cheeky comment with a murmured, 'Son, I was in labour with you for thirty-two hours. You can give me ten minutes to enjoy this.'

Ollie stepped up onto the podium at the front door of the old converted church, and joined his co-founder, Calvin, where they happily waited for the live music to end. Over to his right, an old friend of his mum's was playing piano and singing Christine McVie's vocals on Fleetwood Mac's track 'Dreams'. The girl who was belting out Stevie Nicks' part, bore a starting resemblance to the original American songbird, although she'd confessed to the audience at the start of the song that it was only her second live performance. It was also her first gig since she'd dropped one day out of her working week at Glasgow Central Hospital, so that she could devote time to volunteering and practising her own vocals in the studio that was named after her mother. Stevie Dixon had no illusions of seeing her name in lights, but her late mother's oldest friends had a sneaking suspicion that it would happen. They'd once known someone else who could sing like that, and back in the nineties, she'd packed out bars every night of the week.

Happy to let her moment in the spotlight go, Moira stood at the back of the stage where she was joined by her lifelong pal, former soap actress and wearer of chiffon kaftans, Jacinta McIntyre. Her daughters – Drea and Kara – were Ollie's best mates, brought up as a family that they chose themselves, and she could see them now in the back of the crowd, beaming with pride. Jacinta, however, had her mind on other things. 'I think the documentary team just caught me on a hot mic moment. I was asking the plumber to flush out my pipes. I think it could have been taken the wrong way.'

Moira struggled to keep a straight face. Jacinta had never reached the heights of her lofty aspirations as an actress, but there was no doubt in Moira's mind that she was going to become a reality star of legend as soon as the documentary was released. Moira just hoped that her pipes were flushed and ready.

Over to the left of the podium, Carina and Stevie brought the song into land and the crowd gave them a riotous round of applause. Although, it was Glasgow, so half of the crowd continued to sing for another two verses and a chorus, until Calvin stepped forward and thanked them for their enthusiastic support.

He then invited the guest of honour, a local MP who'd helped them drum up a few grants, to step forward, and address the crowd.

'If he goes on for any longer than five minutes, I'm going to distract him by pretending to faint,' Moira whispered to Jacinta. 'I heard him talking at the switch on of the Christmas lights in George Square last year and it was January by the time he finished.'

The only bonus was that the MP's loquacious address to his non-adoring public gave time for Carina and Stevie to make their way from the stage to her side.

She immediately wrapped the younger woman in the tightest hug. What a blessing that this girl had found her way into their lives, and not just because she'd turned her son's world upside down in all the best ways. He'd been married before, and then had a wonderful short-term romance afterwards, but neither of those relationships had worked, because both were with actresses whose crazy schedules had made it impossible to spend quality time together. Well, that and the fact that his ex-wife had been caught with her tongue down the throat of her co-star. But watching the way Ollie smiled at Stevie now, and the way Stevie blew a kiss back in his direction, gave her hope that this might just be the one that would go the distance. And if it didn't, Stevie would always be a part of her family. They were bonded over old friendships, new love for each other, and the fact that Stevie was a radiographer and that would come in handy for Moira's dodgy knees in the not-too-distant future.

Moira turned her attention to the other half of the Fleetwood duo. 'The voice was sounding pretty fine up there, Posh Pal. If, hypothetically, some bloke who'd been in love with you for years was watching that, I think he'd be blown away by you.'

Carina giggled – yep, giggled. She'd been doing that a lot lately. Ever since her brother-in-law had declared that he did, in fact, adore her and had taken to hanging out with her now that she was spending most of her time back in Hong Kong. Their relationship had yet to go further than friendship, and they'd agreed to keep it that way until her divorce had gone through. Although, her husband had been spotted last weekend in Dubai with the infamous Arabella, who was still almost half his age, so... 'Still keeping it platonic, then?' she checked. Carina nodded to the affirmative. 'We are. But you know... I'm in my Eff You Era, so that's subject to change. Especially now that my girls are on my side.' Carina's daughters, Imogen and Erin, were both out in the crowd somewhere – they'd travelled to Glasgow to support their mum today and spend time with her. 'You know,' Carina went on, 'none of this would have happened if you hadn't decided to go back to Hong Kong. I'm so glad you did.'

'Me too, ma darlin'.' Moira smiled, knowing she would never stop being grateful for the trip that brought Carina back into her life. Or for the twist of fate that helped Stevie find them there. And she'd never stop wishing that some things could have been different. There were so many 'If Onlys' in her life, and the one that truly took a chunk out of her heart was that Lisa hadn't made it back to them. Moira wished she'd sent the letter sooner. Wished Lisa hadn't kept so many secrets. Wished she were here now. But life didn't work out that way and every time Moira wanted to feel her close by, she just had to close her eyes and press play on a recently acquired 1990 recording of her friend.

A restrained round of applause and a few sighs of relief signalled that the MP had finished speaking. Ollie stepped forward to the microphone.

You could hear a pin drop as the much-loved Glaswegian TV star thanked his agent, Calvin, for inviting him to be a partner in this academy. He then thanked the entire squad of music, film and television talent that had committed to volunteering, donating and fundraising for the centre.

He went on to explain the purpose of the academy and the role it would play, providing free acting and singing classes to the kids from low-income areas of the city. 'When I was a kid, I'd have loved to come to a place like this. However, I was lucky. We didn't have much money, or access to theatre schools, but I had a single mother who worked day and night, to give me all the coaching and resources I could ever need. But in doing so, she put her dreams to one side, so that I could chase mine. So my final thanks go to my mother, the incredible singer this centre is named after. Because without her, I wouldn't be standing here. Ladies and Gentlemen, I now declare that the Moira Chiles Academy of Music and Drama is open. Mum, would you cut the ribbon?'

Moira was standing at the doorway, holding a three-foot pair of scissors that the prop department had whipped up last week, and she could barely move because she was so utterly mesmerised and grateful for the words he'd just shared. Thirty years ago, she'd given up the opportunity to develop her rapidly rising reputation in the theatre world, because she didn't want to tour and leave her son. She wanted to be able to come home to him at night. To be present. To take care of him no matter what. And she'd never doubted it was worth it.

'If you don't hurry up and cut that ribbon, I'll bloody do it,' Jacinta whispered in her ear. 'I've got a date with a yoga instructor in an hour and I have to warm up. He's very bendy.'

There was a sudden snigger from a cameraman lurking over to her left, and Moira realised Jacinta had been caught on a hot mic for the second time today. Yep, she was going to be the stuff of reality TV legend.

Containing her amusement, Moira smiled, cut the ribbon, and then waved as the spectators cheered.

At that moment, the doors opened as planned, and Moira stood to the side to allow the hordes of spectators to enter for their first peek at the magnificent facility they'd created.

As they swarmed past her, Moira took in the sight of Ollie and Stevie, hugging in the corner. Of Carina beaming as the MP told her how magnificent she was. Of the photographers who were taking her picture, to be used in the media announcements that would run all day. Of Jacinta, who was now heading for her car, while doing side bends. Of... of...

Moira froze as another face in the crowd, one that she'd first clapped eyes on decades ago, stepped out of the line of people waiting to enter the building and began walking towards her.

Fireworks exploded in her mind as she held her breath, while her whole world rewound to 1990, when she'd walked away from him, breaking his heart and hers.

Now she was standing with two sparkly red cowboy boots rooted to the spot. This time she wasn't walking away.

'I know you,' she said, when he reached her, her smile making it oh so clear that he was welcome.

'I know you, too, Moira Chiles.'

Nate Wilde reached down and kissed her softly on the lips.

'What are you doing here?' she asked, as soon as her racing heart allowed some air back into her lungs.

He pulled back far enough for her to see that he was looking at her the way that only a young guy she'd once met in Hong Kong had ever done.

'You said you wanted to find someone who loved you enough to change their whole life for you. So I was wondering how you felt about that person being me?'

Moira stretched up on to her tiptoes and gave her answer by touching her lips to his for a long, long time.

Thirty-four years ago, she'd left the first love of her life.

Now, she knew the last love of her life was standing right in front of her.

* * *

MORE FROM SHARI LOW

Another book from Shari Low, *One Day and Forever*, is available to order now here:

https://mybook.to/OneDayForeverBackAd

ABOUT THE AUTHOR

Shari Low is the #1, million-copy bestselling author of over 30 novels, including *One Day With You* and *One Moment in Time* and a collection of parenthood memories called *Because Mummy Said So*. She lives near Glasgow.

Sign up to Shari Low's mailing list for news, competitions and updates on future books.

Visit Shari's website: www.sharilow.com

Follow Shari on social media:

- facebook.com/sharilowbooks
- x.com/sharilow
- instagram.com/sharilowbooks
- bookbub.com/authors/shari-low

ALSO BY SHARI LOW

My One Month Marriage

One Day In Summer

One Summer Sunrise

The Story of Our Secrets

One Last Day of Summer

One Day With You

One Moment in Time

One Christmas Eve

One Year After You

One Long Weekend

One Midnight With You

One Day and Forever

One More Day of Us

The Carly Cooper Series

What If?

What Now?

What Next?

The Hollywood Trilogy (with Ross King)

The Rise

The Catch

The Fall

BECOME A MEMBER OF THE SHELF CARE CLUB

The home of Boldwood's book club reads.

Find uplifting reads, sunny escapes, cosy romances, family dramas and more!

Sign up to the newsletter
https://bit.ly/theshelfcareclub

Boldwood

Boldwood Books is an award-winning fiction publishing company seeking out the best stories from around the world.

Find out more at www.boldwoodbooks.com

Join our reader community for brilliant books, competitions and offers!

Follow us
@BoldwoodBooks
@TheBoldBookClub

Sign up to our weekly deals newsletter

https://bit.ly/BoldwoodBNewsletter